PHILANTHROPISTS

Also by Rozlan Mohd Noor

21 Immortals: Inspector Mislan and the Yee Sang Murders
DUKE: Inspector Mislan and the Expressway Murders
UTube: Inspector Mislan and the Emancipatist Conspiracy
Soulless: Inspector Mislan and the Faceless Girl

PHILANTHROPISTS

INSPECTOR MISLAN
AND THE
EXECUTIONERS

ROZLAN MOHD NOOR

ARCADE
CrimeWise

An Arcade CrimeWise Book

This story is dedicated to all frontliners for their dedication and sacrifices during the COVID-19 pandemic. Those who risk and lose their lives so that others may live, the world is forever indebted to you and your families.

First North American Edition 2023

This is a work of fiction. Names, places, characters, and incidents are either the products of the author's imagination or are used fictitiously.

Arcade Publishing books may be purchased in bulk at special discounts for sales promotion, corporate gifts, fund-raising, or educational purposes. Special editions can also be created to specifications. For details, contact the Special Sales Department, Arcade Publishing, 307 West 36th Street, 11th Floor, New York, NY 10018 or arcade@skyhorsepublishing.com.

Arcade Publishing® and CrimeWise® are registered trademarks of Skyhorse Publishing, Inc.®, a Delaware corporation.

Visit our website at www.arcadepub.com.

10 9 8 7 6 5 4 3 2 1

Library of Congress Cataloging-in-Publication Data is available on file.
Library of Congress Control Number: 2022947654

Cover design by Erin Seaward-Hiatt
Cover photography: © Thomas Northcut/Getty Images (vehicle); © Westend61/Getty Images (hand with gun)

ISBN: 978-1-956763-35-5
Ebook ISBN: 978-1-956763-62-1

Printed in the United States of America

PHILANTHROPISTS

1

THE OFFICE OF SPECIAL Investigations (D9), Kuala Lumpur Police Contingent, is quiet, with just a few lights switched on. It is 2:15 a.m. and the investigator on duty, Inspector Mislan Abdul Latif, is leaning back in his chair with his feet on his desk, enjoying a catnap—the long-established posture in which a twenty-four hour investigator catches a little shut-eye between callouts. His assistant, Detective Sergeant Johan Kamaruddin, had earlier told him that he was going to grab some snacks and coffee for them.

They had been on a callout to a crime scene at Jalan Alor, a favorite nocturnal hotspot frequented by locals and foreign tourists alike. An area lined with cheap girly bars, women—mostly Vietnamese, Thais, Filipinas, and Mainland Chinese—plying their wares on the streets, overpriced seafood restaurants, drug peddlers, and scammers. The businesses here are predominantly Chinese-operated, but lately the Middle Easterners and Pakistanis have started inching in. Kiosks selling kebabs, carpets, ornaments, and shisha line the fringes of the nightspot. Jalan Alor is one of the many inner roads running parallel to the main road that operates twenty-four-seven but is busiest from sunset until the early hours of the morning.

The callout was supposedly for an armed robbery. The victim was a potbellied local man in his fifties. He was wearing dark slacks and a light-colored long-sleeved shirt, which looked more like office attire than casual wear for an evening outing. He was intoxicated, and Mislan could smell his stale rancid breath from two yards away.

The investigating officer (IO), whom Mislan guessed was in his early twenties and most probably a rookie, stood next to the drunk man looking exhausted and lost. Mislan signaled him away from the drunk.

The rookie IO briefed Mislan: the complainant claimed he had been walking to his car, which was parked around the block, when he was jumped by two men. One of the men pointed a gun at him, and his accomplice demanded that he hand over his wallet. He refused and the one with the gun pistol-whipped him on the head. He fell to the ground. They then grabbed his wallet and cell phone and fled.

There was some movement in the direction of the drunk complainant. As Mislan turned to look, the complainant, who was walking toward them, tripped over his own feet and hit the ground hard. Mislan heard his assistant, who was talking to the district duty detective, chuckle. Two uniformed constables tried to assist the deadbeat back to his feet but failed. Detective Sergeant Johan told them it was better to just leave him there on the sidewalk until it was time to go.

"Let him sleep it off," Johan told the constables, who were waiting for such an instruction.

"Did he describe what type of gun?" Mislan asked the rookie IO.

"He just said gun," the rookie answered.

"Yeah, I should think so. Did you find out which bar he came out from?"

The rookie shook his head.

"Look, I'm not saying he wasn't robbed or the muggers weren't armed, but I think you should've done a little more inquiring. I mean, just look at him. Look at his clothing. He probably was hitting the booze immediately after office hours. Look around you, look at the others, they're all dressed casually: jeans, polos or crew-neck T-shirts."

The rookie looked around at the crowd and passersby.

"He," Mislan said tipping his head toward the drunk lying on the pavement and snoring like a cow choking, "is plastered. He probably blew all his money in one of the bars and needed an excuse to tell his wife for getting home this late."

Mislan lit a cigarette and offered the pack to the rookie, who declined. Suddenly, the rookie looked dog-tired to Mislan. He spotted a flash of despair in the rookie's eyes, but when he looked up again, it was gone. Mislan noticed that the detective and two uniformed constables were watching them.

"Tell me, did you believe what the guy claimed?" Mislan asked the rookie IO in a softer voice. "He's so hammered, I bet you he can't tell the difference between his dick and a gun. If those men he claimed robbed him had a gun, you think they'd rob a drunk after he blew all his money in a bar?"

The rookie investigator hesitated, then gave a slight shake of his head and looked down at his shoes.

Feeling sorry for the rookie, Mislan asked, "Who told you to call D9?"

"The detective, Murad. He's an old-timer. He told me if it's armed robbery, D9 will handle it."

"My advice is, take the complainant back and let him cool down in the tank. Talk to him when he is sober. You'll probably get another story altogether."

"Yes, sir. Sorry."

"Don't worry about it. I'm sorry for taking it out on you."

As the rookie IO stepped away to give instructions to the two constables, Mislan beckoned Detective Murad over. He was aware of old-timer rank and files taking pride in jerking rookie officers around instead of coaching them and showing them the ropes. Bragging and bullshitting about their length of service and imaginary credentials to hide their laziness and incompetence. His unit has a few of them, and he always wondered how they became detectives in the first place.

He gave Detective Murad a harsh caution for not performing his duties while assisting the IO at a crime scene. He admonished him for giving poor advice to a rookie to call in D9.

By the time Mislan and Johan left Jalan Alor and reached their office, it was 1:45 a.m. Mislan lit a cigarette and bitched to his assistant, "Since when did they start sending rookie officers as IOs to the city?"

Johan shrugged, indicating he had no idea.

"That IO must be regretting his decision to join the police. The brasses should work out a way of easing them into the system."

Detective Sergeant Johan is a rank and file. He joined as a constable and worked himself up the ranks. To Mislan, it was a good and sound approach to ease them into the system. However, as an officer, one is thrown straight into the deep end. Well, not all the officers—only those who were fortunate or unfortunate enough to be posted to the Criminal Investigation Division.

––––––

Footfalls echo in the deserted office, waking Mislan from his catnap. He tilts his head to peek at the entrance and sees Johan coming in carrying two plastic bags of black coffee and a pack of something, probably roti canai. Roti canai with dhal curry had probably made its way into the Malaysian all-hour-food list alongside the national pride, nasi lemak.

Mislan drops his feet from the desk and straightens up in the chair. Just as Johan approaches, the office phone rings.

"D9, Inspector Mislan."

"Sir, Corporal Hamid from Sentul Police."

"Yes, Corporal."

"We got a case, and the IO had asked for D9."

"What's it about?" he asks, feeling a little skeptical after coming back from a faux callout.

"A double murder. Two men shot in a house."

"457, housebreaking and robbery gone bad?"

"Could be, but I was not told by the IO."

"What's the address? Who's the IO?"

"Inspector Shahira Adanan."

2

THERE ARE THREE FEDERAL territories, namely Kuala Lumpur, Labuan, and Putrajaya. Kuala Lumpur is the oldest of the territories, followed by Labuan and then Putrajaya. The city of Kuala Lumpur is divided into five police districts, geographically Cheras to the south, Sentul to the north, Brickfields to the west, Wangsa Maju to the east, with Dang Wangi located in the center. Putrajaya is also a police district within the Federal Territory, yet it is seldom referred to as one by the locals and even among police personnel. The district headquarters is located about twenty miles away from the Kuala Lumpur police contingent in what used to be another state.

Labuan and Putrajaya are part of the federal territory, but to most Malaysians they could well be part of another state. In fact, the physical locations of the two federal territories are in other states, which are Sabah in East Malaysia and the state of Selangor in the west of the Peninsular. When the locals refer to federal territory, or in short FT, they usually mean Kuala Lumpur.

Johan drives the standby car allocated to the shift investigator out of the contingent headquarters. Once he hits Jalan Hang Tuah, Mislan pulls out his phone and taps on Waze. He keys in the destination Taman Sentul Jaya and waits for directions. Waze says it is about seven miles and the journey will take fourteen minutes. How easy it is nowadays to navigate the city. *There is an app for everything, from health, food, directions, everything. No wonder people are getting stupider by the minute,* he mulls. He increases the volume on his cell phone so that Johan can listen to the Caucasian woman's voice directing them.

It is 2:30 in the morning, yet there is a large number of vehicles on the road. It is a city, after all, and they say a city never sleeps. The voice from Waze tells them to turn left and take Jalan Pudu. The Malay word "jalan," meaning road or street, is pronounced by the prerecorded Caucasian voice as "jalang," which in Malay means prostitute. From there, they link up with Jalan Tun Perak to Jalan Parlimen to the Sultan Iskandar Expressway. As they hit the expressway, Mislan lights a cigarette, turns off the air conditioner, and rolls down the window. The rush of cold early-morning wind is invigorating, washing away lingering torpor. As they drive past the National Palace, Mislan wonders if the king and queen actually sleep there. *Probably not. What a waste, all the luxury and no one is enjoying it.* They drive all the way to Jalan Perhentian as the road makes a long right curve connecting to Jalan Sentul. At the intersection, they make a right on to Jalan 1/48B and to their destination on Jalan 2/48B. The voice of Waze announces: "You have reached your destination."

The crime scene is an end lot of a two-story terrace house, which is also the last block on the dead-end road. Mislan remembers when he and his ex-wife were actively house-hunting; his ex-wife said she didn't want an end lot but was fine with a corner lot. At that time, he just couldn't differentiate the two. To him a corner lot is at the end of the row, therefore an end lot. He eventually understood when told of the difference in the price.

The road in front of the end lot is full of police vehicles, and Johan has to park about fifty meters away, next to the monsoon drain. Mislan terminates the Waze app, pockets his cell phone, and steps out of the car lighting a cigarette.

"You're not going in?" Johan asks.

Mislan holds up his cigarette, "Finish my smoke first. Why don't you go in and see if Forensics is done?"

Johan nods and walks toward the front gate with a bright yellow tape stenciled with the words POLICE LINE stretched across it. He shows his ID to the uniformed constable standing guard saying, "D9 IPK."

IPK is short for Ibu Pejabat Kontinjen contingent headquarters. The constable acknowledges and lifts the yellow tape for Johan to enter.

As he straightens up, he asks if the crime scene forensics team is still inside. The constable nods and gestures toward the house. Standing at the front door, Johan sees the investigating officer, Inspector Shahira, and a man in a blue multi-pocket cameraman vest coming down the stairs from the upper floor.

Female Inspector Shahira Adanan is in her early thirties, petite, about five feet tall, and she looks exhausted. She wears a tudung or hijab, which is now common headgear for Muslim policewomen. She has an oval-shaped face with chubby cheeks, giving her a baby-faced look. Her eyebrows lift questioningly as she spots Johan standing in the doorway.

"Morning, ma'am, Detective Sergeant Johan, D9," Johan says without being asked.

"Oh," she says, and her eyes search the living room as if looking for a place where she can park her tired body and give her feet a rest. "Alone?"

"Inspector Mislan is outside, said he'll wait until Forensics is done."

"I think they're almost done." She says it looking at the man standing next to her.

"Yes, we are," the man with the name KHAIROL stenciled on his vest says. Tilting his head toward the stairwell, he asks Johan, "You want to look upstairs?"

"I'll wait for Inspector Mislan."

———

Mislan gives the surrounding area a once-over. He is surprised that there is no crowd of onlookers apart from a few annoyed-looking individuals standing on the other side of the driveway chain-link fence in front of the crime scene. They look like the next-door neighbors, most likely rudely awakened by police sirens or flashing blue strobe lights or loud chatter, or probably a combination of all three. Malaysians are known to be *kepochi*—busybodies—and crime scenes usually draw them in like blowflies to a bloating carcass. Perhaps it is the time of the morning when sleep is at its heavenly state. But that has never stopped Malaysians before from the excitement of being around a crime scene. He glances at his cell phone to check the time. It is 3:01 a.m. He flicks his cigarette toward the monsoon drain, missing it by half a yard.

The development is not new, and mold can be seen on the outer walls. The house shows signs of having been well lived-in, with the expected wear and tear, but is not run-down. Fully grown yellow flame trees line the road, blocking the view from the main road and offering the houses some sense of privacy. The wide and deep monsoon drain running along the main road prevents access into the development except through the road from where they came in. Mislan suspects, *That must be the only road leading in and out of the area.*

Mislan walks toward the front gate, introducing himself to the constable. In the driveway, he notes a black Toyota Vios and a red Yamaha scooter. Next to the front door, he sees several pairs of Japanese flip-flops and an old pair of Nike running shoes. Nothing seems to indicate that this is a family dwelling. The front door and windows are protected with grilles. The door itself is the standard flimsy plywood with the press-button knob fitted by the developer—normally the first item most house buyers would change, but not in this case.

Standing at the front door, Johan introduces him to Inspector Shahira Adanan and vice versa. Mislan steps forward and, seeing Shahira in her tudung, he refrains from offering his hand. Nowadays, it is difficult to know if a Malay woman would accept a proffered hand from a man. In Mislan's view, it is safer to wait for the woman to initiate the handshake rather than him. Since Shahira does not offer her hand, he leaves it at that and gives her a nod of acknowledgment.

The living room can be said to be of a typical rented bachelor house. A few cheap wooden sofa chairs with bright floral-design cushions that need washing if not replacement, and a wooden coffee table with glass top. Mislan counts three aluminum ashtrays overflowing with cigarette butts, empty cigarette packs, one disposable lighter, and a couple of empty drink cans. Three pairs of slip-on shoes are lined up next to the front door. No carpet, no pictures on the wall, just a thirty-two-inch television on a low table.

There is no evident sign of struggle or disturbance, just the type of disarray that comes from untidy housekeeping. Shahira notices the blank expression on Mislan's face.

"It's upstairs. I've checked down here, nothing," she explains.

"Forensics?"

"They're done, packing up."

"What's the story?"

"Two males, both shot twice. Once in the back, once in the back of the head," Shahira says, closing her eyes and inhaling deeply.

"Anything taken?"

"Nothing that I can establish, and there's no one I can ask. The odd thing is we found drugs, quite a lot of them."

"And they were not taken?" Mislan asks, raising his eyebrows. "Interesting. You're calling Narco?"

"I don't know, should I?"

"Your call."

"Let's wait until we're sure those up there are drugs. For now, what I'm sure of is murders, that's why I called D9."

"Fair."

———

They hear footsteps coming down the stairs. Four bleary-eyed men in blue cameraman vests amble down with their equipment cases. They look beat and in a hurry to get back to the office for some shut-eye. Mislan has seen them before at the contingent headquarters but has never worked with them. Khairol hands Shahira three evidence bags, and she signs for them.

"What's that?" Mislan asks.

"Suspected drugs—methamphetamine, amphetamine, ketamine," the man says, like reading from a French restaurant's menu.

"That's a lot of '-mine,'" Mislan says with a chuckle. "You said 'suspected': you can't do a field test to determine it?"

"Best if they're sent to the chemist."

"Why's that?"

"The quantity's large, and if they're confirmed to be illegal sub-stances, that means trafficking, 39B."

"But Shahira said they're dead. Who're we going to charge for the drugs, those corpses?"

"Anyway, we didn't bring the field test kit out with us. We were told it's a murder," Khairol answers with a coy smile.

Mislan smiles back.

"Recovered any bullets?"

"Three, 9mm."

One of the men hands over three evidence bags to Shahira.

"Shells?"

"Nope, searched every inch of the room."

Khairol nods to his team in blue cameraman vests, and they follow him out in single file, waddling like ducks coming back from their evening swim.

Mislan calls after Khairol, "Shahira said four shots, but you recovered three bullets?"

"One could still be inside one of them," he answers without stopping. "Check with the pathologist later."

After the forensics team has left, Mislan turns to Shahira, who looks like she is about to doze off from exhaustion.

"Long night, eh?"

Shahira opens her eyes, taking a couple of long deep breaths to fill her lungs with much-needed oxygen to stay awake. "Third case of the day."

"Lucky you," Mislan jests. "Want to give me what you got?"

"They came through the front door." She starts pushing herself up to stand, jerking her head toward the front door. "The grille was opened using a key, Forensics said probably a master key, and the door was pried open using some tool."

Johan moves to the front door and examines the grille and front door.

"There's a mark on the doorframe, jimmied, probably with a crow-bar or something similar." Johan then examines the grille and says, "Nothing on the grille lock."

"What's 'jimmied'?" she asks.

"Peeled using something like a crowbar. 'Jimmy' is what they called a small crowbar that was used in the olden days," Johan explains.

"A standard grille lockset is easy to open. If I'm not mistaken, a locksmith once told me there're only three groove combinations for the lock. You can also easily make a master key for grille locks," Mislan says.

"Is that so?" Shahira asks, giving Mislan a disbelieving look.

"Yup," Johan replies for his boss. "That's why you see those rich people change to fancy grille locksets. Apart from its aesthetic value, it offers better security."

"They proceeded upstairs, and that was where the two victims were killed," Shahira continues. "You want to go up?"

Mislan and Johan nod.

3

THEY ARE INSTANTLY STRUCK with a vile pungent smell as they reach the small landing at the top of the stairs. Johan notices his boss hesitate for a fraction of a second. Johan squints at him as though asking *Are you OK?* Mislan gives his assistant a tiny smile and continues up the stairs. Right next to the staircase landing is the master bedroom. The strong odor of blood coming out of it is thick and heavy. A stench that reminds Mislan of the time he was slumped in his car with a gunshot wound in his abdomen, just before he had lost consciousness.

A small hallway leads to two guest bedrooms with a common restroom. Shahira takes them straight into the master bedroom. A constable is sitting on the edge of the bed, engrossed with his cell phone. He looks up at them, stands, and puts his phone away.

"What's he doing here?" Mislan asks.

"Guarding the scene," Shahira replies.

"Shouldn't he be standing outside the door?" Johan asks.

"He was when I left him."

The constable slithers out of the room, avoiding eye contact with the officers. Mislan and Johan step inside the room while Shahira stands by the doorway. Mislan reckons she has seen and smelled enough blood for one night. He says nothing and steps closer to the two bodies.

———

The master bedroom is sparsely furnished, another indication of rented premises. There is a queen-sized bed in the center, a light brown two-door wooden clothes closet pushed against the wall, a matching dressing table littered with male grooming stuff, and a red-and-white aluminum towel rack. The bed looks like it has not been made up from the last time it was slept on. The closet doors are wide open. Mislan sees some clothes hanging in it but nothing else. The bathroom light is on and the door ajar. The room has no air conditioner, but the windows are all closed tight. Mislan tells Johan to open all the windows to let in some air.

Two lifeless males, both lying on their sides in a pool of coagulated dark-red blood. They lie facing each other in semi-fetal positions. The blood from the gunshot wounds had stopped oozing. The bullet holes the size of marbles are blackish. The exit wounds under or on their chins are gaping, skin and bones ripped open as if done with a clawhammer.

Each of the deceased was shot twice, as Shahira said: once in the back between or close to the shoulder blades, and once from the back above the base of the skull. The wounds at the skull are difficult to see because of the matted hair from dried blood.

The two victims are shirtless, one wearing a sarong while the other a pair of sports shorts. *Probably their sleeping attire*, Mislan figures. To Mislan, there is something not quite right about their fetal-like positions. He bends closer and notices abrasion markings on their wrists.

"Shahira, you got their particulars?" Mislan asks.

"No. We searched for their wallets but can't find them," she answers, leaning against the doorframe.

"In the other rooms?"

"Searched there, too."

"What about letters, bills?" Johan asks.

"Chinese name, must be the house owner, landlord."

"Where were the drugs found?"

"On the bed, in the middle," she says, pointing to the spot.

"Someone must have put them there, I don't think these guys would do that," Mislan states, more to himself. "By the way, how did we get to know about these killings? I mean, who reported it, the neighbor?"

"No, the Inquiry said they received a call from 999. They relayed it, and MPV was dispatched by Ops to investigate and found this. Lucky me, eh?" Shahira says with a wry pout.

"Lucky you."

"You're not taking this case?" she asks.

Mislan notes the pleading in her eyes. "Have to check with my boss. Why don't you give it to Narco?"

"No way those guys will take it. They said their primary role is the prevention of drug trafficking, not investigating dead drug dealers."

"They got a point there," Johan says with a chuckle.

Mislan takes a closer look at the victims' faces, or what is left of them. Contrary to what most people believe through watching TV, when a person stops a bullet with his head, it is not going to be a black dot on the forehead or face. In real life, the face is usually defaced or disfigured if not blown totally away. The scalp skin will loosen because there is a hole or a tear in it and that will shift the facial structure. Some of the skin will be pulled to one side by tendons or muscles still intact. It is not a pretty sight.

"What do you think," Mislan asks Shahira and Johan, "what nationality or ethnicity?"

Johan steps closer and examines the victims' faces. "Either Malay or Indonesian."

"Shahira?"

"Yes, I thought so too, but hard to say."

"From the skin color, they could be Indian, Malay, Indonesian," Johan adds.

"Hmmm, I guess the landlord can tell us who the house is rented to," Shahira says.

"Yes, he can, but he may not know who was staying here, would he? Our best bet will be the neighbors," Mislan says. "Jo, why don't you go talk to the neighbors while I finish up here?"

They hear men talking and footsteps on the stairs coming up.

"That must be the movers," Shahira says, flashing a smile. "They sure took their own sweet time to come."

"Shahira, you found their phones?"

"Nope, no phones, no wallets, no laptops, nothing. Just clothing and them," she says, head-gesturing to the corpses.

"Let's check the other rooms."

———

The first guest room has a single bed, a plastic clothes closet with a zipper, a table fan, and a porcelain dinner plate that was used both as ashtray and mosquito coil base. The zipper of the plastic clothes closet is pulled down with its flaps hanging by the sides. A few polo and crew-neck T-shirts and a pair of jeans hang in it, nothing else. Another pair of jeans and a bath towel are hung by a nail at the window frame. Mislan pulls the jeans off the nail and checks its pockets.

"I've checked, nothing. Checked all the pants and shirts in the house, nothing."

Mislan drops the jeans and walks to the next room. The room is empty but for a stack of old newspapers and some crumpled plastic shopping bags.

"Who the hell are these people?" Mislan asks himself.

"Drug pushers, traffickers, most likely." She holds up the three evidence bags.

"How much is there, you guess?"

"Two and a half, three pounds, maybe more."

"That's a lot of shit to leave behind."

"You think the killers were looking for these?" she asks, holding up the exhibit bags containing the drugs.

"You said it was on the bed, in plain sight. If they were, the killers must be blind or stupid."

Shahira laughs.

"But they shoot good."

4

The drive back to the office is shrouded in silence. Mislan seems deep in thought, smoking and staring out the window. The dashboard clock shows 5:12 a.m. Johan asks if his boss is OK. Mislan nods without turning his head.

About eight months back, his boss was the victim of a botched murder attempt. He was shot while on his way home. He took a hit in the stomach and was lucky to survive. The doctor said the bullet missed his major organs. When he arrived at the hospital, he was going into hypovolemic shock due to massive loss of blood. If the residents around the area had not called 999 and if the MPV personnel had waited for the ambulance instead of immediately ferrying him to the Kuala Lumpur Hospital Emergency and Trauma Center, Mislan would not be sitting next to him now. No one knew how long he had lain slumped in his car drenched in his own blood. No one knew what was running through his head before he lost consciousness. Even after all these months, Mislan had not spoken of it to anyone, not even to him. He had ignored all advice that he get professional help. Even the head of Special Investigations tried to persuade him to see a psychologist. To get her off his back, Mislan said he would think about it. Johan knows the inspector is stubborn; he cannot force the issue, but one day when his boss is ready to talk, he will open up. Until then, he will wait.

Since he came back on active duty, Johan noticed minor changes in his boss's behavior. Not noticeable unless you have been as close as they were. Like this morning when they were walking up the stairs at the crime scene. There was a moment of hesitation when the tang of dried blood hit them. The tiny pause was unnoticed by Shahira, but he had noticed it. He'd seen similar hesitation at other bloody crime scenes they visited. Then it would be followed by a long silence and chain-smoking. The attempted murder did something to him emotionally. Johan is sure of it, but until his boss decides to talk about it, he will stand by him. Show that he is here should Mislan ever need to talk.

———

At the office, they head straight for the makeshift pantry, which consists of an old work desk and four plastic stools stacked at the far corner next to the emergency exit. Johan pours the coffee he had bought earlier into mugs, unwraps the roti canai, and pours the dhal curry into a bowl. Mislan lumbers over after placing his backpack on his desk.

"You're not eating?" Johan asks as he tears the roti canai, dipping it into the dhal. Roti canai is the Indian flatbread dish that had long since become an all-day Malaysian staple.

"No, it's cold and tough, leathery."

"We should all chip in and get a microwave."

"Like they would," Mislan says, referring to the rest of the investigators and their assistants. "You know how police officers are, if we can't get it for free, then we don't need it."

Johan laughs.

"What did the neighbors say?" Mislan finally asks.

"The neighbor, Mok Ah Kau, said he doesn't know who rents the house. He knows the owner is Chinese because they met several times before. That was when they'd just bought the house. The owner never stayed there, always rented it out. Before our vics stayed there, the house was rented by an Indian family. The family moved out about six or seven months back. Then the house was rented to the new tenants. Who, he doesn't know."

"Does he know where the landlord lives?"

"No, but he thinks the landlord once mentioned Kepong."

"The vics, does he know them?"

"Seen yes, know no. According to Ah Kau, many men went in and out of the house at odd hours. Malay, Myanmar, Indon, but all the times only men, never women. They talked Malay and some languages he doesn't understand, sometimes loudly like they were arguing. Ah Kau said their presence made him uncomfortable, and he cautioned his family to stay indoors whenever these men came. 'Don't be *kepochi*, don't be busybodies,' he warned his family."

"Sensible measures."

"Are we taking this case?" Johan asks.

"You want it?" Mislan asks his assistant.

"It's interesting."

"Interesting, how?"

"Oh, before I forget, the entire Mok family, all six of them, didn't hear any gunshots. Now that's an interesting point. The second, nothing seemed to be taken, I mean what was there to steal if it was a 457? There was nothing worth taking except for the bundle of drugs. And that's the third thing, why didn't they steal the drugs? They were in plain view on the bed, according to Inspector Shahira."

"Three out of maybe five or six, not bad," Mislan jests with his assistant. "Soon you'll be as good if not better than me."

Johan laughs. "What are the others?"

"I'll tell you if ma'am says we take on the case, otherwise no point in racking our brain for a case that's not ours," Mislan says with a sly grin. "In the meantime, why don't you put your thinking cap on and see if you can put your finger on the other two or three anomalies? I need to get some shut-eye before the morning prayer."

The morning prayer is a daily meeting chaired by the unit head. The outgoing shift investigator will brief other investigators in attendance on the last twenty-four hours of callout cases. The meeting is short and sweet, and the unit head will disseminate any information or general instructions or assignments, if any. As Mislan is the outgoing investigator, he will be required to brief the morning prayers. How the meeting got its moniker, no one actually knows.

Draining his tepid coffee, Mislan grabs a face towel from his backpack and heads to the restroom. He washes his oily face with soap and towels off. His face always feels hot and oily when staying up all night. He takes a leak and returns to his office for a short nap at his desk.

The D9 investigators don't have a private office of their own. They share a common office space like a squad room with other investigators and their assistants. He leans back in his chair, takes off his shoes and lifts his feet onto the desk. With arms folded across his chest and eyes closed, he tries to be as comfortable as he can. Ever since his son Daniel moved to stay with his ex-wife, and Dr. Nur Safia, or Fie for short, stepped out of his life, Mislan has dreaded spending the night at his apartment. The apartment is too empty, his life too solitary, and all he has left are the office and the cases he works on. Johan is the only one he has as a friend and partner, but Jo is Jo. He has his own life to live. After the attempt on his life, he feels he has no one he can talk to, *really* talk to like he used to talk to his ex-wife or Fie, or even Kiddo, his son. He has bottled up the trauma of being shot, of breathing in the pong of his own blood, of experiencing near-death, of the fear every time he gets into the car alone to go home. The attempted murder is being investigated by D9 Selangor, the neighboring state. To date, they have not made any headway.

He still has nightmares of the incident, still feels the slippery blood over his stomach when he showers and the nauseating choke in his throat. The pain in his stomach is like a burning ulcer that accompanies each nightmare.

Today, smelling the pungent dry blood and seeing the two bodies, he imagined it was him. Shot execution-style.

5

AT 8:30 A.M. SHARP, the head of Special Investigations, Superintendent Samsiah Hassan, starts the morning prayer. Mislan, the outgoing shift investigator, is the first to go. He updates the attendees on the callout cases for the last twenty-four hours: three robberies and one double murder. The three robberies are being investigated by the respective district's investigating officers and the double murder of the yet-to-be-identified victims is on the table for grabs. He lays out the summary of the double murder case.

"Quoting my assistant, it's an interesting case," Mislan says, ending his briefing.

"And because Jo said it's an interesting case, we should take a closer look at it," Samsiah says in jest.

The rest of the officers chuckle.

"Yes, ma'am," Mislan replies, hiding a smile.

"See me after this and we'll discuss it. Anyone like to raise anything?"

The officers shake their heads.

"Just a caution. I'm sure you all have heard of the virus going around, the coronavirus pandemic. It's a strong possibility the government will implement some sort of strict preventive measure. It all depends on what is happening in China, particularly in Wuhan, which is under strict lockdown. The virus, which was first detected through visiting Chinese tourists, is now spreading locally at an alarming rate. Locally infected clusters have been confirmed, and the rate of infection is alarming. I need you to exercise caution and advise personnel under your supervision accordingly. My PA is trying to secure face masks from Logistics for the unit. In the meanwhile, I suggest if possible to get your own face masks from a pharmacy for your daily use."

"First we have the COVID-19 pandemic, then a political coup by a backdoor government. I tell you this country is headed for big trouble," Inspector Tee moans. "No way in hell this backdoor government can handle the situation."

"Tee, I will not tolerate any political talk in my unit. We serve the people, no matter who the government is. Do I make myself clear?" Samsiah admonishes firmly. "And that goes for every one of you. Keep your political views to yourself."

The officers go dead quiet.

"Until we receive specific instruction on this coronavirus issue, we shall continue as usual." Superintendent Samsiah stands, indicating the meeting is over. She signals for Mislan to see her in her office.

"You want Jo too?" Mislan asks.

"Might as well bring him along."

After Superintendent Samsiah leaves, some of the officers sneer at Tee for his political comments.

"Tee, you PH supporter *meh*?" Inspector Reeziana asks. PH stands for Pakatan Harapan, a coalition of several political parties that won the last general election before it was overthrown by the so-called backdoor government of disgruntled PH members.

"Sure *lah*, sure DAP," Inspector Khamis says. DAP stands for Democratic Action Party, a PH coalition party that is Chinese-dominated.

"I know which political party Mislan subscribes to," Reeziana says. Before any officer answers, she says, "I-Don't-Give-a-Shit Party." She lets out a hearty laugh, followed by several of them.

———

Mislan and Johan take their seats as Superintendent Samsiah finishes whatever she was writing. She closes the file she is working on and turns her attention to the two officers.

"So, Jo, Mislan said you'd like us to take a closer look at the Sentul double murder. To quote him, you said it's an interesting case."

Johan flashes a grin.

"Enlighten me, please."

"We got the callout at—"

"I said enlighten me, not brief me," she says, cutting Johan off. "Mislan has done that during the morning prayer. Tell me why you think the case is *interesting*."

Mislan smiles as his assistant purses his lips, stealing quick glances in his direction.

"Tell ma'am what you told me," Mislan encourages him.

"Well," Johan starts nervously, "to me, there're three things that don't seem to fit. One: although four shots were fired, two into each victim, none of the next-door neighbors, and mind you there're six of them in the family, heard any gunshot." Johan inhales deeply and rushes on, "Two: there was nothing in the house worth stealing if it was a housebreaking and robbery under Section 457. Three: about three pounds of drugs were found in the middle of the bed in clear sight where the victims were killed. If it was a 457, why weren't the drugs taken? They were the only valuable thing in the house."

Johan stops speaking, catches his breath, and turns to look at Mislan and back to the head of Special Investigations.

"That's it?" Samsiah asks.

Johan nods, saying, "But Inspector Mislan said he felt there were five or six things that do not fit."

Superintendent Samsiah raises her eyebrows curiously. "Did he?"

"Yes, ma'am," Johan says, beaming, pleased that the attention is now shifted to his boss.

"And you can only come up with three," she says, pulling the detective sergeant's leg.

"Yes, ma'am. Inspector Mislan is an officer, so he has to have more than me," Johan replies with a chuckle.

They laugh with him.

"Well?" Samsiah asks Mislan. "What other things don't add up?"

"To me, Jo's points are strong enough to pique our curiosity, sufficient to give it a closer look. That's except for the neighbors not hearing
anything. The neighbors are Chinese, and you know how they don't
like to get mixed up in anything not concerning them, especially if it
involves the police. So for them not hearing anything, it must be taken
in that prospect."

Superintendent Samsiah nods her understanding of the stereotypes
of various Malaysian ethnicities. The Chinese always avoid the spotlight
when it does not directly involve them or when no gain is to be made.
The Malays on the other hand just love to be the center of attention in
any situation; involving them or not, gain or no gain. The Indians—
well, they are in the middle, perhaps a little skewed to the Malay fond-
ness of the limelight.

"To add to Jo's observations are the bodies' positions." Mislan takes
out his cell phone, scrolls to the photos he took of the victims, hands the
phone to Superintendent Samsiah, and waits while she scrutinizes them.
When she hands it back to him, he continues, "They were in an almost
fetal position facing each other."

"And that tells you?"

"They were on their knees when they were killed, execution-style.
Look at the position of their hands, at their back pinned by their shoul-
ders. Usually, the hands would be stretched out like breaking a fall.
Even their legs were not stretched out like if you're killed while standing. In my opinion, the vics were on their knees when they were shot."

"Interesting deductions," Samsiah says.

"Here." Mislan hands her his phone again. "Photos of the vics' wrists.
See the light yellowish markings. It looks like rope burns or ligature marks
made by something when their hands were tied behind their backs."

"But their hands were not tied behind their backs when the police
arrived," she states rather than asks.

Mislan and Johan nod.

"I guess the killers must have untied them," Mislan offers.

"But no ropes were discovered?"

Mislan shakes his head. "Next, each vic was shot twice, once in the back
of the head and another in the back between or around the shoulder blade."

"That tells you?"

"I don't know yet, but it's interesting. I would've thought the shot to the back of the head was enough to do the job. My question is: Why the second shot? It would only bring unwanted attention. I mean, why one gunshot more than necessary to do the job? More shots, more noise."

"Agreed."

"Overkills point to emotional or personal vendetta motives. Killing to vent anger or satisfy revenge."

"So you think the killers knew the vics?"

"I don't know. Anyway, why kill both of them in the same room? One of the vics was staying in the back room but was ushered to the master bedroom and they were killed together there. Wouldn't it be easier just to kill him in his room?"

"Perhaps they were in the room when the killers broke in."

"Perhaps but unlikely."

"Why unlikely?"

"The vic staying in the back room smokes, and I don't think the vic occupying the master bedroom does. There was no ashtray found in his room, the master bedroom. On top of that the windows were closed. There was no TV in the room for them to watch together, the TV was downstairs. Their rooms aren't air-conned, so why were the windows closed?"

"OK, go on."

"The closets in both rooms were wide open, and the odd thing is that there were no bags or suitcases to be found anywhere in or on the closets, under the bed, or in the whole house. Have you known people who don't have bags or suitcases in their house? The IO, Inspector Shahira, said no personal documents, wallets, cell phones, or laptops were found. Nowadays, who doesn't own a cell phone?"

"Hmmm."

"Forensics, D10, recovered three 9mm bullets and said one may still be in one of the vics but no casing. Inspector Shahira said they searched the entire room."

"You're thinking the killers picked up their casings."

"Most probably, and that tells me these guys are careful, knowledgeable in crime scene forensics techniques. Most people think that Ballistic can only match bullets to a gun. What most people don't know is that bullet casings or shells are also used to match the gun used. The unique characteristics like the ejector or firing pin marks can be matched to a gun. In fact, casings are better evidence as there is a chance of lifting a print from them, unlike from a bullet. Also unlike bullets, casings don't get damaged. Bullets usually get damaged on impact, which can render them useless for ballistic analysis. I read that Ballistic have more data on casings than bullets."

"I didn't know that," Johan admits.

"Either the killers know the facts you just said, or they learned them from crime stories on TV," Samsiah says. "OK, I can understand them recovering the casings, but why take the vics' personal belongings like wallets and phones?"

"I don't know, but if I'm to guess, I would say the vics aren't local, and taking their personal belongings will make it very difficult if not impossible for us to identify them."

"OK, Jo. I'm convinced, and good observations. I'll inform Sentul Police that we'll be leading the investigation."

6

As he and Mislan head back to the office, Johan is beaming with pride at the outcome of the meeting. In the many years he has been with the unit, this is the first case they will be leading based on his request and case observations. Assisting Inspector Mislan has been a challenge and sometimes borderline career-suicidal because of the inspector's maverick approach in getting closure. Then again, Johan guesses that was the only way to approach criminal investigation, with all the obstacles and interference an investigator has to wade through.

In the eleven years they have been together, Mislan evolved from being his boss to a friend, an elder brother he never had. They stuck together through thick and thin, stood shoulder to shoulder against adversaries, covered each other's backs in gunfights, and respected each other's personal space and private lives.

Entering the office, a few officers and their assistants are gathered around Inspector Tee's desk chatting and laughing. Seeing them, one of the officers beckons them over.

"What's up?" Mislan asks.

"So, Jo, did you get the *interesting* case?" Reeziana asks.

"You're looking at the lead," Johan announces proudly.

"Ma'am bought your *interesting* theory," Tee says, showing a thumbs-up. "Well done."

"Lan, what do you think of this coronavirus pandemic?" Khamis asks. "I read on Facebook, the shit is everywhere. Saw one posting where a motorcyclist dropped dead at a petrol kiosk."

"You know better than to get news from Facebook," Reeziana chides. "Check out KKM, the Ministry of Health portal, OK?"

"Yeah, go ahead and trust the government's bullshit. They'll hide everything from the people until they cannot hide it any longer. Social media is the best unfiltered news source," Khamis snorts. "Especially now with the new PN government."

"What's PN?" asks Mislan, who always stayed away from politics.

"Perikatan Nasional, the coalition between Barisan, PAS, and the breakaway Bersatu, the backdoor government," Tee sneers.

"I told you, Lan doesn't give a shit about politics. He doesn't even know who the ruling party is, and I bet you he doesn't even know who our new prime minister or minister of home affairs are," Reeziana says. "All he knows and cares about is his case."

The officers and their assistants laugh.

"I joined the police force, not a political party," Mislan answers. "In my book, politics is a cesspool with a bunch of people given gold cards to steal with impunity."

"I second that," Khamis says.

———

COVID-19 was first detected in Malaysia in January 2020. The infected were Chinese tourists but the then-government under Pakatan Harapan (PH) didn't bar further Chinese tourists. The government was economically very dependent on China, so the prime minister and minister of finance were fearful of antagonizing their Chinese counterparts.

The spread of COVID-19 intensified in West Peninsular Malaysia. On top of that, the government approved a Tabligh Jumaat religious gathering of thousands of Muslims in Sri Petaling, just outside Kuala Lumpur. This gathering infected hundreds of participants, and the virus spread all over the country. By early March, cases of infection had run into the thousands.

While the country was being ravaged by the virus, the political landscape was also ravaged by the few same-old-same-old players. Allies within the ruling coalition PH started plotting against each other. There was a breakaway, and the prime minister resigned. Some from the former prime minister's party immediately formed a coalition with the opposition, calling themselves Perikatan National (PN). They had an audience with the king, and a new government was formed. The former deputy in the ex–prime minister's party, who teamed up with the opposition, was appointed the new prime minister. The voters who voted PH into power just two years previously now termed PN the "backdoor government."

———

It is 10:15 a.m., and Mislan tells his assistant to go home, get some rest, and come back to the office around 3:00 in the afternoon. They'll go over the case and plan their moves.

"I'm sure Shahira has knocked off for the day. We need to see her and get copies of whatever she has. You've got her number?" Mislan asks.

"No, but I can get it from the station."

"Try and set a time we can meet up with her."

"OK, I will give her a call. What time's good?"

"Around 4, and it'll speed things up if she can have all the copies ready by then. Jo, if you pass any pharmacy on your way home, can you get some face masks? The pharmacy at my place ran out."

"Sure. See you at 3."

———

Driving out of Kuala Lumpur Police contingent headquarters, Mislan heads toward Jalan Imbi with Berjaya Times Square on his right. At the junction he makes a right onto Jalan Kampung Pandan. From there he hits the Middle Ring Road 2 (MRR2) all the way to the junction of Jalan Ukay Perdana. He makes a U-turn under the overpass back to MRR2 and up Jalan Wangsa 1. Since the attempt on his life, Mislan has avoided using Jalan Ukay Perdana to go home, especially at night.

He knows the probability of the killers using the same road for a second attempt is unlikely, but he just does not feel like driving by the spot where he almost lost his life.

His cell phone rings; it is Johan.

"Yes, Jo."

"Inspector Shahira will be in her office around 4:30 this afternoon. I told her it's OK, we'll meet her there."

"Good."

Since his son moved out to live with his mother, the three-room apartment had seemed too large for him alone. Several times he thought of getting a cat as a companion but pushed the idea aside. When he was still married, they had two cats named Putra and Prince. His ex-wife took them with her when she left. That is the trouble with divorce: amicable or hostile and painful. The wifey gets to take everything— kids, household items, pets —and leave you with the heartache and the kitchen sink. Anyway, there is no way he can care for a cat by himself. It would probably starve to death or run away the first opportunity it got. The only spaces he uses in the apartment are his bedroom to work and sleep and the kitchen to make coffee. He rarely cooks now; most of the time he will get takeout from a McDonald's or mamak restaurant. Mislan is not a fussy or big eater. He always says he eats to live, not lives to eat. He decides to stop at My Makan Café and get a pack of nasi lemak.

After showering and having his brunch, Mislan tries to get some sleep. After the incident, his habits changed. He now double-bolts the front door when he is home and does not remove the clip from his Berretta 9mm pistol before putting it in the drawer. It was indeed a life-changing experience.

———

Inspector Shahira is waiting in her office when Mislan and Johan arrive. Unlike his office, which is a general open space shared by all investigators and their assistants, Shahira shares a private room with another investigating officer. The office is small but very tidy and organized. Female officers tend to keep tidy and homely offices; it is just their nature.

Mislan takes the single guest chair in front of her desk and Johan pulls the guest chair from the empty IO's desk. He notices an open box of cupcakes. One of them is half-eaten. Shahira follows his line of vision and smiles.

"You want one?" she offers, holding up the box to Mislan and Johan.

Mislan declines, but Johan takes one.

"They're really good. Got them specially made by a friend," she says as she takes another bite of the cupcake.

"Any update?" Mislan asks.

"Nope," Shahira answers, swallowing and shaking her head. "D9 taking the case?"

"Looks like it. Did you manage to get any ID from their prints?"

"Nothing, no record in our system or National Registration. I made copies of the report and crime scene photos," she says, tapping a file. "That's about all I've got for now. The bodies were sent to GH, but I haven't checked when the autopsies will be conducted. You want to attend?"

"Yes, there's something I need the pathologist to look at."

Shahira raises her eyebrows questioningly.

"The markings on the victims' wrists," Mislan clarifies. "The bullets and drugs?"

"Sent to Ballistic and Chemist. Copies of requests are in the file."

"Is that area inhabited by foreigners?" Johan asks.

"Why?"

"The neighbor said some Myanmaris, or whatever the Myanmar nationals are called, visited the house," Johan replies.

"You can say they're everywhere now, I mean the foreigners. Bangla, Myanmar, Indon, Nepalese, Thai. The Selayang wholesale wet market is the biggest employer of foreign labor and is close by, so I'm sure Sentul is infested with them. I'm sure you heard of the Myanmar refugees demanding that Selayang be given to them," Shahira says in disgust. "They got the cheek to tell Malaysians to vacate Selayang and hand it over to them. Who do they think they are!"

"Let's not get into that, OK?" Mislan suggests.

"Sorry. You think the victims are foreigners?"

"You said no record from NRD. What else could they be? Have you informed Narco?"

"Yes. As I said, they're not biting."

"Who is Narco chief here?"

"ASP Thomas."

"You traced the landlord?"

"I've assigned a detective to check with the Land Office for the title deed."

"Any detective assigned to this case?" Johan asks.

"No one specific, but they're all told to look into it," Shahira replies, sounding disappointed. "By the way, what made D9 decide to lead?"

Mislan lays out the observations made by his detective sergeant and himself of the crime scene, the anomalies and curiosities.

"Wow, you guys got all that just by looking at the crime scene," Shahira remarks. "I'm impressed—no, I'm super impressed."

Mislan and Johan laugh at Shahira's expression.

———

While Mislan enjoys his nicotine break by the car shed, Johan disappears to chat with some of the detectives. Ten minutes later Johan reappears, and Mislan tells him to drive to the crime scene.

"What's there?"

"I'd like to look at it in daylight. Maybe walk through the house one more time. What did you find out?"

"Nothing much. One of them said that area is crawling with foreign workers, mainly Bangla and Myanmar. A lot of complaints over the years by the local residents, but the numbers kept growing. What Inspector Shahira said was probably right, the close proximity to the Selayang wholesale wet market."

Recently, there has been a lot of hoo-ha about the Rohingyas, a sort of xenophobia fueled by irresponsible individuals on social media. Mislan doesn't know what sparked it, but the hostility is obvious. Malaysians have always been hospitable and charitable. The Rohingyas and other foreign immigrants had been living harmoniously among Malaysians for years. Then suddenly, this outburst of hostility.

As they approach the housing development, Mislan notices several sundry shops that look to him as being operated by Bangladeshi or Myanmarese people, most likely the Rohingya from Rakhine state. Several foreign-looking women are milling outside dressed in bright flowery dresses and tudung. A few are carrying babies or toddlers on their hips. Parking in front of the crime scene house, Mislan notices an abandoned shed partially hidden by a shady tree and hedges at the end of the road.

Stepping out of the car, he walks over to the shed.

"Jo," he calls, "come take a look at this."

Johan approaches and stands beside his boss. It is an open shed with zinc roofing and no wall, probably an abandoned car shed. The floor is hard earth. In one corner closest to the hedges, there are some flattened cardboard boxes arranged for sitting or sleeping. Cigarette butts, tinfoil, half-bent spoons, burnt-out candles, and empty drink cans are scattered next to them. Johan points.

"Drug den. There, can you see the disposed syringes, candles, and spoons? Hotel California."

Mislan looks at his assistant questioningly.

"The Eagles, you know the song 'Hotel California'? The master's chamber."

Mislan nods. "Oh. Worth paying a late-night visit, see if it's still in use."

"I'll get Sentul standby detectives to check it out."

————

As they turn to walk to their car, they see a blue Mazda CX 5 SUV pull up behind their vehicle. Mislan grabs Johan's arm, signaling for him to hang back. They pretend to chat while keeping an eye on the SUV. The driver kills the engine, and an oversized Chinese man in his mid-forties steps out. From the passenger side emerges a similarly heavyset Chinese woman, also in her forties. They walk over to the D9 officers' car, giving it a good look inside and out. Satisfied it's empty, and no one hiding in it, they walk to the front gate of the crime scene house.

Mislan nods to Johan, and they step apart from each other and walk to the two individuals.

"You take the woman, I'll take the man," Mislan says.

"Why don't you take the woman?" Johan asks.

"Because you're better with women," Mislan says with a grin.

"Yeah, right."

The two individuals walk through the gate and the officers step up to it, blocking their exit. The two turn to look at them, with surprise but mainly fear on their faces.

"Excuse me," Mislan says, "may I know what you're doing here?"

"I'm the house owner," replies the woman defiantly. "Who are you *ah*?"

"I'm Inspector Mislan, and this is Detective Sergeant Johan. This is a crime scene. Do you have permission to enter the premises?"

The two look at each other, then back to the officers.

"We need permission, *meh*?" asks the woman, defiance turning to confusion. "This is my house."

"Yes, but it's a crime scene. Do you see the yellow tape with the words POLICE LINE across the front door? What are you going to do, take it off?"

They look at the front door and then back at the officers, now unsure of their response.

"You said you're police, show me your ID," the woman says, a hint of defiance returning.

The two officers show their authority cards and in return ask them for their identity cards. The man takes his out from his wallet and the woman from her purse, handing them over to Mislan.

"Mr. Tan, who was the house rented to?" Mislan asks.

In the meantime, Johan snaps a photo of the two identity cards and WhatsApps it to Inspector Shahira, with a note saying the woman is the landlord.

"A Malay man, Ismail Sabri. I have his details back at my shop," Tan says, speaking for the first time.

"Do you have a business card?"

They both hand him their cards: *Tan Kim Tong Hardware, Kepong.* Mislan hands them over to Johan, who again snaps a photo of them and WhatsApps it to Inspector Shahira. He returns the identity cards and pockets the business cards.

"But Ismail doesn't live here, does he?" Mislan asks.

"He said his workers stay here," Mrs. Tan replies.

"Have you met the workers?" Johan asks.

Mr. and Mrs. Tan shake their heads.

"Did Ismail say what nationality his workers were?" Johan asks.

"He said Malay from Kelantan."

"Do you know what Ismail does for a living?"

"He owns a stall in the Selayang wet market."

"What made you come here today?" Mislan asks, curious.

"My wife heard over the news of the killing in this neighborhood. She called her friend staying across the road and was told it was in our house."

"When was this, the news?"

"The five o'clock news, Chinese news."

"OK, why do you need to go inside?"

"We just want to see if anything is damaged or stolen," Mr. Tan says.

"Guess you can follow us. Don't touch anything and stay close to us," Mislan instructs.

"OK, thank you."

"After this, I need you to contact Inspector Shahira from Sentul Police. She needs to record your statement. Detective Sergeant Johan will give you her number."

———

In the daylight, the living room looks shittier than Mislan remembers from last night. Cigarette butts, snack wrappers, and crumpled paper are strewn carelessly on the floor and under the settees and coffee table. The walls are marked by handprints and cracking paint. Mrs. Tan almost faints when she steps into the house. Her face contorts as if a knife was plunged into her chest.

"*Aiyo!*" she cries out. "Like this one ah my house."

She dashes to the back of the house and comes back with a broom.

"People or animal stay here, look!" she exclaims, starting to sweep the floor.

"Mrs. Tan, please stop. Don't do anything until you get clearance from Inspector Shahira," Mislan tells her firmly.

"Look, look how they spoil my house!"

"I understand, but this is a crime scene, and until it is returned to you, it has to remain intact."

Mr. Tan says something to his wife in Chinese, and she goes back to the kitchen to return the broom.

"Sorry, Inspector," Mr. Tan apologizes and adds, "you know *lah* women: they love their properties more than their husbands."

"It's OK, but I don't recommend you go upstairs. It's a little messy."

"They break things?"

"No, it's all bloody."

"Oh . . ."

"Is this house rented furnished?"

"No, just beds and one closet in the master bedroom."

"Then there's nothing that's worth stealing?"

"No, I suppose not."

"You can have my word that the house is intact, nothing broken or damaged except for the front door lock."

"Thank you."

———

Mislan and Johan proceed upstairs. The smell of dried blood hits them as they're about to reach the top landing. With the windows shut since they left the scene, the air is stale and clammy. Again Johan notices the slight hesitation in his boss's step, almost missing the landing. Johan raises his hand to break his boss's fall, but Mislan recovers quickly enough to plant his feet on the landing.

"You OK?" Johan asks.

Mislan nods without saying anything.

Standing at the master bedroom doorway, Johan asks what they are looking for.

"I don't know, just wanted to be sure we didn't miss anything. Jo, can you open the windows?"

Mislan stands in front of the clothes closet and examines its contents. Again he pats every shirt and trouser to feel for something in them; nothing. He senses someone at the bedroom door and sees Mrs. Tan standing there. Her face ashen, jaws gaping and eyes bulging, staring at the patch of dry blood. She utters something in Chinese, repeating "suwei" several times, which Mislan knows to mean "jinxed" or "cursed." Probably she's saying the house is now cursed, and no one would want to rent it anymore—loss of revenue.

"Mrs. Tan, I told you not to come up," Mislan says, stepping toward her.

Mr. Tan appears by her side, apologizes to Mislan, and drags her away, talking to her in Chinese. Mislan waves his apology off and turns back to what he was doing.

"Jo, help me push the closet away from the wall."

Together they move the closet from the wall and check the back— nothing, just cobwebs and dust.

"Can you try and see the top?" Mislan asks.

"I'll need to get a chair or something to stand on."

"If you stand on the bed, can you see the top?" Mislan suggests.

"Let's try."

"Anything?"

"Just dust."

They examine the guest rooms and come out with nothing.

"Who the hell are these guys?" Mislan sighs. "Even if they're wet market workers, I'm sure there'd be something in the house to indicate who they were. Family photos, girlfriends, friends, anything. Let's check the kitchen."

The kitchen is bare; no stove, fridge, pots, pans, or cooking utensils. Not even a knife or things to make coffee or tea. Under the sink, a large plastic shopping bag filled to the brim with Styrofoam containers and the oil-paper wrappers commonly used to pack meals. Beside it is a stack of empty drinking water bottles.

On exiting the crime scene, they reattach the police barrier tape to the front door and ask Mr. Tan to WhatsApp them the details of the renter, Ismail Sabri, when they get back to their shop. Mislan reminds Mr. Tan to call Inspector Shahira, too.

7

THE SUN IS SETTING when Mislan and his detective sergeant leave the crime scene. The roadside food stall at the turnoff leading out of the housing development is open. Mislan tells Johan to stop for a cup of coffee and to do some poking. The instant Johan pulls up by the stall, half the customers pay for their drinks and meals, taking off on motorbikes and bicycles. Johan glances at his boss, mouthing the word "PATI," meaning "foreign immigrants without permits"—illegals.

"They can spot police the moment they lay eyes on us," Mislan says with a smile.

"I think the first training they received from their employers upon arrival in the country was—How to Spot a Policeman."

The two officers laugh, step out of the car, and take their seats at one of the makeshift tables. Johan waves the operator over, and they place their orders, one iced black coffee and one iced tea. The operator asks if they want anything to eat, and both decline. The stall looks unhygienic, smelling of the stench from the monsoon drain next to it. The operator himself looks like he hasn't stepped under a shower for the past week, with his clothes unwashed for the same length of time. When he brings their drinks, Johan asks him if he is a local.

After pretending not to have heard the question, turning his head to other customers as if he heard a nonexistent order, the operator admits he isn't a local.

"Bangla?" Johan asks.

"Rohingya . . . Muslim."

"Where's your UNHCR card?" Mislan asks.

"Sorry, boss, not get yet."

"Whose stall is this?" Johan asks.

"My boss, Malay man."

"What's his name, his phone number?" Johan insists.

"Sorry, boss, left at home," the operator says, shaking his head.

"Bullshit!" Johan snaps. "What's your name?"

"Mohib."

The officers are aware they're being watched by several customers. Mohib is starting to get nervous and jittery. The officers feel that to continue questioning him may put his life in danger. Johan tells Mohib to give them his cell phone number. He hands Mohib a ten ringgit note to pay for their drinks, which he knows will require the operator to go to the counter for change. He softly tells Mohib to write his phone number on a piece of paper and give it to him together with the change. Mohib nods. When the stall operator hands back his change and cell phone number, Johan asks what time the stall closes.

"Around 1 or 2 a.m. Start at 6 p.m."

"I'll call you after you close or before you open, so that people don't see you talking to us."

———

On the drive back to the office, Johan makes a call to Sentul police. He asks to be connected to the standby detective. He informs the standby detective of the abandoned shed at the end of the road, and asks if they could check it out at midnight.

"Anything in particular you need us to check on?" the detective asks.

"See if the place is an active den. If it is, ask the ones there if they saw or heard anything last night."

"If they did?"

"Hold them and inform me, doesn't matter what time."

"OK, Sarge."

As his assistant is terminating the call, Mislan asks him what the odds are that the detective will follow up on his request. Johan smirks.

"Have some faith, will you?" Johan jests.

"Unlike you, I don't have much of it to spare anymore. Now I give it sparingly. Why don't you ask our standby to check the place out?"

"I'll check to see if they can spare the time."

————

They reach the office at 7:40 p.m., and only Inspector Tee is around. He has a green surgical face mask over his mouth and is engrossed in his laptop. Seeing Mislan, Tee points to his desk saying there is a pack of face masks for him and Johan.

"You're required to wear them, ma'am's instructions," he says.

"To wear them or to wear them correctly?" Mislan asks.

Tee gazes at him questioningly.

"You wear the mask to cover your mouth and nose, not just your mouth. The way you're wearing it is like wearing underwear covering your balls with your dick hanging outside," Mislan says with a laugh.

"Yeah, right."

Setting down his backpack, Mislan takes the pack of face masks and hands some to Johan.

"You keep them. I bought some on my way home earlier. They're in the car, totally forgot about them," Johan says.

"How's business?" Mislan asks Tee.

"Slow, just the way I like it."

Mislan's phone rings; it is Inspector Shahira informing him the autopsy will be conducted tomorrow around 10 a.m.

"You're attending?" Mislan asks.

"No, I've got a court case. Can you attend for me?"

"Sure. I need to speak with the pathologist anyway. Anything specific you want me to ask the pathologist to look at?"

"No."

Mislan tells his assistant to knock off and get some rest. Johan tells him he wants to check on the standby detectives, see if they can swing around to Taman Sentul Jaya to check on the abandoned shed.

———

Mislan is having one of his frequent nightmares when his cell phone rings, mercifully yanking him out of it. It is his assistant, saying the standby detectives Syed and Aziz have picked up a druggie from the shed. He may have some information about that night. The druggie is currently detained at the office. The phone screen shows a time of 1:45 a.m.

"I'm on my way to the office," Johan says.

"OK, I'll meet you there."

Terminating the call, Mislan takes a sip of cold coffee to wet his throat, splashes water on his face, steps into jeans, and puts on a polo shirt. Lighting a cigarette, he grabs his handgun and backpack. Driving to the office on the quiet lonely road, he reflects on the nightmare he was having. He was lying in the hospital bed, with Johan, Fie, his ex-wife Lynn, and Daniel by his side. They'd just been informed by the doctor that he wouldn't make it. Dr. Safia and his ex-wife, Lynn, were verbally attacking Johan, while his son held his hand, tears rolling down his cheeks.

"Why didn't you inform me?" Fie asked angrily. "Why did you wait until he was dying?"

The same was demanded of his assistant by his ex-wife, Lynn, who added, "Don't you think his son has the right to know, to be with his father?"

Mislan could see the two women were furious, and his assistant was distraught because of their accusations and blame-throwing, but he couldn't speak, couldn't defend Johan, and couldn't answer for him.

"Inspector Mislan insisted he didn't want any of you to be notified. He doesn't want any of you placed in danger. He said the killer is still out there and may be watching. With you coming around to visit him, your lives will be in danger," Johan answered apologetically. "I'm sorry. He made me promise."

He doesn't know if Dr. Safia and his ex-wife accepted his assistant's explanation because he was awakened by the ringing of his cell phone. In a funny way he feels disappointed he doesn't know the ending of the dream—what happened to Dr. Safia and his ex-wife. That would have been the first time they met—would they become friends?

———

Parking his car, Mislan receives a WhatsApp message from Johan saying they are in Interview Room One. Stopping at his office, he sees the shift investigating officer, Inspector Tee, napping and decides not to wake him. He quietly drops his backpack, puts on a face mask, and takes a spare one for his assistant. He isn't taking any chances, especially with a druggie whose immune system is weak. Entering Interview Room 1, he finds a scrawny Malay male who is about forty or maybe younger—it's hard to tell with addicts, with their bodies eaten away by drugs. He smells like rotting fish, and Johan is sitting across him without a face mask. Mislan hands the face mask to his assistant and picks up the identity card belonging to the druggie from the table. His name is Adham Baba, thirty-two years of age, hailing from Kota Bharu, Kelantan.

"So, you bought the Mcdonald from the doctor?" Johan says as Mislan takes a seat beside him and indicates to his assistant to put the face mask on.

"Yeah, we call him the doctor 'cos he hangs around the clinic across the road," Adham answers.

"Why are you asking him about buying McDonald's?" Mislan is baffled.

"It's not the fast food, it's the drug. They call it 'Mcdonald' without the s, one of the three Ms—Molly, Mcdonald, and Magic Mushroom," Johan explains. Seeing his boss's confused look, Johan adds, "I'll explain later."

Adham listens with interest and asks, "You guys aren't from Narcotic, are you?"

Johan gives him a shut-the-fuck-up stare. Mislan lights a cigarette, and the druggie asks if he can light one too. Johan points to the NO

SMOKING sign on the back of the door. The druggie indicates Mislan with a snide slant of his head as if saying, *He can.*

"He's my boss," Johan says simply in response. "Now tell us what you saw that night."

"You mean the night the two guys got bumped off?" Adham says, his eyes shifting back to Mislan.

"Yes, the night the two guys got popped. You tell me a good story, maybe my boss here will let you smoke," Johan tempts him.

"That night I scored some Mcdonald from the doctor. See, earlier I sort of stumbled into some cash and decided to treat myself."

"What time was this?" Mislan asks.

"I don't know, not like I have a watch," Adham replies, holding up his wrists for the officers to see.

"OK, go on."

"Then I went to my resting place, you know, the place where your people picked me up for no reason. I wasn't doing anything illegal, that's where I rest for the night."

"Then what?" Mislan snaps.

"I was resting, minding my own business when this car light shone into my place. Damn rude, don't you think? First I thought it was the Narcotic pricks doing roundups, so I snuck into the bushes next to my pad. After a moment the headlights went off, but no one came to check out my place. I watched from the bushes and saw two men came out. They went to the gate of that house, and I couldn't see them anymore from where I was hiding. So, I thought it must be a late-night deal going down or something, and I got back into my pad to rest."

"That's it?" Mislan asks, sounding disappointed.

"Can I smoke?" the druggie asks.

"Yeah, go ahead," Mislan says.

Adham takes a bent cigarette from his pocket and lovingly strokes it several times. When it straightens and looks like a smokable cigarette, he asks for a light. Mislan pushes his disposable lighter across the table. Adham lights his cigarette, and before the druggie can put the lighter into his pocket, Mislan asks for it back.

"Then what happened?" Johan asks.

"After, I don't know, thirty minutes, maybe less, I noticed movements at the gate, and I saw the two men coming out. One of them was carrying a bag, like a backpack but quite big. Like the Bangla use for traveling. The last man looked up at the house before he entered the car."

"Then?"

"Then they were gone."

"Did you get the car number, make and model?" Mislan asks.

"The lights were shining toward me, how could I see the number? Then when the car turned to leave, it was dark."

"What about the make, color?"

"It was a . . . what do you call it . . . S, S—"

"SUV," Johan prompts.

"Yes, SUV, black. Like Toyota Harrier or Lexus."

"What about the men?" Mislan asks.

"Eh?"

"The men, tall, short, fat?" Mislan prompts, "Malay, Chinese, Indian?"

"About his size," Adham says, chin-gesturing to Johan. "What race, I don't know, can't see their faces, and they wore black." He takes a last drag on his cigarette, or maybe the cigarette butt, drops it to the floor, and adds, "They wore caps, black caps."

"Did you hear anything when the men were inside the house?" Mislan continues.

"Like what?"

"Loud shouting or noise."

"No, my pad is too far to hear them. Ohhh," the druggie says, dragging out the syllable, "you mean like bang-bang?"

"Yes, did you?"

"Nope."

"When all this happened, had you taken your Mcdonald?" Mislan asks.

"Yes."

"So you were high, hallucinating," Mislan suggests.

"You really don't know shit about the shit, do you? The shit don't make you hallucinate, the shit makes you sharp, alert and energized. It's when you don't get your daily dose that you lose all the good qualities in life." Adham grins ruefully, "You should give it a try, may help you think better."

Mislan and Johan laugh.

"You know the two guys that were killed?"

"No way, I know pushers, but those guys were way above street pushers, they're dealers. Big-time, I heard. People like me or pushers aren't in their circle of friends, if you know what I mean."

"Are they locals?"

"I don't know, but I heard they're Myanmar, Rohingya."

———

When Mislan and Johan return to their office, Inspector Tee is nowhere to be seen. *Must be on a callout,* Mislan guesses. Johan makes two mugs of coffee and brings them to Mislan's desk.

"What do you make of the info?" Johan asks.

"Interesting but nothing to work on. Jo, why don't you chat with the stall operator? The SUV had to come in through the junction and pass the stall. Maybe he remembers seeing the SUV."

"It's too late now, he's probably closed. I'll give him a call in the morning."

Mislan lights a cigarette.

"You think it's a drug war or something?" Johan asks.

"Could be, but I don't think so. If they were drug-related killings, why were the drugs not taken? That'd be the reward, don't you think?"

"The druggie said one of them was carrying a backpack when they came out. What do you think was in it?"

Mislan shrugs.

"Any guesses?"

"Nope."

"They were dressed in black with black caps, like a raiding party in a movie."

Mislan laughs. "Yeah, like a movie raiding party."

8

THE KUALA LUMPUR GENERAL Hospital (KLGH) is on a triangular piece of prime land fronting Jalan Pahang, Jalan Pekeliling, and Jalan Raja Muda. One can access it through any of these roads. KLGH is one of the oldest general hospitals in the country. When Mislan was growing up with his grandmother on Jalan Raja Muda, originally named Princes Road, GH was already in existence. He remembers playing field hockey in the open-air stadium that used to be called TPCA but has changed its name to something or other. New extensions and buildings have been and are still being added to the old hospital main block. Health is big business nowadays.

From where they are coming, Johan decides to drive through Kampung Baru onto Jalan Raja Muda into the hospital compound. Like in most government establishments, finding parking is murder. Johan decides to park by the roadside in front of the police post, now upgraded to a station. He pops into the station, identifies himself, and informs the corporal on duty that they are going to the Medical Forensic Department and that his car is parked in front.

He leads Mislan through the Emergency & Trauma Center, passing through a maze of corridors and out on the other side of the building.

"How do you know all these rat routes?" Mislan asks, amazed.

"My MPV days. Used to come here a lot getting details of accident and injury cases and visiting the morgue," Johan answers without breaking his step. "The morgue used to be over there, but now with the new label of Medical Forensic, they moved to that building. Perhaps they needed more space and to create a professional image. I know you prefer HUKM, but this place here is just as good."

Hospital Universiti Kebangsaan Malaysia (HUKM) is a teaching hospital under the National University of Malaysia. Dr. Safia, or Fie, was Mislan's lover after his wife left him and was a pathologist in HUKM. Johan remembers about a year ago, after the conclusion of their case monikered Soulless, she vanished without a goodbye. When asked, his boss just shrugged it off. Even when he was shot, Johan wanted to track her down to inform her, but Mislan insisted he didn't want her to be told. His excuse: the killer was still out there, and he didn't want her endangered. Johan avoided mentioning that she was the reason his boss preferred HUKM to KLGH..

As they cross to the Medical Forensic building, Mislan's cell phone rings. The caller is Rotziah, or Audi for short, an annoyingly persistent television investigative journalist with Astro Awani.

"Yes," Mislan answers.

"Inspector, how are you? Long time no hear," Audi says in her usual cheery manner. "I heard you're the lead in a double murder case."

"What else you did hear?"

"Your publicity-junkie OCCI gave a press statement yesterday evening saying it was drug-related, a drug deal went bad. Is it true?"

"Since he said it, why didn't you ask him during the press conference?" Mislan asks mockingly.

"You know better than to question his statement. I'm sure you have lots of experience in that area," Audi replies.

Mislan can hear her chuckle.

"I don't have anything at the moment, why don't you hassle Inspector Shahira from Sentul Police?"

"OK, thanks, but I still want to hear from you."

At the Medical Forensic building, Johan introduces himself to the receptionist and asks if she could check the schedule for their case. He gives her the case number and she tells him Dr. Mariam will be performing the autopsy in Room 3.

Autopsy Room 3 is at the end of the floor, and as the officers enter the room, they are smothered by the omnipresent smell of antiseptic. Johan notices his boss cringe as the smell hits them. He figures it reminds his boss of his stay in the ICU. A naked body except for the crotch area, which is covered with a piece of white cloth, lies on the cold stainless steel autopsy table. An attendant making last-minute arrangements looks up at them.

"May I help you?" he asks.

"I'm Detective Sergeant Johan, and this is Inspector Mislan from D9. We're here to witness the autopsy of the Sentul double murder."

"You may stand over there, Dr. Mariam will be here shortly," the attendant says and continues working.

The side door opens and a woman dressed in green hospital attire, with a full-body plastic apron, wet boots, surgical gloves, bandanna, mask, and protective goggles, enters. It seems to Mislan like she went a little overboard with the PPE, perhaps because of the COVID-19 pandemic. The attendant nods toward the D9 officers and tells her where they are from. Dr. Mariam is probably in her forties; it is difficult to judge with the PPE covering her face. She is slightly on the heavy side and speaks with a firm commanding voice. Probably was an army cadet during her college days. Mislan steps forward and introduces himself and his assistant.

"According to the autopsy request, Inspector Shahira is the investigating officer," Dr. Mariam says, stepping to the autopsy table.

"Yes, she is, but D9 is leading," Mislan says, moving closer to her.

"D9, that's Special Investigations, isn't it? What's special about this case?"

"At the moment it's all circumstantial, we're still digging."

"Any special thing you want me to examine? Inspector Shahira did not indicate anything."

"If possible, could you examine the wrists? I thought there were abrasion markings on them," Mislan requests.

Dr. Mariam lifts the deceased's right wrist, examining it closely.

"The request listed them as John Does. Have they been identified?" Dr. Mariam asks as she examines the wrists. "Raman, bring me the camera," she instructs the skinny Indian attendant. Dr. Mariam points to the part of the wrists where she wants photos to be taken, and Raman the attendant snaps them.

"Doc, can you view the other one too?" Mislan asks.

"I usually do one at a time, but since you seem to be in a hurry to be somewhere else, OK. Raman, bring in the other body."

As the skinny attendant leaves the room, Dr. Mariam says, "Yes, these are contusion marks, looks like ligature marks, probably caused when the wrists were tied together. Let's see if the other John Doe has similar markings." Dr. Mariam pulls the magnifying glass that is attached to a flexible arm, switches on the light, and examines the wrists more closely. "There are some tiny impressions, like groove markings, embedded in the skin. Wonder what could've caused them."

———

Leaving the hospital, Johan makes a detour through Kampung Baru to Jalan Raja Muda Musa. Mislan asks where they're going. His assistant says since it is close to lunchtime, they might as well have lunch before going back to the office. There is a famous Nasi Padang Asli restaurant on Jalan Raja Muda Musa. Kampung Baru, which translates literally as New Village, is a Malay Reserve. This means only Malays can own the land within it. The area is serviced by a maze of narrow roads, some accessible only by motorbike and on foot. The dwellings are a shamble, with many made from brick and wood. Nothing featuring traditional Malay design. Now more and more modern-design concrete ones are being built to replace the old wooden dwellings or squeezed in between them. Most of the houses are in close proximity to one another, with the windows giving a view into the neighbor's house.

Mislan remembers a documentary of Kampung Baru on *Nat Geo* featuring the traditional Malay architecture and cuisine—well, it is not entirely true now. Probably what makes Kampung Baru special is its location, nestled in the heart of a bustling city surrounded by modern structures like the Twin Towers only a stone's throw away. But the whole area is now populated by outsiders, mainly from the East Coast and Indonesia. As far as Mislan knows, the original inhabitants of Kampung Baru, those he grew up with, have long since moved to more modern housing estates or satellite towns.

"OK. You spoke to Mohib the stall operator?" Mislan asks.

"Yes, he said around the time he was closing up, a vehicle drove by heading in the direction of the crime scene," Johan answers.

"That'll be about, what, 1 a.m.?"

"Yes, he closes his stall at 1. After about thirty minutes or so, the same vehicle passed by exiting the housing development. He doesn't know what make or model of the vehicle, but it's a black SUV."

"Number?" Mislan asks, not really expecting a positive response.

"No, he didn't catch it."

"So the druggie was telling the truth," Mislan admits aloud. "Black SUV, two men in black, one carrying a bag when they left the scene. What could all that mean?"

"Dr. Mariam said the shot to the back of the head was the kill-shot. Then why the second shot?" Johan asks, puzzled.

"I don't know, a ritual maybe."

"Eh?"

"Jo, we need to know more about the vics. By knowing them, hopefully we can know the motive for the killings. I need you to chat with the Sentul detectives and see what we can learn. I'll pay Narco a visit, see if they have something on the vics."

The lunch crowd at Nasi Padang Asli restaurant is growing. Mislan and Johan share a table with two other customers. They decide not to be served but to serve themselves from the dishes arrayed buffet-style. Mislan has taken beef rendang, half a salted egg, and some fried eggplant with chili. Johan, on the other hand, heaps his plate with every dish that can fit on it. Mislan looks at his assistant's plate with amazement.

"I love the food here, everything is so good," Johan says when he notices his boss's gaze. "Just had to taste every dish I can without overflowing my plate."

The waiter comes over, makes a mental calculation of the food they are having, asks for their drink orders, writes the price of the meal on a tiny piece of paper, and places it on the table. Mislan has to admit Johan was right: the dishes do taste good.

———

Back at the office, Mislan makes a call to Chew, the forensics supervisor based at the Federal Crime Forensic Department. Chew has worked several cases with him, and they have a good working relationship, full of mutual respect.

"Chew, how're you?"

"Inspector, nice to hear from you again. Busy as usual but otherwise fine, thank you," Chew says in his soft-spoken voice. "How may I assist you?"

"I don't know if you can, because it's with Ballistic."

"Oh."

"Anyway, if you know those guys, I just need you to ask them about the bullets in the Sentul shooting. There were three bullets recovered at the scene, another one will be submitted later after the pathologist cuts it out of the victim. All I need to know for now is: Are all the bullets from a single gun?"

"I read about the case, two days back, right? You're the lead?"

"Yes."

"I know the super there. Let me give him a call. Let you know soon as I find out."

"Thanks, Chew."

"No problem, stay safe."

"Yeah, you too."

Mislan notices since the COVID-19 pandemic, "stay safe" seems to be the new normal in parting words, just like the parting words of "Sawadee Kap" when he was in Thailand.

———

Johan is away in Sentul trying to dig up any information he can get from the detectives there. While waiting for his assistant to return, Mislan decides to visit the Narcotic Criminal Investigation Division (NCID), which is on the sixth floor of the old building where D9 is housed. He takes the emergency staircase down, and as he walks down the corridor to the NCID office, he spots a familiar face emerging from the elevator lobby.

"Hey, Mislan," Inspector Kumar calls, "where're you headed?"

"Your unit."

Inspector Kumar gazes at him questioningly. "Meeting?"

"No, just a courtesy call," Mislan teases with a chuckle. "Need to speak to someone about the drug activities in Sentul."

"Sentul is under my watch. What's it about?" he asks, sounding rather wary.

Police officers are very territorial and suspicious creatures, especially when it comes to inter-division matters. Instead of working together, they are always super alert and defensive when officers from other divisions start poking their noses into their territory. Their first impression is that the officer is trying to find fault, to hang blame on them for whatever.

"Let's go to your office and talk," Mislan suggests.

Mislan can feel the anxiety oozing from Kumar as they walk to his office. Kumar has an office to himself. Once inside, he asks what Mislan wants to know about Sentul.

"You heard of the shooting a couple of nights back, Taman Sentul Jaya?" Mislan gets straight to the point.

"I read the case summary, two men right?"

"Yes, and the IO found three packs of drugs."

"Yeah, methamphetamine, amphetamine, ketamine."

"Do you know of these people, I mean the victims and their activities?"

"They've not been identified yet, right?"

"No, but do you have any intel on the trafficking activities in that area?"

"What do you need to know?"

"Any info on drug trafficking within and around the area that may assist me in identifying the victims."

"You know I can't do that without my boss's authorization," Kumar answers, wary of Mislan's request.

"OK, I'll get my boss to talk to your boss," Mislan says, standing up. At the door, Mislan turns to Kumar, flashes a smile, and says, "Look, I'm not using the info to make money."

Stepping out of the office, Mislan hears Inspector Kumar shout *"Fuck you!"* after him.

———

Walking up to his office, Mislan makes a call to his assistant.

"Jo, you still in Sentul?"

"Yes, talking with detectives here. Anything?"

"Can you swing over to Selayang and meet the tenant of the house? I'll WhatsApp you the address and phone number."

"Sure."

"Ask him who was staying in the house, and get their particulars."

"Done."

9

BACK IN THE OFFICE, he finds Inspector Reeziana, the shift investigating officer, is by herself. She looks up from her computer and points to the emergency staircase, their unofficial smoking area. Police buildings have long been designated smoke-free zones, which is absurd as most police officers are smokers—*at least the ones that are really working*, according to Mislan's hypothesis. Closing the door behind them, Mislan takes out a cigarette and hands the pack to Reeziana.

Lighting up, she asks, "What's eating you?"

"The case and the asshole at Narco," Mislan says, tilting his head and blowing out smoke like a steam locomotive chimney. "It just doesn't add up. The vics were killed, in my opinion executed, but nothing was taken except their personal belongings."

"Which asshole?"

Mislan shakes his head, not wishing to name names. Reeziana lets it slide.

"If you say it's an execution, I think it does add up. The killers went there to execute the vics, not rob them. So they did what they were supposed to do and that's it. Like pros."

"Yes, but why take their personal belongings—trophies?"

"No, not trophies. To buy time. If we don't know their identities, it makes it difficult for us to look for the motive. Takes away our starting point to conduct inquiry. In a murder investigation, the vic is where we start digging, where we connect the dots, establish leads. If we don't know the vics' identities, their families, friends, or associates, where do we start?"

Mislan sighs. "But why leave the drugs? It was in plain sight."

"My guess is, drugs are not their domain. How much do you think the drugs are worth, ten, fifteen K? That's a lot, but not like a hell of a lot. And if drugs are not their thing, they'll have to ditch them to a third party, which can link them to the killings. Fifteen K is not worth getting caught for murder."

"You think they take the vics' personal belongings to show proof to their client that the job was done?" Mislan asks.

"No, that wasn't the reason. As I said, the reason is to rob us of a starting point. I think your best lead for identifying the vics is through the landlord; he has to know who was staying in the house."

"It was rented to a Malay guy, Ismail Sabri, who runs a stall at the Selayang wholesale wet market. Jo's locating him. Hopefully, we can get some leads as to who the vics were."

———

The front desk clerk pokes his head into the emergency staircase landing, informing them Superintendent Samsiah wishes to see all officers and assistant investigators in the meeting room in five minutes. Reeziana asks the clerk what it is about. The clerk just shrugs and leaves them.

"What do you think?" Reeziana asks. "Did you do something to piss her off?"

"Not yet, but why do you think it's me every time ma'am is pissed off?" Mislan asks, annoyed by her assumption.

"Only you have the talent for that," Reeziana answers with a grin. "Not to mention the guys up there," she continues, jerking her head to the ceiling.

Mislan knows she's referring to the Office in Charge of Criminal Investigation, or OCCI to them, Senior Assistant Commissioner of Police (SAC) Baharuddin Mohd. Sidek. Mislan had stepped on the OCCI's toes several times, and if not for Superintendent Samsiah's firm way of standing up for him, he would have lost his job several times over.

"What can I say, I'm blessed," Mislan answers with a swagger.

Other officers and their assistants are already seated in the meeting room when Reeziana and Mislan enter. They all look alien and funny with their face masks on.

"Afternoon, doctors," Mislan jokes.

Before anyone can respond, Superintendent Samsiah appears behind him.

"Funny, very funny, Lan," Superintendent Samsiah says. "And why are you not wearing your face mask? Apart from being against policies and procedures, are you also immune to COVID-19?"

"No, ma'am."

"Then for the sake of the others, please put on your face mask," Samsiah instructs firmly.

Mislan leaves the meeting room and comes back wearing a face mask, to be greeted by smiles and grins hidden by the face masks of the officers and assistants. Mislan is surprised to see Assistant Superintendent of Police (ASP) Ghani, head of Special Projects, and his lapdog assistant present; probably a raid is in the pipeline.

"All the assistants are here except for Jo. Lan, where is he?" Samsiah asks.

"He's locating the house's tenant in Selayang."

"Selayang's in Selangor, can't you get them to assist? I don't want to get a call from their OCCI about us poking our nose into their state."

"I told Jo to get assistance from Selayang police," Mislan lies. It totally slipped his mind that the Selayang wholesale wet market is located in the State of Selangor.

Unlike in the United States or some other parts of the world, Malaysian police jurisdiction is nationwide. There is no such thing as federal, state, or district police jurisdiction. However, for the purpose of accountability, administration, and effectiveness, each state oversees the personnel and crimes within its own boundary. And it is a matter of policies and procedures as well as courtesy that personnel from one state do not just cross over to kick down doors without the host state being informed or involved. Bureaucracy—to Mislan, it is inhibiting and a load of crap.

"The wholesale wet market? Lan, message him now and tell him to put on his face mask. That place is one of the virus hotspots," Samsiah instructs.

Mislan nods and pretends to message his assistant on his phone.

"There is a strong possibility that the government, based on the advice of the Health Ministry, will be imposing a lockdown, or in this case Movement Control Order, MCO. The force has been put on notice and this'll involve the GD. Stations will be very short-staffed as most of them will be deployed to man roadblocks to enforce the MCO."

The officers and assistants look at each other. The GD mentioned refers to General Duty, uniformed personnel.

"From what I've heard, and this is not official yet, all nonessential businesses will be closed. That means no more late-night teh tarik or roti canai and nasi lemak. This information is not to be shared with your friends or acquaintances. It's for you to start buying your daily needs because you won't be able to do it like normal working people. Do you understand me?"

The officers and assistants nod.

"You are to wear your face mask at all times in the office or when on callout. Sanitize your hands when you enter or return to the office. Mislan, do you hear me?"

The head of Special Investigations stresses the last question, staring at her most incorrigible officer where policies and procedures are concerned.

"Yes, ma'am."

"Good. For now until otherwise informed, IO scheduling is as per roster. When the MCO's announced, officers and assistants that are not required to be in the office are to work from home. Your cell phones shall be active 24/7."

"When's it starting, this MCO?" Reeziana asks.

"I have a feeling it'll be sooner than later. Whenever it is, make your arrangements from today."

10

MISLAN'S CELL PHONE RINGS. It's Chew from Crime Forensics, telling him that from the preliminary examinations of the bullets recovered at the crime scene, they're from two different guns. All the bullets were 9mm. Ballistic hasn't completed the full examination, and once completed, they'll be able to tell him more.

The information gets Mislan thinking. *If it was an execution, why were two guns used? Were the victims executed simultaneously, one gun, one man? If so, why the second shot to the back? Except for the one bullet still in the victim, how do I know which bullet came from which victim? Would the Ballistic guys swab the bullets for traces of DNA to be matched with the victims? Probably not.*

Johan walks through the office door, all sweaty and smelling like he had slept with fish and chickens. When he passes Inspector Reeziana's desk, she remarks, "Eeuw, where the hell have you been?"

Johan frowns at her remark.

"Shouldn't you shower before coming in?" Reeziana jests.

Johan plonks onto a chair in front of his boss's desk. Mislan stares at him in anticipation.

"The minute I stepped into the marketplace, they made me. Their eyes never left me for a second," he gripes.

"Who?"

"The Rohingyas, who else? The place was crawling with them. When I walked between the stalls, they purposely stepped hard into puddles to splash me. Not a word of apology. They pretended to freshen the fish and chicken tables with water and splashed me again. It was bloody unnerving, and the worst part was when they shouted to each other in their language. By the tone, I knew it had something to do with me being there. Hell, that place made the hairs on my back stand up. It was like being in another country, the people, the language, the stinking smell."

Mislan laughs.

"We started it with our xenophobia, so what do you expect in return, a warm welcome and a hug?"

"Remember what Inspector Shahira said?" Johan asks.

"About what?"

"The Rohingya demanding that we all get out of Selayang and hand it over to them. Damn, from what I saw, Selayang's already theirs unless the government does something about it," Johan sneers.

Mislan ignores his assistant's remarks arising from his anger at how he was treated by the workers at the wholesale wet market.

"Did you get to locate the tenant?"

"Yes."

"And?"

"Ismail Sabri, age fifty-six, lives in Rawang, a fat man with a faded skullcap. He was a chicken wholesaler for almost two decades, since the old market. He said the house was rented under his name for one of his ex-workers by the name of Ajimullah Islam, a Rohingya refugee. About six months back, Ajimullah quit his job and asked if Ismail could lend his name to rent a house in Taman Sentul Jaya. Ajimullah wanted to start his own business and bring over his family: mother, wife, and children. He claimed that the house owner would only rent to locals, not refugees. So Ismail lent his name to the tenancy, charged Ajimullah an extra two hundred ringgit above the cost of rental. So far the rent payment has been prompt." Johan pauses, taking a deep breath, and turns to smell his sleeve before cupping his nose at his own odor.

"Doesn't he know it's dangerous, not to mention stupid, to lend his name to a tenancy agreement? What if the tenant defaults or does something to the house?" Mislan is amazed.

"I did ask him, but as usual I get the 'we-are-Muslim-we-got-to-help-each-other' bullshit."

"Well, when stupidity can't be explained, blame it on religion."

"Anyway, I showed him the vics' photos, and he pointed to this as Ajimullah," he continues, showing Mislan the photo on his phone. "He doesn't know the other vic."

"Does he have this Ajimullah's cell phone number?"

"Yes." Johan refers to his notepad. "I tried calling, but it's off."

"Have you checked out this Ismail?"

"I asked Rawang Police to check up on him. I'll call them later to see if they have anything on him."

"What about his other workers, do they know Ajimullah?"

"I don't know, I didn't ask. I mean, the way they acted, I doubt they'd talk to me."

"We need to talk to him again, find out more about the vics."

"In that case, I suggest we go there in the early morning. They start around 4 in the morning and close around 3 p.m."

"I'll meet you here around 4, 4:30 this morning. We'll get one of the standby detectives to come along."

It is almost 5 p.m. Mislan updates his assistant on Superintendent Samsiah's instructions and suggests they knock off for the day, do some grocery shopping, and get some rest.

"Yeah, I heard talk about this imminent MCO from some of the guys I hang out with. Did ma'am say when it would be implemented?"

"No, but she said it may be soon. Anyway, just keep it to yourself and stock up on necessities. And don't forget to wear the face mask, especially when ma'am is around," Mislan says with mirth.

On his way home, Mislan stops at the Giant supermarket close to his apartment to buy some eggs, bread, cigarettes, and a can or two of sardines. He is shocked to see the large crowd and the long queue. Although most of the customers are wearing face masks, they pay no heed to the much-talked-about "social distancing" of three feet apart. Walking in, he sees that almost all the shelves are empty. No bread, no eggs, no canned food, no instant noodles, no cookies, no toilet rolls, no most of everything. He picks up a pack of Nescafé and looks for sugar. No sugar. *Shit*, he curses under his breath, *so much for the secrecy of it all*. He guesses it is not only the police who got the heads-up on the impending MCO. After queuing for fifteen minutes at the express checkout counter, he asks for five packs of Sampoerna Hijau cigarettes. While waiting for the cashier, he notices the condom stand is also empty. *Malaysians are prepared for the lockdown, got their priorities right for home entertainment.*

After going home and showering, he makes a mug of black coffee and toasts two slices of bread. He spreads butter on the toast and sprinkles some sugar on them. Taking the coffee and toast to his bedroom, he switches on the television. Mislan is not a movie person; he only watches sports and news on TV. Most of the time he leaves the TV on so he can hear voices, which gives the illusion of not being alone and takes away some of the loneliness.

He notices a crawler on the TV screen saying the prime minister will be making a special announcement regarding COVID-19 at 8 p.m. *That has to be the MCO announcement*, he thinks. *The news must have leaked, hence the panic buying.* He takes a bite of toast and washes it down with coffee. Taking out his notepad, he goes through the notes on the Taman Sentul Jaya killings:

Two victims, identity unknown, one confirmed by tenancy holder as his ex-worker Ajimullah Islam, a Myanmar national, UNHCR Rohingya refugee.

Both victims shot twice, identical pattern, once to back of the head, once between shoulder blades.

Two different 9mm guns used but unsure if one gun was used on one victim & another gun on other victim or both guns used on both victims.

Three bullets recovered outside the bodies and one bullet recovered from a body.

Victims' belongings like cell phones, wallets & laptops (if any), were missing, believed removed by the killers.

About three pounds of illegal drugs were recovered from crime scene, placed in clear view on bed of one of the victims.

Pathologist confirmed abrasions which look like rope burns on both victims' wrists. There were minuscule impression marks on the rope burn markings, can barely be seen with naked eyes. Pathologist cannot say for certain what caused the impression marks.

Adham, a druggie, saw two men arrive in black SUV around 1 a.m. and go into the house. They came out about 30 minutes later carrying a backpack. The druggie could not tell their ethnicity or what they look like, only that they were about five feet, seven inches tall (about Johan's body build).

The druggie's info corroborated by the roadside stall operator Mojib, who claimed a black SUV entered development about the same time and left about 30 min later.

Anomalies:

No one, not even neighbor, heard any gunshot fired by the killers.

Why vics' car and motorbike not taken?

"Shit, Lan, you dumb asshole. The car and motorbike could lead you to their identity," Mislan chides himself. He dials Inspector Shahira's cell phone number, and after three rings, she answers.

"Shahira, Mislan, sorry to call you after office."

"No problem, what's up?"

"The car and motorbike at the scene, have you checked the owners' registration?"

"Oh, my God, I totally forgot about them."

"Where're they now?"

"At the station, the exhibits store."

"Can you get one of your men to check with JPJ?" Mislan asks. JPJ being the motor vehicle department in Malay.

"I'll do it first thing tomorrow morning."

"Thanks."

"How's the investigation going?"

"Not as well as I would like," Mislan replies, sounding frustrated.

"Keep knocking, and I'm sure something will come up soon."

The new prime minister, also known as the backdoor prime minister by PH supporters, comes on as scheduled and, as Mislan guessed, announces that a fourteen-day Movement Control Order (MCO) under the Prevention and Control of Infectious Diseases Act 1988 and the Police Act 1967 will be implemented nationwide. During the MCO, only essential businesses such as food retailers and petrol stations will be allowed to operate for limited hours daily. Restaurants, not roadside stalls, are allowed to operate, but there will be no inside dining allowed, only takeout. The same goes for government offices, only essential duties are allowed while the rest are to work from home. The MCO will take effect the day after tomorrow. He warns the public that stern action by the police will be taken against those who breach the order. He also advises the public not to go on panic buying and assures them that there will be sufficient food supply.

"Too late," Mislan says to the prime minister on the TV.

Mislan thinks about Daniel. How he and his mother will cope with the lockdown. Will they have enough food? Will he understand why he is not able to go to school and play with his friends? Will they be safe from the virus? He misses his son very much, misses his innocent laughter, misses his inquisitiveness, his smell, his hugs, and everything there is to miss about him. He speaks to his son regularly, but it isn't the same, can never be the same as when they are together. Once he tried video-calling with his son, but he noticed the uneasiness in Daniel's eyes and voice. Probably his mother was watching him, and since then he only calls.

His thoughts shift to Dr. Safia. Wherever she is, she must be very busy. Her exposure to the virus as a frontliner must be high. *Where the hell is she?* he wonders. The last he heard from her was about a year back when she sent him the song "Say Something."

Mislan's cell phone rings, distracting him from his thoughts. It's Johan asking if he heard the announcement.

"Yeah."

"So you know, there'll be no more nasi lemak sotong in the morning," Johan jests. Mislan's favorite breakfast.

"Hmmm."

"OK, night, see you at 4."

It is 4:10 a.m. The heavy downpour has just stopped when Mislan pulls into Kuala Lumpur Police contingent headquarters. He decides to wait in his car and makes a call to his assistant.

"Jo, I'm downstairs."

"Coming. Inspector Reeziana is giving us Detective Aziz but not the standby vehicle," Johan sighs.

"No problem, we'll take my car."

He sees his assistant and Detective Aziz emerge from the building, both not wearing face masks. Driving out, Mislan asks his assistant to call Rawang Police and ask if they can spare an MPV to back them up at the wholesale wet market.

"You're expecting trouble?" Johan asks.

"Don't know what to expect, but better safe than sorry."

Johan makes the call and is told the MPV will be waiting at the main entrance to the market.

"That may not be a good idea," Mislan says. "The MPV presence there will alert them, and our guys may disappear. Tell Rawang to instruct the MPV to wait for us at Selayang Police Station. We'll go to the market together."

Johan makes the call to Rawang Police to change the rendezvous location. Selayang wholesale wet market is about ten miles north in a town under the Police District of Rawang, Selangor. In the early days, the original settlers there were the Minang, originally from the Minangkabau highlands of Sumatra, Indonesia. When they arrived in the peninsula, most of them settled in the Negeri Sembilan state, but some made their way up north to Selayang and formed their village there. But modern Selayang has been invaded by the Rohingyas, and the entire area is crawling with them. Just as Chow Kit in Kuala Lumpur was overrun by Indonesians about two decades back.

As it is 4:15 in the morning, the traffic is low. Mislan decides to cut across the city and heads for Jalan Kuching, which will take him all the way to Selayang passing Taman Wahyu. It takes them less than twenty minutes to reach their destination. An MPV is parked and waiting in the compound of Selayang Police Station when the team from D9 arrives. Johan approaches the patrol car and asks if they are assigned as their backup. The driver nods and starts the engine. Mislan drives to the wholesale wet market, which is about nine minutes away, with the MPV on his tail.

––––––

The dashboard clock shows 4:50 a.m.; the sky is dark, and the air damp and humid. The shower earlier caused puddles in the potholes on the road leading to the market building, and the stench hangs in the air. The market is buzzing with workers carrying, pushing, or pulling bundles and huge baskets of farm produce, live chickens, sides of beef, and so on. It is a sort of organized chaos with calls, chatter, and shouts in languages mostly alien to the officers. The market is a large single-story structure, with a high roof and no walls. The concrete floor is wet, slippery, and patched with puddles of water from the fresh produce. It is a large open space with concrete tables marking each stall.

Johan looks at his boss and grins as if saying, *"Told you."*

"Where's the stall?" Mislan asks, ignoring his assistant's mocking grin.

"The chicken section around the corner," Johan replies, pointing to the south end of the building.

The officers skirt around the edge of the building, doing their best to avoid the pools of water while at the same time watching where they're headed. It's tricky, as the lighting is poor outside of the building and the tiny drains are overflowing with dark, smelly water. Johan points to a passage between two concrete tables.

"Over there," he directs.

Mislan notices that the men working in the area where his team turns to enter have stopped whatever they were doing and are observing them. It's the usual reaction when police enter any area where their presence is not an everyday affair. In their case, their numbers and the two uniformed policemen are certainly work-stoppers. He hears a few shouts, probably to other workers deeper inside informing them of the team's presence. He notices some of them moving toward the passage and some in the direction his team is heading. *Most probably driven by curiosity,* he figures.

"Jo, observe but don't react," Mislan tells his assistant.

Johan turns to look left and right, then back to his boss. Mislan can see the apprehension on his face.

"Keep your cool, we don't want trouble," Mislan says calmly.

———

At Ismail's chicken stall, Johan introduces his boss and asks which of his workers is Ajimullah's friend. Ismail calls to one of his workers who is tasked with slaughtering chicken. A dark-skinned man in his mid-thirties, well-built, about five feet, seven inches tall, walks over. His plastic apron and hands are bloodied, and he smells of chicken shit and blood. Mislan observes he is still carrying the slaughter knife, a sharp six-inch blade, in one hand.

About twenty yards away, a large crowd has formed a semicircle around Ismail's chicken stall. They are keeping a safe distance from the center of attraction. They're watching and softly chatting with each other, still unsure of what is happening or what is going to happen.

"What's your name?" Johan asks.

"Azara," the man answers. Before Johan can ask further questions, he defiantly says, "I'm a Rohingya refugee under UNHCR."

Most of the Rohingya refugees seem to be of the opinion that as UNHCR-registered refugees, they are insulated against any law of the country. A stereotypical mentality regarding most Western institutions, especially when dealing with developing and underdeveloped countries. This mentality has been passed on to the Rohingyas. While Johan questions Azara, Mislan keeps his eyes on the crowd.

"You know Ajimullah?" Johan continues, ignoring Azara's claim of being a UNHCR refugee.

"Last time when he work here."

Hearing the name Ajimullah, the crowd starts to get loud. One of them starts a chant, but it is not echoed by the rest and dies off. Mislan doesn't know what was being said or shouted by the crowd, but it didn't sound friendly. Someone in the crowd shouts something to Azara, which to Mislan sounded like encouragement for defiance or to shut up.

He isn't surprised by the crowd's calls to Azara not to cooperate with the police. In the prevailing hostile situation and predicaments some Malaysians have put them in, it's the natural reaction.

"How long did you know him?" Johan asks.

Azara doesn't answer; his eyes are fixed on the crowd. Mislan suspects the earlier shout was for him to stop talking to the police. Johan repeats his question, a little louder and firmer. The crowd responds by jeering, shouting, and moving closer. Mislan hears the word "police" shouted several times. He sees Azara's hand tighten on the slaughter knife until his knuckles turn light brown. He gazes at his assistant and eye-gestures toward Azara's hand. Johan gives a slight nod of acknowledgment.

Tension is thick in the foul-smelling air. Mislan has two options: back down or stand firm and get *them* to back down. He instructs the two uniformed constables to stand in front of the crowd, hoping the M16 ArmaLite assault rifles across their chests will scare them. It does have that effect but not as much as he hoped. He reminds himself that these people are no strangers to guns and authorities. Back where they came from, police or military clampdowns and brutality were daily affairs—that is, if you believe the reports by foreign media. The Malaysian police must seem like kindergarten teachers compared to their Myanmarese counterparts.

"Let's take him back before things get out of control," Mislan says softly to his assistant.

Johan tells Azara to put the slaughter knife down on the concrete table. Azara stares at the detective sergeant and slowly raises his hand, the blade pointing toward him. Johan lifts his shirttail and places his hand on the pistol grip at his waist. Azara's eyes widen at Johan's move and the expression on the detective sergeant's face that says *"Don't even think about it."* He steps to the table and puts down the knife as Johan moves behind him. In one swift move, Johan grabs his right hand and cuffs it. Before Azara can react, he grabs the other hand and cuffs them together.

"What're you doing? I'm UNHCR refugee. You cannot arrest me!" Azara says angrily.

Seeing one of their own being handcuffed, the crowd erupts loudly. Insidious-sounding calls incite the crowd and are reciprocated by some of the men intimidatingly holding up and waving meat choppers, knives, and drag-hooks. The noise is overwhelming. The crowd is turning into a hostile mob. The two uniformed constables look at Mislan for instructions as the crowd inches closer. Without warning, Mislan draws his Berretta sidearm and fires two shots into the air. The gunshots pierce through the hooting and jeering, silencing the hullabaloo. They momentarily freeze, then like goats scamper away in panic. Detective Aziz, who is video-recording the crowd with his cell phone, is skirting behind Johan for a better angle. The explosion from the two shots startles him; he trips over something, and plunges into a tub of water filled with chicken feathers. Luckily, he has the wits to hold his hand and phone out of the water.

Laughter and cheers erupt from the crowd at Detective Aziz's expense. It somewhat defuses the mounting tension and lessens the threatening shouts. Mislan seizes the moment and barks instructions to the two constables to break up the crowd. A man breaks through the crowd and steps up to Mislan. He introduces himself as Rafee, the committee leader for the wholesale foreign workers.

"Good, please tell your people to disperse," Mislan says firmly. "The next shot may not be a warning shot."

"Why are you arresting him?" Rafee asks, pointing to Azara.

"It's none of your business. Tell your people to break up."

"I'm the leader—"

"I said tell your people to break up, or I'll tell my men to shoot those that are carrying weapons," Mislan says firmly, cutting off Rafee midsentence.

"We're UNHCR refugees, you cannot arrest us," Rafee says defiantly.

"Don't bet on it," Mislan replies. Turning to the uniformed policemen he barks, "Shout three warnings to disperse. If they fail to disperse after that, shoot those that are armed."

Rafee has no doubt that this officer means what he says. He immediately shouts to the crowd in their language. Some murmurs are heard from the back of the crowd, but to the relief of the two constables, the crowd starts to melt away.

Grunting aloud, Detective Aziz pulls himself out of the tub, drenched and covered in feathers. He smells of chicken shit, but other than that, nothing is bruised except perhaps his ego.

"Why is he arrested?" Rafee asks when the crowd has dispersed.

"For investigation," Mislan replies, signaling to his men to start walking back to their cars.

"What investigation?"

"Nothing that you need to know about."

"I'll complain to UNHCR, you cannot arrest refugee," Rafee says intimidatingly.

Mislan replies with a wide smile.

"What's your name?" Rafee asks.

"Inspector Mislan."

"OK, I'll make a complaint and make sure you lose your job. I have powerful people in politics, in UMNO, in PAS, PKR."

"Good for you."

At their cars, Mislan initially thinks of instructing the MPV to ferry the chicken-shit-smelling Detective Aziz and the arrestee Azara back to his office. Then Johan reminds him that the MPV would need authorization to cross state borders. Mislan decides he doesn't need the hassle. He already has more than enough on his hands with the discharge of his firearm. They get hold of some plastic sheets and old newspapers to put on the back seat and jam the two chicken-shit-smelling guys in.

The normally twenty-minute drive is done in ten minutes flat with all windows rolled down and Mislan chain-smoking all the way.

11

BY THE TIME THEY pull into the Kuala Lumpur Police contingent head-quarters, it is 6:15 a.m. The building is still deserted when Johan and Detective Aziz quickly escort the arrestee in. The guards at the lobby give them a nasty glare as they wait for the elevator. Mislan stays back at his car, turns the air-conditioning on, and waits for the air to blow out the rotting smell from the interior. After about ten minutes, he decides that is the best he will get until he can send the car for inside-out washing.

Walking into the elevator lobby, Mislan can smell the odor left by the two men. Entering his office, he is confronted by Inspector Reeziana about bringing back a smelly arrestee.

"You should have taken him to Sentul Police, it's their case anyway," Reeziana stresses. "This stink will be around for days."

Mislan flashes her a smirk.

"I bet you there'll be complaints from the entire building. Just wait until ma'am hears about it."

"Here, have a ciggie, it'll kill the smell," Mislan says, throwing her his pack.

Johan comes into the office and tells him the arrestee is in Interview Room 2, which is the farthest down the corridor. Detective Syed is with him. Johan had asked Detective Aziz to go home and shower before coming back.

Lighting a cigarette, Mislan tells his assistant he needs to lodge the report for discharging his firearm and for detaining Azara.

"Give me fifteen and I'll join you."

Malaysian police are armed by the force. Officers and detectives carry firearms 24/7. However, discharging one's firearm while apprehending or in pursuit of a criminal is not something deemed acceptable by the force. Several officers and personnel had been charged in court due to public pressure, and some were sentenced to prison. *Why the hell do you arm your personnel if they're not allowed to lawfully use the firearm in discharging their duties?* Mislan used to question.

After completing the report in the Integrated Police Reporting System (IPRS), Mislan puts on his face mask and joins his assistant in Interview Room 2. Johan has already started the interview, and Mislan takes a seat next to him, switches on his digital recorder, pushes it on the table, and lets his assistant continue.

"You and Ajimullah grew up in the same village?" Johan asks.

Azara the arrestee nods.

"Verbally answer yes or no for the recorder," Johan says, pointing to the digital recorder.

"Yes."

"So you know him well."

"Yes."

"After he quit his job at the market, what did he do?"

Azara shrugs, indicating he does not know.

"I said answer with words, not with body language," Johan stresses.

"I don't know."

Johan takes out his refugee card from his wallet, and Azara's eyes widen.

"What're you doing with my card?" Azara asks. A glimmer of fear flashes in his eyes.

"I think this is a fake," Johan says, turning the card in his hand. Passing it to his boss, he asks, "What do you think, boss?"

Mislan takes the card, examines it, and nods, saying, "It's fake. I think we should refer this case to Immigration and let them handle him as an illegal."

"It's real, I'm a refugee. You can check with UNHCR," Azara claims, his voice taut with fear.

"OK, here is the deal. You tell me all you know of Ajimullah and we'll forget that you're an illegal and that you pulled the knife on me," Johan says, looking straight at the arrestee's face.

Azara stares back at the detective sergeant. Johan can see in his eyes that he is unsure about snitching on his friend, a friend who probably had helped him when he first arrived in the country.

"Ajimullah is dead, so he would not know you snitched on him," Johan adds to soothe his guilty conscience. "You're alive, probably married with kids, and you'll be charged in court as an illegal and deported back to your country."

"UNHCR will protect me," the detainee replies boldly.

"Listen here, Malaysia is not a signatory to the UN convention on refugees. As far as our law is concerned, you're all illegal immigrants. UNHCR can do nothing about it," Mislan says. He lights a cigarette, stands, and says to his assistant, "Send him to the lockup, and we'll let Immigration handle him." He moves toward the door.

"Wait, wait, I'll tell you what you want to know about Ajimullah," Azara pleads.

———

By the time the interview is over, it is 7:45 a.m. The office is already whirring with complaints of the smell. Inspector Reeziana is holding center stage, and Mislan's name is mentioned several times. As soon as Mislan and Johan enter the office, they are bombarded with questions on what they think they were doing.

"Doing our jobs," Mislan replies with a smile. "Sorry, but we get our arrestee on as-is-where-is basis."

"You could at least have stopped by his house and let him change into something more appropriate," Inspector Tee says.

"He's not here for a job interview, OK?"

Superintendent Samsiah stands in the doorway, asking what is the stinking smell. "Did someone hide a dead chicken in his drawer?"

The officers look tellingly at Mislan. After the mystery is explained and they all have a good laugh at Detective Aziz's mishaps, Superintendent

Samsiah suggests they get a few cans of air freshener to spray the office and interview room.

———

After the morning prayer, Mislan and Johan are summoned by Superintendent Samsiah to her office. In there, they find Assistant Superintendent of Police (ASP) Amir Muhammad from the Integrity and Standard Compliance Department (ISCD) seated in one of the guest chairs. ISCD is the Royal Malaysia Police equivalent of Internal Affairs in the US police. Mislan and his boss have had some dealings with ASP Amir before on compliance issues. ASP Amir had always acted pragmatically and fairly. Both Superintendent Samsiah and ASP Amir are wearing face masks, a new normal that Mislan has yet to subscribe to.

"Mislan, Johan, how have you been?" ASP Amir asks in a voice muffled by the face mask.

"Been better, sir," Mislan answers.

Johan replies with a polite nod and smile.

"I suppose you're aware why Amir is here," Samsiah says to her officers.

Mislan and Johan shake their heads.

"Let me just briefly update you. Earlier, I was called by the OCCI," Amir begins.

At the mention of OCCI, Mislan closes his eyes, inhaling deeply and letting out a heavy sigh. Superintendent Samsiah and ASP Amir look at each other, amused.

"Anyway, there were a few individuals from the Selayang wholesale wet market when I arrived. I suppose you know why they were there."

"I can guess," Mislan says.

"I'm sure, but Mislan, before you say anything, have you seen the video that has gone viral on social media?" Amir asks.

Mislan and Johan look at him blankly.

"I'm guessing you have not," Amir continues. "Here," he says, passing his cell phone to Mislan.

Mislan and Johan watch the twenty-second video of Mislan firing two shots into the air and shouting to the boisterous crowd to back off. Mislan hands back Amir's cell phone and grins.

"Not bad eh?" Amir remarks with a tiny smile.

"Perhaps before I say anything, it may help if you watch the video taken by Detective Aziz at the market prior to the incident," Mislan suggests.

"You have a video?" Amir asks.

"Yes. Jo, can you email it to ma'am so that we can watch it on her laptop?"

Johan nods and emails Detective Aziz's video to Superintendent Samsiah. She opens her email, retrieves the video, turns her laptop so that Amir has a good view and presses Play. Instantly, the room is filled with threatening shouts in a language they do not understand. The screen shows men in their work clothes waving meat choppers, knives, and drag hooks at the uniformed policemen. The camera pans from side to side, capturing as many of the men in the crowd as possible. Then it moves to Johan and the arrestee. They see the arrestee holding up the knife, pointing it at Johan. A few seconds later, the voice of Mislan shouts for the crowd to back off, followed by two gunshots. At that point, the camera goes berserk, pointing first to the ceiling, then to the side and the floor, followed by all over the place before it ends.

"What happened?" Amir asks, puzzled.

"Aziz tripped and fell into the tub for cleaning chickens," Johan says with a chuckle.

Samsiah, Amir, and Mislan laugh.

"Amir, I'm sure from the video it was obvious the officers' lives were threatened and in danger," Samsiah says, troubled by what she saw. "There were, what—fifty, seventy of them? Some of them carrying weapons and acting in a threatening manner. I'm of the view Mislan acted with reasonable cause to safeguard their safety, to prevent a blood-bath, my officers' blood."

"Yes, I agree with you ma'am, but"—Amir rolls his eyes upward to indicate the OCCI—"you know him. How he desperately wants

Mislan's head." Amir lets out a chuckle. "Ma'am, can you forward the video to me?"

"He wants mine too," Samsiah says wryly. "He can try, but he's not getting Mislan's or mine, not on this."

Amir laughs.

"The sad part in our job is we can't viral a video that protects our actions," Amir sighs. Turning to Mislan, he asks, "Are you writing the arrestee up for criminal intimidation against Johan?"

Mislan shakes his head. "He has tons of info on drug dealing, the Myanmar connections. I'm thinking he's more useful to us, Narcotic, if we cultivate him. Let the charge hang over his head to keep him in line."

"Good thinking, but you may have increased the possibility of you getting roasted," Amir says. "Let me see how I can get around this with you-know-who. Perhaps if this arrestee's info is good and Narcotic makes several big busts, that'll satisfy his appetite for publicity."

"Thanks, Amir," Samsiah offers, ending the meeting.

Mislan's cell phone rings; it is Audi, the investigative journalist. Before he can inform her he is in a meeting, she says, "Great video."

"I'm in a meeting," Mislan says and terminates the call.

"Lan, you and Jo are done with the arrestee?" Samsiah asks.

Mislan and Johan nod in sync.

"Can I hand him over to Narcotic?"

Again, Mislan and Johan nod in sync.

———

After ASP Amir Muhammad leaves, Superintendent Samsiah asks Mislan and Johan to update her on the interview. Mislan briefs her that the two victims were identified as Ajimullah Islam and Fatama Hok by the arrestee. The three of them grew up in the same village in the Rakhine state. About eight years back, the two victims landed on Langkawi island. While in Langkawi, they hooked up with the Thais connected with the Golden Triangle Myanmars in the drug business. Taking advantage of their refugee status, they made their way to Kuala Lumpur. To blend in with the Rohingya community, they got themselves work at the wholesale market. They worked separately with different wholesalers for several years. At the market, they familiarized themselves with the drug business and local distribution syndicates. According to the arrestee, they made friends with lorry drivers from Thailand delivering fresh fish. That's how the drugs were smuggled in, under crates of fish and vegetables. Because fish and vegetables are perishable produce, they weren't kept waiting for long. The lorries are also dirty and smelly, so they weren't thoroughly inspected by customs. They only conduct a 100 percent check if they get a tipoff.

About six months back, the two men quit their jobs, and Ajimullah managed to convince Ismail to lend his name to rent a house—the crime scene.

According to the arrestee, the victims were dealing in heroin and meth smuggled from the Golden Triangle by a Thai-Myanmar syndicate. They were not mere street peddlers but big-time suppliers to the Rohingya and local pushers.

Superintendent Samsiah raises her eyebrows.

"Traffickers, 39B," Samsiah says, referring to the section of the Dangerous Drug Act 1952.

Mislan nods.

"The arrestee claimed they kept huge amounts of cash from their transactions in the house," Mislan says.

"Logical. They'd have a hard time explaining the money if they banked it, wouldn't they?" she says. "How much was the arrestee talking about?"

"He said a lot, and when pressed for a number, he said maybe two hundred to three hundred K," Johan replies.

"That's enough of a reason. People do get killed for much less," Samsiah says. "So you think the motive was robbery?"

"Yes and no," Mislan answers, pursing his lips.

"Explain."

"Yes—there was no money recovered by Inspector Shahira, and the druggie we interviewed did claim that one of the men coming out of the crime scene was carrying a large backpack." Mislan pauses, craving a cigarette.

Superintendent Samsiah reads her investigation officer's pleading expression and says, "No."

"No what?" Johan asks.

"Your boss is thinking of smoking—no," she says, followed by a tiny chuckle.

"You're cruel," Mislan jokes. "If it's a plain killing, I can accept it was robbery. The thing that puzzles me is, it was not a killing. It was an execution. And don't give me that crap that it was a drug deal gone bad, like what the guy up there was saying. If so, you think they'd leave the drugs on the bed? Well, I haven't heard of drug dealers passing up drugs yet."

"What makes you think it was an execution?"

"The pathologist Dr. Mariam confirmed there were contusions, that's abrasions in layman's terms, like rope burns on both the vics' wrists. She also said there were tiny impression markings on the abrasions, for which she doesn't know the cause. I'll talk to Chew from Crime Forensics and see if he can figure it out."

Superintendent Samsiah remains silent as she digests the information.

"Dr. Mariam said the shot to the head on both vics were to the parietal bone, I think that's what it's called, meaning to the top back of the skull downward. The vics were approximately five feet, six or seven inches tall. According to the druggie, the men he saw coming out of the vics' house were slightly taller, more like Jo's height. The only way to shoot the vics on the back of the head downward was if the vics were positioned lower, like on their knees."

Superintendent Samsiah acknowledges Mislan's view with several slow nods.

"You have a hard nut of a case," Samsiah says. "Any theory about the execution?"

Mislan shakes his head.

"OK, for the moment until something else surfaces, I'll go along with your theory of robbery and execution. Now you may go and have your nicotine fix."

12

LEAVING THE HEAD OF Special Investigations' office, Mislan heads straight for the emergency staircase landing. He lights a cigarette and returns the call to Audi the journalist. She answers on the first ring.

"Great acting," Audi says. "I wonder how your publicity junkie boss will react, I mean you stealing his limelight."

Mislan can hear the investigative journalist laughing her heart out. *Damn this woman, she does not even bother to close the mouthpiece.*

"Look, I was just grilled by ISCD."

"Woah, that was superfast. So, you're in hot soup?"

"Not if you're willing to do me a favor," Mislan hints.

"Hmmm, I can be convinced, but what's there for me in return?"

"What do you want?"

Audi may be a pain in the ass with her persistent nagging, but she is a real journalist. They already collaborated on a couple of Mislan's cases, sharing information and sources. In return, she got an exclusive on each case. The inside stories that the publicity junkie OCCI chose to ignore, for whatever reason.

"The Sentul double killings, exclusive. You know I like the dirty and gory stuff."

"OK, but not at this moment."

"Why not?"

"Because I've got nothing. That's why."

"Don't give me that 'I-got-nothing' bull."

Mislan inhales deeply, saying nothing.

"Really! You really got nothing?" Audi asks when Mislan does not answer her.

"Yup."

"OK, but I get it when you have something."

"Deal."

"Yes, Inspector, how may I be of assistance?"

———

At that afternoon's press conference Q&A by the OCCI, Senior Assistant Commissioner Baharuddin Mohd. Sidek, Audi raises her hand to catch his attention. As with all his press conferences, he is flanked by his PR officer and, in this instance, ASP Amir. The photo session is of the utmost importance for the OCCI, not the substance of the subject released.

"Yes," Baharuddin says, pointing at Audi.

"Sir, you said action will be taken against the officer for unlawful and unprovoked firearm discharge."

"Yes, in accordance with our ISC procedures. For those that don't know, ISC stands for Integrity and Standards Compliance. I've already instructed the head of Contingent ISCD to initiate the inquiry."

The OCCI turns to ASP Amir, flashing a smile. Audi notes a minuscule hint of satisfaction in the smile, as if saying "*His ass is mine.*" Audi is sure the OCCI meant Inspector Mislan's ass.

"Sir," Audi continues, "have you, your PR or ISCD officers viewed the *longer* viral video of the incident that led to the inspector discharging the warning shots?"

The question catches the OCCI off guard. He turns to ASP Amir and then to his PR officer, ASP Theresa, inquiringly. ASP Amir hides a smile, but ASP Theresa displays a classic expression of being dumbfounded.

"Miss?"

"Audi."

"Yes, Miss Audi, there're so many videos going viral. You cannot expect me to view them all, can you?" Baharuddin replies evasively.

"But with the many viral videos, you and your officers did manage to notice the short video you showed us."

"The video was highlighted to me by the representative of the wholesale wet market," Baharuddin snaps. "It was taken by one of them and uploaded to social media."

"Yes, I saw it too on YouTube, but I also saw another video that was uploaded and went viral. Go to YouTube and search for *Police Officers Surrounded by Angry Illegal Immigrants Mob*," Audi says sarcastically.

Audi notices the sudden red flush of anger on the OCCI's face and embarrassed blush on ASP Theresa's.

"Which station did you say you were from?" the OCCI asks.

"I did not, but since you asked, I'm from Astro Awani," Audi says boldly.

The OCCI knows not to mess with Astro Awani, as it's one of the news channels with the most viewers. He raises his hand to stop any more questions, thanks the media, and makes a hasty retreat followed by his PR officer.

ASP Amir hangs around the podium observing the media crew filing out. As Audi walks by, he stops and pulls her aside.

"Where did you get the video from?" Amir asks, his expression calm and pleasant.

"It's on YouTube," Audi answers innocently.

"Is it?" Amir says, looking at her and trying not to smile. "I was surfing it this morning and didn't see it. For your info, I did actually see it this morning—but not on YouTube."

"Where?" Audi asks, playing dumb.

"Ooo," Amir says, dragging out the syllable, "from the assistant of the inspector implicated."

"You mean Detective Sergeant Johan? Well, I can promise you that I didn't get it from a detective sergeant," Audi says, holding up two fingers to her temple and flashing a wide smile. "Scout's honor."

"I believe you. So now it's on YouTube?"

"Yes, it's there."

"You may have just saved an officer's career. Thank you," Amir says and walks away.

———

Mislan's cell phone rings; it's Audi telling him mission accomplished.

"You should've been there. The look on his face was worth it all. Now you owe me big-time," she says, giggling.

"OK, thanks."

"Aren't you interested to know how it went down?" Audi asks, sounding disappointed.

"Nope."

"Not even a little curious?"

"Nope."

"Darn!" Audi cusses, followed with hearty laughter. "By the way, the ISC officer stopped me and asked about the video on YouTube."

"What did you say?"

"He said he saw the video, shown by Jo this morning. So I told him it wasn't Jo that gave me the video."

"Did you tell him where you got it from?"

"No. He said I probably saved an officer's career. I had a feeling he suspects, if not actually knows who."

"I don't want the OCCI to start gunning after Jo. He doesn't know anything about this."

"Don't worry, we have a deal and I'll keep to my end of it."

"Thanks."

———

Mislan tells his assistant to knock off, as they will be on a twenty-four shift tomorrow. Leaving the office, he drives through Kampung Pandan and notices the general duty personnel setting up a roadblock on the opposite main road leading into the city. A tent equipped with stand fan, field tables, and chairs—it looks to Mislan like the MCO is going to be a long-drawn-out affair. Going through Ampang Hilir, the high-end residential area where the expatriates live, he passes the house, the crime scene of his infamous case monikered the Yee Sang Murders. He hits the Middle Ring Road 2 and makes a left toward Ulu Klang. Just before the slip road U-turn, another roadblock is being erected. *The government must be really serious about enforcing the Movement Control Order.*

He stops at the Petronas petrol kiosk to tank up and finds a long line of cars waiting for their turn. "Shit, this MCO is already getting to be a nuisance," he moans. As he waits in line, he peeps at the entrance to the Giant supermarket. The line is all the way out around the building. No way is he going to wait in line just to get a loaf of bread and a dozen eggs. He'll stop by a 7-Eleven or KK Mart. After waiting almost fifteen minutes, he gets to tank up. Driving down the ramp, he slows in front of a 7-Eleven. The line is just as long. He drives farther up to KK Mart; it's the same. "Fuck," he swears under his breath, "stupid panic-buying."

Giving up on his intention to buy bread and eggs, he makes a U-turn to the Thai restaurant and orders a fried rice takeout. While waiting for his order, he asks the operator if they will be open tomorrow during the MCO.

"Don't know if we can," the woman replies. "No clear directives from the government."

"Isn't food an essential business?" Mislan asks.

"Sundry shops and supermarkets, but I'm not sure about restaurants and stalls."

"That may pose problems for those that don't cook."

"You know *lah*, this new government, they don't think about the people. They only think about themselves. If we can't open, how to survive, pay rent, pay workers?"

Mislan lights a cigarette and steps away. He is not into politics and doesn't even like talking about it. To him, politicians are the biggest bullshitters and unscrupulous gold diggers to walk the earth. They lie, cheat, and promise you the moon and stars, and while you fantasize about the promised future, they rob you blind.

He makes a call to his assistant.

"Jo, you at home?"

"Close, why?"

"Any sundry shops around your place?"

"A few."

"If there's no long line, can you buy me a loaf of Gardenia sandwich bread and a dozen eggs? The people at my place here are panic-buying, and the lines are crazy."

"Sure, anything else you need?"

"That's it for now. Bring them to the office tomorrow, I'll pay you then. Thanks."

———

Mislan feels exhausted, having been awake for more than fourteen hours from 4 in the morning. After showering and making a mug of coffee, he sits at his workstation in the bedroom and makes a call to Daniel. After three rings, his son answers.

"Hi, kiddo," Mislan greets him.

"Hi, Daddy."

"How are you?"

"Daddy, Mummy said I can't go to school tomorrow."

"Yes, kiddo, it's because of the virus . . ."

"COVID-19, I know."

"Has Mummy bought food for the house?"

"Yes, yesterday. Mummy bought a lot of Maggi," Daniel says, sounding happy. "Mummy said I can have Maggi every day."

"No, kiddo, it's not good for you, OK."

"OK, Daddy, bye."

"Love you, kiddo."

"Love you, too."

Terminating the call, Mislan sends a WhatsApp text to his ex-wife: *Pls don't allow kiddo to eat maggi every day, thks.*

His ex-wife replies: *No laa was just teasing him.*

He calls Inspector Shahira and inquires about the victims' vehicles she was supposed to check on.

"Sorry, forgot to inform you the result. This MCO has roped in all of us to handle roadblocks."

"So what's the result?"

"The Toyota Vios is registered to its previous owner. Let me check. . . . OK, Indra Rani d/o Kalimuthu. She traded in the car to Wah Hee Used Car, and it was sold to a Rohingya. They cannot register the transfer of name as the Rohingya is not officially legal. The same for the scooter—it's still under the name of the previous owner. The transaction was in cash, so the used-car dealer didn't keep any records."

"No records?"

"Nope, none. It's a common practice by used-car dealers. No record of sales, no income tax."

"What about road tax and insurance?"

"Everything is now online, so I guess the new owner just continued renewing it."

"Shit. Thanks, Shahira."

"No problem, sorry for not letting you know earlier."

———

Mislan switches on Al Jazeera News; it talks about COVID-19. Flipping to CNN, the same, Sky News the same, nothing but COVID-19. It's depressing. The song "American Pie" comes to mind: "*This'll be the day that I die.*" To date, over 7,500 have succumbed to the virus globally. China is leading the infection count, but European countries such as Italy, France, Spain, and the UK are fast catching up. The same goes for America.

He flips to Astro Awani and leaves it there, half-listening to it. The host is interviewing a panel of men discussing the pandemic and the government's measures to flatten the curve. "Flatten the curve" and "social distancing" are the new buzzwords on the tip of every government spokesperson's tongue.

The host asks what the government is doing to assist those who aren't able to work, especially the daily wage earners and stall operators during the fourteen-day lockdown. One of the panel members says the government has come up with a multibillion-ringgit package to assist them, and the prime minister will be making the announcement soon.

Mislan smiles listening to the reply, lights a cigarette, and takes out his notes on the Sentul double murder. He reviews the notes, going over each scribble methodically. When he comes to the tiny marking on the victims' wrists, he pulls the photos from the file in his backpack. The pathologist had given him four photos, for each of the wrists of the men. He chides himself for forgetting to send them to Chew of Crime Forensics for closer examination to figure out what caused the marks.

As he's examining the photos, his attention is drawn to the announcement of today's upcoming news by a female newscaster. She reads: "Police officer fired warning shots to disperse hostile mob." Eager to watch the news that will be aired at 8 p.m. to see the reaction on the OCCI's face, Mislan closes his notes. There will be nothing much he can think about until after the news. He props up the pillows against the bed's headboard and stretches out.

The tension and tiredness dissipate as soon as he lies back and rests his head. His thoughts wander to his son, and his hand automatically reaches over to the side where Daniel used to sleep. He closes his eyes, trying to imagine his son beside him, and in a matter of seconds, he is asleep with the television blaring on.

———

It was late at night and Mislan made a right at the traffic lights under the overpass heading onto Jalan Ukay Perdana. About one mile down the road he stopped at the traffic light next to the Bistaria Residensi housing development. He heard a motorbike coming from behind, but it stopped just a few yards before reaching his car. Glancing at the rearview mirror, he saw the pillion rider coming off the motorbike and walking slowly to his car on the driver's side. Mislan thought with all the road construction and diversions going on in the area, they were probably lost and about to ask for directions. The man knocked on his window, and in that fleeting moment, Mislan asked himself: If they were asking for directions, why not ride up beside his car? Why stop behind?

As the window rolled down the man raised his hand and pointed a gun at him. Instinctively, Mislan engaged the reverse gear and stepped on the gas. The car leapt backward as the man fired two shots. He felt a sharp ripping, burning sensation in his stomach. He lost control of the car, and it came to a sudden stop when it rear-rammed the concrete barriers lining the road. Taking deep breaths, he pulled his gun and fired three shots in the direction of the man who was running toward him. From somewhere to his side, he heard a motorbike rev its engine, and he fired another shot in its direction. The motorbike stopped, and he saw the shooter getting on it, and they disappeared into the night.

Mislan felt his trousers, slimy and sticky with blood. He opened the door and half-slumped out of the car. His breathing was short and labored, his throat was dry, and his head was spinning. He tried to crawl out of the car, but his legs would not move. He thought of his cell phone on the passenger seat, but he was certain it must have flown off the seat when his car backed into the concrete barriers. Half-slumped from the door of his car, he accepted that this was the end of it all: the end to his misery, the end to his loneliness. He started to lose consciousness, and everything around him turned darker and darker. He knew that, at this hour of the night, Jalan Ukay Perdana was usually deserted, and the chances of him being rescued were slim. Suddenly, the pain was gone and the world was pitch-dark and silent.

Mislan did not know how long he was out. When he regained consciousness, he heard voices, far and distant voices. He tried to open his eyes, but the eyelids were too heavy. He recognized one of the voices: his boss, Superintendent Samsiah. She was saying it was quick thinking of him to react by reversing the car instead of driving forward, which was what people in his situation would normally do. By reversing, the shot trajectory lowered from the chest to his stomach. Also by reversing, he had a clear view of the shooter and was able to return fire. His action prevented the shooter from finishing him off.

Mislan vaults to a sitting position on his bed. He instinctively touches the scar on his stomach. The ulcer-like pain is burning and his stomach growling. *Another one of those nightmares.* He checks his cell phone for the time, and it shows 2:15 a.m. The TV is airing a repeat of the interview of the government panel about the MCO. He reaches for the remote and switches it off. He realizes he has not eaten the fried rice he bought earlier and is starving. He remembers his late mother telling him that sleeping on an empty stomach will make you have bad dreams. He doesn't know if it's true, but he definitely doesn't want the nightmare to return. Getting off the bed, he walks to the kitchen, makes himself a mug of coffee, and sits at the dining table to eat the cold fried rice.

13

As usual, Mislan leaves his apartment at 6:30 a.m. to make the ten-mile drive to his office that normally takes him about fifty minutes. Exiting the housing development, he's pleasantly surprised at the absence of vehicles on the road that is ordinarily lined with cars all the way to the Middle Ring Road 2. The stretch on MRR2 that is constantly jammed due to the massive overpass construction is clear of vehicles too. Mislan is delighted. Something he never dreamed of experiencing in his lifetime of living in a city plagued with too many cars and an infrastructure that can barely accommodate them.

Passing through the Ampang Point commercial area, he sees the shops are all closed. The food stalls on the islet in front of the row of shophouses are also closed. *The MCO will adversely impact the livelihood of many.*

Turning into Kampung Pandan, Mislan is stopped by uniformed policemen manning a roadblock. It feels strange seeing all of them with face masks and a few even wearing surgical gloves. He lowers his window, and the police corporal bends forward to ask where he's heading.

"D9, IPK," Mislan replies, showing his building security tag.

The corporal, whose name tag stitched onto his uniform identifies him as Bujang, takes a closer look at the tag, says, "Thank you, sir," and waves him on.

"Thank you," Mislan says, thinking with the name Bujang, the corporal is probably from Sarawak.

Driving into the contingent compound, Mislan is again pleasantly surprised at the many empty parking spots on a weekday. He normally has to make a big circle right to the back of the building to get a spot. Not today. Only a few officers and personnel are at the elevator lobby, and all of them wear face masks and stand apart from each other.

As he enters the office, sleepy-eyed Inspector Reeziana greets him and asks what it's like outside there.

"Ghost city," Mislan answers.

"That bad, eh?"

"Better than any Raya holiday I've ever experienced in KL."

Kuala Lumpur is the commercial hub of the country. Most of the people who work and live in it were not born there. They migrated from all over the country, and during the Raya or Chinese New Year holidays, these people go back to their hometowns. The city is deserted, and tourist spots are taken over by the foreign migrant workers.

Johan arrives carrying a plastic bag and hands it to his boss.

"Bread, eggs, and two packs of cigarettes," Johan says.

Mislan hands him a fifty-ringgit note.

"The front desk says ma'am wants the morning prayer to be held in here," Reeziana says. "Social distancing."

"Good, then we're allowed to smoke," Mislan says with a sly grin.

"You wish."

———

At 8:30 a.m., Superintendent Samsiah enters the investigators' office. Seeing her wearing a face mask, Mislan quickly puts his on but not quick enough for her not to notice. She stops at his desk, looks straight at him, and proclaims, "If you wish to die from the virus, that's your choice, but you will not do so at the expense of my men. Do you understand me?"

"Yes, ma'am, sorry."

Superintendent Samsiah walks to Johan's desk and leans her butt against it, facing the office. "Ghani, why don't you sit over there," she says, pointing to Reeziana's assistant's desk. "From now on, we'll have our morning prayer here to adhere to social distancing. I'd like for it to be short and sharp. Any matter to be discussed at length shall be conducted in my office. Any questions?"

ASP Ghani, the head of Special Projects, as well as Inspector Khamis, Inspector Tee, Inspector Reeziana, and Mislan—the four investigators—shake their heads.

"Yana, go ahead," Samsiah starts the meeting.

"Business is bad, only one armed robbery. The victim, a cigarette stand vendor, was robbed by several individuals believed to be Indonesian along Jalan Tiong Nam 4. The victim, also an Indonesian, suffered two stab wounds to the right side of his abdomen. He is now in GH and said to be stable. Dang Wangi is conducting the investigation. I believe the victim and robbers knew each other, but he is not talking. I guess they'll settle it between them."

"I guess the bad guys too are busy panic-robbing," Khamis jokes.

"Good. As you're aware, the stations will be bogged down by MCO roadblocks. They won't be able to provide us with uniformed personnel backups unless absolutely necessary. I've worked out our own backup rotations. Special Project shall be the first backup team on call, followed by the team on rest day."

All heads turn to ASP Ghani in dismay. It is an unspoken consensus among the investigators not to get Ghani's team involved in their investigation. Ghani is known for his take-no-prisoners approach. Noticing her officers' concerns, Superintendent Samsiah continues.

"As backup, your team will comply with the decisions and instructions of the investigating team." She turns to Ghani and says, "Do you understand?"

ASP Ghani nods, but it is clear he is unhappy with the last remark as he outranks the investigators.

"Lan, you're on today, right," Samsiah says rather than asks.

Mislan nods.

"For your info, there'll be no court sitting, so that'll give all of you the opportunity to revisit investigations of active cases on your plates. I also expect with the MCO there'll be a drastic drop in the crime rate."

Superintendent Samsiah pushes herself off Johan's desk, indicating the end of the meeting, and pans the office looking at each and every officer before saying, "OK, that's it. Stay safe."

A murmur of "Thank you, ma'am" follows her out of the investigators' office.

————

Johan and the other assistants come back into the office. The officers gather around the pantry, except for ASP Ghani, who somehow never seemed to fit in—also because he has his own private office. They make coffee and tea for themselves, and Mislan lights a cigarette before passing the pack to Reeziana.

"You guys had breakfast?" Mislan asks.

They shake their heads.

"I thought of getting some on the way here, but all the stalls were closed," Tee says.

"Mamak restaurants are open," Khamis offers.

"Not my taste," Tee replies.

The officers and their assistants talk about the MCO, the pandemic, and the devastating economic impact on the country. Mislan excuses himself, signaling for Johan to follow him to his desk.

"Jo, can you scan these for me? I need to pass them to Chew," Mislan says, handing him photos of the wrists.

"You're going there?"

"No, I'll email them to him, remember social distancing?" Mislan says with a laugh.

After Johan leaves, he makes a call to Chew.

"Hi, morning, Inspector," Chew answers on the first ring.

"Morning, Chew, you sound cheery. What's up?"

"What's there not to be cheery about? For the first time I enjoyed a clear drive to the office, the air unpolluted and no new case from last night."

Mislan laughs. "I'll be emailing you the photos of the victims' wrists taken by the pathologist. Can you try and match the markings to anything that could likely cause them?"

"I'll give it a shot."

"Thanks."

―――――

During the MCO, the crime rate does seem to drop significantly. For the whole day, not even one callout is received by D9. Mislan is bored sitting in the office with nothing to do. And it's only 1:30 in the afternoon. The rest of the officers and assistants have long gone home to rest.

"Jo, you have any mates in Narco?" Mislan asks.

"Yes, but not here, Penang," Johan answers from his desk. "Why?"

Mislan lights a cigarette, shrugging as if saying "Never mind." Johan can see his boss is restless. He's a man of action, but the Sentul double murder hasn't offered anything they can pursue.

"You want to go to Selayang and poke around?" Johan asks.

"No, I don't think the guy up there has cooled his heels yet. He's probably still trying to nail my ass on the market incident. Going there may just give him the hammer."

"So, what do you want to do?"

Mislan form his lips in an O shape trying to blow smoke rings, but it comes out in puffs of cloud. "Can't even blow fucking rings," he snorts, giving up. "I don't know, how about lunch?"

"Anything to stop you from brooding." Johan stands up and walks to his boss's desk, ready to leave.

"Wait a minute, I thought restaurants can only do takeout," Mislan says, looking up at Johan standing in front of his desk.

"Yeah, I forgot," Johan answers with a grin.

"Fucking MCO."

―――――

Mislan says he wants to research the modus operandi of the Sentul double murder, and Johan volunteers to go out and see if there are other halal restaurants apart from mamak that are open to pack lunch for them. After Johan leaves, he logs on to the Integrated Police Reporting

System (IPRS). It captures all police reports or First Information Reports (FIR) that empower the police to initiate investigation under the special powers provided by the Criminal Procedures Code (CPC).

Apart from the report itself, the IPRS contains a brief summary, the modus operandi, suspect or suspects (if any), and other information that may assist in solving the case. After trying several keywords, he is rewarded with a case in Seremban 2 that happened about a month back. The MO was quite similar to his case:

The perpetrator or perpetrators entered the house, a double-story shop-house, through the front by prying the door open. The grille gate was unlocked using what is believed to be a master key. The victim was killed in the master bedroom. In this case, the victim, a Malaysian-Chinese, was shot once in the back of the head. A .32 bullet was recovered inside the victim. No mention of drugs recovered. No bullet casing recovered. The neighbors claimed they did not hear any gunshot from the house. No suspect. The case was classified as murder under Section 302 of the Penal Code, and the investigating officer is ASP Rohimmi Noor of Seremban 2 Police.

Mislan lights another cigarette, excited by his discovery. He rereads the report, beaming like a child at his birthday party. Although there are dissimilarities, his gut feeling says the killer or killers were the same perpetrators as in his case. Mislan needs to speak to the IO, needs to clarify certain facts that weren't in the report. He prints a copy of the report, logs off, and places a call to Seremban 2 Police asking for ASP Rohimmi.

The operator tells him ASP Rohimmi is not currently in the office, and Mislan asks for his cell phone number. He dials the number, and after several rings it goes into voice messaging.

"Sir, I'm Inspector Mislan from D9, IPK KL. I'm calling about the Seremban 2 murder. Can you please return my call?"

Seremban 2 is a satellite town northwest of Seremban, the capital city of Negeri Sembilan. It is roughly forty-one miles or fifty minutes away from Kuala Lumpur via the North-South Highway.

He needs to get copies of the investigation, the crime scene photos, the ballistic reports, witness statements, and especially the autopsy report. Mislan thinks he can drive down and be back again at the office in about two and a half hours.

With the IPRS printout, he goes to Superintendent Samsiah's office. Superintendent Samsiah is engrossed in reports when he knocks lightly on the open door. She lifts her head, closes the file she's reading, and beckons him in.

"Yes."

"Ma'am, I need you to see this report," Mislan says, taking a seat and pushing the printout toward her.

"Been busy, I see," she says, lifting the printout.

Mislan smiles and waits for her to read.

"Interesting," she says, putting it down. "And you're here because . . . ?"

"Can I go to Seremban 2?" Mislan asks with a sly grin.

"Is KL not keeping you busy enough that you want to expand your area of coverage?" Samsiah jests. "Have you spoken to the IO?"

"He's not answering his phone, but I left him a message."

"Did it cross your mind he may be busy managing a roadblock with this MCO?"

Mislan grins. The truth is it did not.

"I suggest you wait for him to return your call, which I'm sure he will when he's free. Then you give him a brief of your case. Only after you've done that do you ask him if you could have copies of his documents and say you'll make available to him your documents. If he's busy, he can leave it at the inquiry for you to collect. Likewise, you'll leave yours for him there too."

"Yes, ma'am. So that's a 'no' for me to go to Seremban 2 today," Mislan says, followed by a chortle.

"Yes, it's a no, and why are you not wearing your face mask?"

"I'm confident my boss is not a carrier of COVID-19," he answers cheekily.

"Thank you for your unfounded confidence in my immune system, Dr. Mislan, but I'm not as confident as you are of yours. Please put on your freaking mask, Lan."

"Yes, ma'am. Sorry, ma'am," Mislan answers with a bashful smile, making a hurried retreat before the head of Special Investigations can continue her admonishment.

———

Johan is at the pantry when Mislan comes back from his boss's office. Two packs of rice and iced black coffee are on the table.

"I got us nasi kandar," Johan says as he unwraps his pack of rice.

"From Kudu?"

Johan nods. "You should see the queue, it goes all the way to the back of the restaurant. MCO or no MCO, that place is making a ton of money."

"We're Malaysians, and eating is our passion."

Using their hands, they savor the famous Kudu Restaurant's nasi kandar. As they eat, Mislan updates his assistant. He tells him about the dead end on the Toyota Vios car and Yamaha scooter. Johan nods, saying that it's common. A lot of the Indonesians do the same when buying vehicles. Mislan then tells him about his discovery of the Seremban 2 case reported in IPRS, and pushes the printout toward him. Mislan watches his assistant frown, put down the report, and look at him inquiringly.

"You think it's the same guys as in our case?" Johan is doubtful.

"You don't?" he asks with his mouth full.

"The caliber's different. Ours was 9mm, and here it's .32. And there was no mention of drugs."

Mislan nods. "But look at the similarities. The grille was unlocked using what they believe to be a master key, the front door jimmied, the shot to the head, no casing recovered, no vic's personal belongings, and no one heard the gunshot." Mislan takes a sip of his iced black coffee. "No mention of drugs doesn't mean they weren't there."

"What do you mean?" Johan stares at his boss and adds, "You're saying our people took them?"

"I'm not saying anything, I'm just saying if it wasn't mentioned, it doesn't necessarily mean it wasn't there," Mislan answers, followed by a chuckle.

"Yeah, right."

They continue eating in silence for a bit.

"Ma'am denied my request to go to Seremban 2," Mislan says.

"With good reason, I'm sure."

"I need to talk to the IO and get ahold of their investigation documents."

"You know ma'am is the last person that'll stop or obstruct an investigation. What exactly did she tell you?"

Mislan looks at his assistant and laughs.

"You're always on her side, aren't you?"

"I'm not on her side, I'm on the side of common sense," Johan says with mock seriousness.

———

ASP Rohimmi Noor of Seremban 2 Police returns Mislan's call. Mislan again introduces himself and tells him he's the lead investigator for a double murder in Sentul. He tells ASP Rohimmi that after reading the IPRS report, he believes there are similarities between the cases. In brief, he describes the similarities and asks if they can exchange copies of their investigation papers.

"I don't see why not, if it can help solve the cases," Rohimmi answers.

"Can we meet tomorrow? I'll drive down to Seremban 2," he suggests.

"I'm caught up managing the MCO roadblock and will only be back at the station by around 4 in the evening, and that's if nothing major happens."

"Perhaps we can meet earlier. I'll swing by your roadblock."

"Yes, that'll work. We can exchange the IP copies then."

"Thank you, sir. Looking forward to meeting you."

As Mislan terminates the call, Superintendent Samsiah appears at the office doorway. She heads straight for Mislan's desk.

"Just stopped by to give you good news," she says, waving an acknowledgment to Johan.

"You're making us breakfast tomorrow," Mislan jokes.

Superintendent Samsiah and Detective Sergeant Johan laugh.

"I'm serious, all the stalls are closed," Mislan says, putting on a serious face. "You know I cannot function without my nasi lemak."

"Now is a good time to start eating healthy," she suggests. "Amir just called to inform us that your Selayang market incident was NFA by ISCD. They deemed it as a justifiable and lawful discharge of firearm in the line of duty. The video taken by Aziz somehow magically found its way onto YouTube to clear your action." Superintendent Samsiah gazes at Mislan and slowly pans to Detective Sergeant Johan. "Here's the best part: it was that reporter, what's her name, Audi, that raised it during the OCCI's PC. How coincidental was that?"

The NFA mentioned by Superintendent Samsiah is a police term for "No Further Action," meaning the case is closed until, of course, new incriminating evidence surfaces.

Mislan puts on the best shocked expression he can conjure, and Johan stares at an imaginary speck on his shoes.

"I don't want to know anything about it—just be careful not to be caught, especially when you rope in outside help."

Mislan chooses not to acknowledge her advice, for to do so would be an admission, but through the corner of his eyes, he sees his assistant nodding in earnest.

"Ma'am, the Seremban 2 IO, ASP Rohimmi, agreed to meet me tomorrow. Can I go with Johan?"

"Where're you meeting him?"

"At one of the roadblocks he is managing. He'll WhatsApp me his location when I'm close by."

"Fill out the movement request," Samsiah says. "OK, I'll see you guys tomorrow. Good night and stay safe."

Mislan and Johan stare at her back in disbelief as she walks out of their office. This is probably the first time in the history of D9 that they're seeing her leave the office before 7 p.m.

Nights are usually the busiest time in a twenty-four shift. For whatever reason, nighttime attracts the thugs, drunks, psychopaths, rapists, and general scum and entices them to do what they do. Perhaps due to the misconception that the darkness will conceal their activities.

Tonight, however, is draggy. Mislan doesn't receive a single callout. About the only predicament he and his assistant face is what to have for dinner. They resolve the issue by Johan going to the 7-Eleven to buy a bottle of strawberry jam to eat with the bread he bought earlier for his boss. Then Johan spends the rest of the night liking and commenting on posts on his social media.

Mislan has never been into social media. His ex-wife and Dr. Safia have accounts but not him. *Why do I need to see what other people eat, where they go for vacation or what their children look like?* he used to tell his ex-wife when she suggested he get on Facebook. *Or who is dating who?* After a while, his ex-wife gave up. When Dr. Safia tried to encourage him, he just nodded at her suggestion and left it at that.

Johan is the total opposite; he is into all that stuff: Facebook, Instagram, Twitter, and whatever else is out there. Johan once showed him his Facebook account, and he had more than a thousand friends or followers or whatever they term it, mostly female. *Who the hell has the time to chat with one thousand friends?* Mislan asked himself.

14

THE MORNING PRAYER IS short as there is nothing for Mislan, the outgoing shift investigator, to report. Superintendent Samsiah suggests they monitor the frequency of callouts in the next few days. Should it continue this way, perhaps a couple of the officers should volunteer to assist the general duty personnel at roadblocks. Districts are facing a shortage of officers to rotate for all the roadblocks. Inspector Reeziana and Inspector Khamis immediately volunteer, saying it would be interesting out there.

"OK, let's see how it goes," Samsiah says. "That's it, stay safe."

After she leaves, the officers and assistants gather around the pantry. Inspector Khamis, Reeziana, Mislan, and a couple of the assistants light up under the disapproving gaze of Inspector Tee.

"You guys better stock up," Khamis says, holding up his cigarette, "these are nonessential items. They won't be restocked."

"No shit," Reeziana quips. "Don't the fools know that cigarettes are the most essential of items? Without cigarettes, there'll be mental illness and nicotine withdrawal–induced violence all over."

"Yeah, right," Tee sneers.

Mislan and the other smokers laugh.

"Jo, you want to go home and catch some sleep before we go to Seremban 2?" Mislan asks his assistant.

"Just need to shower and change, that's all," Johan replies.

"What's in Seremban 2?" Reeziana asks.

"Don't know for sure, but there may have been a similar case to Sentul, about a month back."

"Cool."

"OK, Jo, after you shower and change, why don't you swing by my place? It's easier to go from there."

————

They take the Middle Ring Road 2 until the Sungai Besi Town exit that merges onto the Sungai Besi Expressway. The road is mostly empty except for a few vans and trucks delivering dry goods. From there they take the UPM/Sri Serdang/Kuala Lumpur/Johor Bahru exit onto the North-South Highway. As they drive, Johan fervently updates him on the human cost of the crisis. It is only the second day of the MCO, and some businesses are already making their employees go on no-pay leave during the period. People are worried this will eventually result in them losing their jobs and livelihood. Social media is full of postings calling for the government, the elected politicians, to assist their constituencies, and all they said was: *We're looking into it.* According to Johan, some nongovernmental organizations, associations, and caring individuals are gearing up to step in and assist the people instead of waiting for the government.

After about twenty-five miles of listening to Johan's litany, Mislan takes the Seremban/Labu exit. He asks his assistant to Waze the directions to Persiaran Utama S2/1.

"Where on Persiaran Utama?" Johan asks.

"I don't know, ASP Rohimmi said the roadblock is on that road. We'll just drive down the road, and I'm sure we'll run into them."

"OK, make a right here. That's Persiaran Utama."

Mislan makes a right and the female voice from Waze tells him to continue driving straight for four miles. He lights a cigarette and lowers the window.

"Have you had your breakfast?" Mislan asks.

"Just coffee."

"I'm hungry. You think there's a shop we can get something to eat?"

"You mean at the roadblock?"

Mislan nods.

"If it's on this road, I doubt it. You want to make a detour and look for a restaurant?"

"No. Let's hope they have something to eat at the roadblock."

————

They see a roadblock about five hundred yards ahead. Several uniformed policemen and women are standing by the red "Police Check" stop sign. Mislan stops the car and asks the police corporal if ASP Rohimmi is around. He points to the tent and asks what it's about. Mislan introduces himself and is asked to park by the side where a police Land Rover and sedan are parked.

They walk to the tent and spot ASP Rohimmi with a few uniformed policemen having brunch. To his delight, he sees a stack of plastic food packs and a large hot drink dispenser on a table at the deep end of the tent. *What a godsend*, he says to himself, glancing at his assistant, who is stifling a grin.

Mislan introduces himself and his assistant to Rohimmi but does not proffer his hand; no unnecessary human contact is the new normal. Rohimmi is in his late forties, bald, and stout. He has a deep manly voice, a warm and friendly attitude, and a constant smile. From his dialect and generous hospitality, Mislan guesses he must be from a northern state, perhaps Kedah.

"Come, come," Rohimmi invites them. "Have you eaten? We've got a lot of food. The people around here are very kind. Every day they send us food, saying we don't have time to look for it ourselves."

Two uniformed policemen stand, offering their chairs to the D9 officers. A policewoman brings two packs of fried noodles, and another brings two paper cups of coffee.

"Eat," Rohimmi invites. "There's plenty more where that came from."

"Thanks."

As the two D9 officers dig in, the assistant superintendent of police takes out an e-cigarette and starts vaping. Vaping is something Mislan cannot understand—if you want to smoke, then smoke. Why the need to smoke something fake? It's like masturbating instead of real sex. He grins, thinking, *Who cares what he smokes? The fact remains he smokes, and so can I, what a great start to the day.*

"How's traffic coming here?" he asks while sucking on the e-cigarette. He exhales a plume of strawberry-scented smoke.

"Hardly any, except for goods vehicles," Johan answers. "How about here?"

"The same, but you still get a few dickheads trying to bluff their way through."

Johan looks toward the roadblock and sees a car and two motorbikes being stopped and the driver and riders questioned.

"So, what do you do?" Mislan asks.

"For now, nothing; we just record their particulars and let them off with a caution."

"Will that contain the situation?" Mislan asks skeptically. "I mean, the people from breaching the MCO?"

"Doubt it, but that's the instruction from the top."

Mislan finishes his noodles and lights a cigarette. Rohimmi hands him a large brown envelope, and Mislan does likewise. Both extract the contents for a quick look. Johan watches as the two officers eagerly digest the investigation documents while puffing intently on their cigarettes.

"It says here the bullets recovered were 9mm," Rohimmi points out. "In my case, it was a .32."

"Yes, but the MO similarities are uncanny. The entry where the grille door was opened using what Forensics believed to be a master key. I mean there was no sign of it being peeled or jacked out, which is common in housebreaking. Then the front door, which was jimmied using possibly a crowbar."

Rohimmi scrutinizes the report by Crime Forensics (D10) and nods.

"What got my attention were two things. One is the victim's phone and wallet were missing and seemingly nothing else. Second is the killshot, which is to the back of the head. Here, look at the autopsy report." Mislan highlights the report to him, pointing to the Cause of Death (COD). "And this says ligature markings on the victim's wrists."

"Sorry, I missed that. What do you make of it?"

"I believe the victim's hands were bound behind his back. The abrasions were caused when he was shot in the back of the head, due to the body spasm or whatever it is termed."

"But the victim was not bound when we found him." Rohimmi is baffled.

"Same with mine. Again, I believe the killer took off whatever was used to bind the victim's hands, the same way they picked up the casings."

Rohimmi gives him slow, thoughtful nods. "You think they're professional hit men?"

Mislan and Johan nod.

"Looks like it."

They hear a loud reprimand coming from the roadblock. A policeman is barking angrily at a motorcyclist carrying a woman with a child sandwiched between them. Rohimmi excuses himself and walks over to the roadblock. The two D9 officers take the opportunity to refill their paper cup with fresh coffee. After a while, he comes back with a smile. He sits and explains: as a father himself, the policeman was annoyed that the parents took the child out with the virus around.

"Understandable," Johan says.

For a moment, Mislan thinks about his son. Is Daniel confined at home, or is he out playing with his friends?

"So, you feel the MO is identical, and these killings were committed by the same perpetrators," Rohimmi continues. "In other words, you're saying these men go from state to state to kill. Possibly contracted out by unknowns."

"Could be," Mislan agrees. "So far, I only managed to track your case, which shows some similarities in MO. So it's hard to say with certainty for now. Your victim, was there a background check done on him?"

"Just the routine check to establish his identity, why?"

"Just a hunch. Is it possible to request a thorough check? I mean, Secret Society, Narcotic, and all."

"Yes, but it may take some time, what with these MCO deployments and being short of personnel."

Mislan nods his understanding. "Oh, one last thing, who reported the incident?"

"Gerakan." ASP Rohimmi meant "Bilik Gerakan," or Operation Center.

Mislan nods but says nothing. That is one of the things about his case that puzzles him—the call to Malaysia Emergency Response Services. *Why the call to 999, why not call the police station? It could be that the 999 number is well-known to all and not everyone knows the telephone number to the nearest police station. Or perhaps the caller doesn't want to be involved in a police investigation, but that's stupid because the call made to 999 can be traced back to him or her. Maybe the caller doesn't know that fact. What is most important, it proves that someone knew about the killing, probably heard the gunshot or witnessed it. Otherwise, why would he or she call 999?*

It puzzles him, but at the same time, he's ticked off for not paying attention to it when he was informed by Inspector Shahira. When they get in the car, he decides to run it by his assistant.

"Jo, ASP Rohimmi said the incident was called in to 999," Mislan says. Johan nods.

"Inspector Shahira said the same of our case."

"Yes."

"Doesn't it strike you as odd?"

"What, the call?"

"Yes, why call 999 and not the police?"

"Probably he doesn't know the station number."

"Then why not go to the police station?"

"I don't know, too far or just doesn't want to be involved?"

"That's what I initially thought, but 999 calls are recorded and can be easily traced back to the caller through the phone number."

"If the phone is registered to the caller; otherwise it's not so."

Mislan nods. "How did the caller know of the shooting?"

"What do you mean?"

"The caller called 999 to inform them of the incident. How did the caller know there had been a shooting?"

"What are you getting at?"

"What I'm saying is: someone knew of the shooting, and that some-one called to report it to 999. The neighbors didn't hear any gunshot in both cases, but somehow someone knew."

"So you're saying the neighbors lied?"

"Possible."

"Maybe someone, a friend, came to visit and saw the bodies. He or she freaked out and ran off. Then he or she called 999."

"Hmmm, in both cases?" Mislan says, looking at his assistant. "You're such a believer in coincidences, aren't you?"

———

For the drive back, Johan takes the wheel. Mislan asks him to pull over at a petrol kiosk as he needs to use the restroom. Coming out from the restroom, he enters the shop and comes out with five packs of cigarettes. Johan gives him a stare as Mislan enters the car.

"Didn't you hear what Khamis said? These are nonessential items and won't be restocked by the suppliers," Mislan explains.

"Perhaps this is a good time to stop smoking," Johan suggests.

"Ma'am thought when I was hospitalized, it was a good time to stop smoking. Well, I didn't, and now you think this MCO's a second chance for me." Mislan chortles. "Think again, buddy."

"We're thinking about you, your health," Johan says with a tiny smile.

"Thanks, my health will be worse if I don't smoke," Mislan retorts, sniggering. "Same goes for the health of those around me."

Driving out back to the highway, Johan asks, "Why don't you ask Inspector Khamis to buy your cigarettes? I heard he gets his supplies from the Aceh shops at Jalan Raja Bot. Smuggled cigarettes at a cheaper price."

"It doesn't carry our government's seal," Mislan says, letting out a hearty laugh. "And that makes them bad for your health."

Johan gives his boss a wry gaze.

They ride in silence until they approach the Sungai Besi Toll Plaza and Johan asks if they're heading for the office or his apartment. Mislan tells him to drive to his apartment. Johan takes the slip road and heads for the MRR2 and to Bukit Antarabangsa.

Before Johan leaves, Mislan asks him to check with Malaysia Emergency Response Services (MERS) to find out who called to report on the Seremban 2 and Sentul cases.

"Are you on to something?" Johan asks, intrigued.

"Maybe, but I'm not pinning much hope on it."

15

FOUR DAYS PASS WITH no word on the inquiry into the victim's background from ASP Rohimmi Noor of Seremban 2 Police. Mislan is restless; his case is going nowhere. The only consolation is there are no new cases for the entire Special Investigations team. The MCO is the most effective crime prevention tool ever implemented. Either that or the coronavirus is scaring off the villains. Whichever the reason, Mislan and the investigation team are thankful but bored as hell.

During the daytime, the office is quiet. Personnel are distancing themselves from each other and are glued to social media for current news and information. At night, it is ghostly, even eerie at times. The phone doesn't ring, and there is hardly any human activity.

Inspector Khamis and Reeziana have volunteered to be assigned to the districts, where they'll assist at roadblocks. That leaves only two investigators on shift rotation, Inspector Tee and him. The rotation is simple: one day on, one day off.

A couple of days earlier, Johan's check with MERS yielded the following information:

According to the MERS log, the call for the Seremban 2 killing was received at 1:44 a.m. from a Chinese male who claimed to be Tan Yu Beng. The MERS operator recorded the report and then informed the relevant agency. In this case, it was the police's Operation Center.

The MERS log recording of the call for the Sentul double murder was received at 1:35 a.m. from a Malay male claiming to be Daud

Abdullah. MERS acted accordingly. In both the cases, the calls were made to 112 instead of 999 because they were made using cell phones. The number 999 is for landlines, but the term remains the most common one locals use to mean an emergency call.

A check with the cell phone service providers revealed that the number used to report the Seremban 2 killing was a postpaid one registered to the victim, Chai Lai Meng. Whereas the cell phone number that reported the Sentul double murder was a prepaid number belonging to a person unknown to Mislan or Johan. The name Hadassah listed as the prepaid owner sounded foreign, and upon checking the address that had been given, it was found to be fake. Johan, however, recognized the number to be one used by one of their victims—Ajimullah. This new discovery burst his theory that someone must have known or witnessed the incident and made a call to 999.

In both cases, the cell phones of the victims were missing. In the absence of any indication they were taken by others, Mislan theorized the killers must have taken them. *But why? To make the calls to report their death? What was the point?*

Mislan pondered and tried to make sense of the killers' actions. *Were they trying to say something, make a statement? But what? And to whom—the investigator? To screw with his head? Why call MERS, knowing their calls would be logged and recorded? Why call immediately after the killings? Why the need for the incidents to be discovered immediately?*

Too many questions and not enough answers. He lights a cigarette and consoles himself. *These are psychopaths, they don't need reasons.*

———

Morning prayer has been suspended by the head of Special Investigations until things are back to normal. Every 8:30 a.m., the outgoing shift investigator will brief her and the incoming shift investigator in her office.

Terminating the very short meeting, Superintendent Samsiah asks Mislan to stay back. She waits for Inspector Tee to leave the office.

"How have you been keeping? I know you're staying by yourself, are you eating well?"

Mislan nods.

"Where are you getting food from?"

"The restaurants up at my place are open for takeout."

"Good. How's your case coming along?"

Mislan shrugs.

"Not going anywhere, eh?"

"Looks like it."

"Want to kick it around? I've got a lot of time on my hands. Where's Jo?"

"Glued to his phone, Facebook or something. I really don't know how he does it."

"Unlike you, Jo is a people person, he's young and available. So he's got a lot going for him, and what better place to go hunting if not on social media."

Mislan sighs, not following his boss's reasoning.

"What's puzzling you about your case?"

"You already know all there is to know about it, but the latest is we tracked the calls to MERS. Both the killings were called in to 999—well, in these cases 112."

Superintendent Samsiah nods.

"Both times, the calls were made immediately or very soon after the killings, using the vics' cell phones."

Superintendent Samsiah arches her eyebrows.

"The question is, why use the vics' cell phones and why shortly after the killings?"

"Hmmm, that's definitely puzzling," she agrees. "And what's the best theory you came up with?"

"That these people are lunatics and lunatics don't need reasons," he answers, grinning.

"Don't underestimate psychopaths, Lan. Research has shown psychopaths to be highly intelligent people. They're great planners, very organized and meticulous. Some of them have high IQs. What differentiates them from us is their criminal means and motives, their lack of empathy toward others."

"Are you describing me?" Mislan jokes.

"You can be said to be a borderline case," she says, followed by a hearty laugh. "That's why you're good at what you do."

"I'll take that as a compliment."

"OK, so these killers made the calls to 999 using the vics' cell phones shortly after their deeds because they're psychopaths," she says, pursing her lips. "How do you know it was the killers making the call?"

"The vics' phones were missing when the IOs arrived at the scene, so the probability they were taken by them is compelling. That is if it's read together with the missing vics' wallets and other personal belongings. I mean, apart from us, the forensics guys, and the killers, who would search a bloodied corpse for its belongings?"

"The items may not have been on the victims' person. OK, for argument's sake, I grant you your assumption, although I think many more individuals can be added to your list. Perhaps they do it because they want to witness the action. You know, see the police arrival, the crime scene team and so on."

"Could be, but what's there to see? They were in dwellings. Unless they join the police team, they're not seeing anything."

"True."

"When I was a district IO, I attended a bomb call response training. You wouldn't believe what they code-named a bomb call."

Samsiah narrows her eyes at him, as if asking *What?*

"Ops Bunga," he says, followed by a laugh. Operation Flower. "I suppose they think when a bomb goes off it'll look like flower-shaped fireworks. Anyway, at the training, we were taught to observe the surrounding area to identify suspicious onlookers or characters. Usually in a bomb-hoax call, the caller would hang around to enjoy the commotion, the panic he or she created. That I can understand, but in these cases, what was there to see or enjoy? They've already seen firsthand what they did."

"Maybe they want the police to be the first on the scene," Samsiah suggests.

"For what reason?"

"I don't know, maybe they want the police to find something. That if the crime was discovered by the others or the public, that something would be removed, taken, stolen. And in the Sentul case, the drugs."

"OK, that makes more sense, but what about the Seremban 2 case?"

"It's not good of me to think this, but what if there were drugs and the responding personnel took them without reporting?" she says, not looking pleased with herself.

"Stole the drugs?" Mislan remarks, his eyebrows raised. "That's interesting, and something that can't be entirely dismissed. I asked ASP Rohimmi to do a thorough background on the vic, with D7, Narco included. He has yet to revert."

"What're you witch-hunting for?"

"Now that you've mentioned it, the probability of drugs being at the scene. The vic drug link."

"Let me speak to Narco, see if they can speed up the background for you."

"Thanks, ma'am."

"Anything else you need to kick around?"

"That's enough for one day, my head is already spinning."

After Mislan leaves, Superintendent Samsiah makes a call to ASP Amir Muhammad at ISCD. She asks if he can spare some time to meet with her. Then she makes a courtesy phone call to the head of Narcotic Criminal Investigation Division, Negeri Sembilan Police contingent headquarters.

16

On his way home, Mislan decides to make a detour to Kampung Baru in search of breakfast and possibly some other food items. He comes upon two roadblocks where he has to identify himself and tells a fib about his reason for being out and about. Driving around the familiar roads, he can't help but feel strange at the creepy desolation of the surrounding areas, areas that had always been swarming with people. Empty stalls lined the roads, stalls that usually sell breakfast dishes from every state of the country. Stalls that are constantly packed with customers for sit-down meals or takeout. Passing by the famous Jamek Mosque and seeing the main gate closed is something he would never have envisaged. He wonders how long this pandemic will last. The more pertinent question: How long will people last before experiencing financial ruin?

Giving up on finding breakfast, he heads toward Jalan Pekeliling and hits Jalan Ampang, stopping at Ampang Point mall to get a McDonald's set. During the MCO, he supposes he has to get used to fast food. At the entrance of the mall, his temperature is taken by the security guard, and sanitizer is sprayed on his hands before he is allowed in. Another new normal. Except for pharmacies and food outlets, all other shops are closed.

The queue at McDonald's is long. A group of food delivery guys from Grab, Food Panda, and many others are given preference and are picking up their orders. Business couldn't be more booming.

It's a joke how the government takes care of the large corporations but doesn't give a rat's ass about killing the small businesses that operate stalls, Mislan reflects with a sigh.

———

Lying in bed, Mislan watches the news. For days it has been filled with stories of the pandemic, the infected, and death tolls worldwide. America might become the new epicenter. The US president is pointing fingers at the World Health Organization, accusing it of not being transparent and for being China-centric. He threatens to stop US funding to the WHO.

Malaysia too made international news but for the wrong reasons. Al Jazeera News reported that the Malaysian Women, Family and Community Development Ministry had asked housewives to mimic the voice of the Japanese cartoon character Doraemon when speaking to their husbands. This would allegedly comfort the husbands and avoid domestic violence. Doraemon's voice sounds to Mislan like a high-pitched nasal tone with silly giggles. If a housewife is stupid enough to follow the minister's suggestion, the husband would probably get her committed to the loony bin.

He turns off the TV, but he isn't sleepy. Last night he managed to get a lot of sleep as there was not a single callout to attend to. He gets up from bed and calls Chew of Crime Forensics.

"Hey, Chew, can you talk?"

"Inspector, sure," Chew replies, cheery as ever.

"The impression on abrasions, did you manage to match them to anything?" he asks with expectation.

"I tried comparing it to many things that might cause similar impressions, but nothing is conclusive," Chew answers apologetically.

"I see," Mislan says, disappointed.

"The closest I came up with, but it may not hold up as evidence in court, is something like a cable tie. The inside of a cable tie is threaded so that once you pull the strap to tighten the cable, it cannot come loose."

"You mean like plasticuffs, the plastic straps used in place of hand-cuffs?" Mislan asks excitedly.

"I don't know, I haven't examined a plasticuff before."

"We use them for large roundups where a lot of cuffs are required. It's double-loop. I'll try to get ahold of one and send it to you."

"That may help. You guys have it at the office?"

"No, we don't use them, but I think the Federal Reserve Unit does. They usually do crowd control, riot dispersal, and group arrests. Never mind, I'll get hold of one and send it to you."

————

After talking to Chew, Mislan calls his assistant. Detective Sergeant Johan answers on the first ring.

"Jo, are you home?"

"No, I'm at Dang Wangi Police."

"What're you doing there?"

"Just catching up with some of my old MPV buddies. Anything?"

"I need you to get hold of a plasticuff. Like the kind the FRU use. I want to pass one on to Chew, Forensics."

"I think the District Light Strike Force uses them. Let me check and call back."

The District Light Strike Force is made up of general duty person-nel that the officer in charge in a police district will deploy to break up small illegal gatherings like industrial strikes without a permit. They're usually equipped with the basic personal protective equipment (PPE) like shields, helmets, face protection, elbow and knee paddings, tear gas, pepper spray, batons—and, Mislan supposes, plasticuffs too.

Fifteen minutes later, Johan calls saying he has gotten hold of a plasticuff. Mislan asks if he can send it to Chew at Crime Forensics, and Johan says he will. He then calls Chew to inform him that Johan is on the way there.

————

His mind shifts to the cases. In both, the neighbors claimed they didn't hear gunshots. That could mean two things. One, the neighbors lied to avoid getting involved with a criminal investigation. But what were the chances that neighbors in two separate cases claimed not to hear anything? Two, the killers used gun suppressors or silencers.

Malaysians do not have the constitutional right to carry arms, concealed or openly. Permission to own and carry firearms is heavily regulated and controlled. Except for the security forces and certain government enforcement agencies, ownership of firearms is licensed. The license is renewed yearly and may be revoked by the police without offering any reason. Firearms are regulated by the Arms Act 1960 and the Firearms (Increase Penalty) Act 1971. Under the latter legislation, a person convicted of using firearms in the commission of a criminal act faces the death sentence.

As for gun suppressors or silencers, they are totally banned—but that does not mean there are none in the country.

Mislan has heard that shooting through a plastic bottle or wrapping a damp towel over the gun can act as a blast suppressor. He remembers seeing an old spy movie where the shooter wrapped a damp towel over his gun to kill a person in a room. He couldn't remember what level of noise was made by the gun, but he supposed it worked because he also can't remember anyone kicking down the door to arrest the shooter. He can't recall having seen shooting through a plastic bottle before.

He logs on to YouTube and searches for "gun suppressor." To his surprise, there are hundreds of videos about suppressors: various types of handgun suppressors, rifle suppressors, assault weapon suppressors, and DIY suppressors. He spends hours viewing them.

There is this one video that interests him. It is about a suppressor nicknamed Hush Puppy. According to the video, the silencer was specially designed for the SEALs. The SEALs wanted a suppressor for their clandestine operations that would barely make a sound. The video showed one about seven inches long, and when a 9mm handgun was fired using it, there was hardly any blast. It just went, *puff.* The video also showed the stripped parts of the suppressor, which he doesn't understand. He downloads the video onto his cell phone.

If the killers were determined to get their hands on suppressors, they could easily get hold of them, he figures. Even if they didn't want the risk of bringing the suppressors into the country, they could easily get a machinist to fabricate some for them.

After hours of video-watching, his eyes are tired and watery. He logs off and lies on the bed, closing his eyes. His mind wanders to Dr. Safia. A woman with whom he found friendship, companionship, understanding, and maybe, just maybe, even love. He vividly remembers the first time they made love. It was at her apartment, the night his boss called to give him the news of the killing of Four-Finger Loo, a blueblood triad member.

The evening before the killing, Mislan had sought the assistance of a former D7 officer, Inspector Song from Petaling Jaya Police, to arrange a meeting for him with Four-Finger Loo, an ex-Tiger general. Mislan needed to establish whether the triple murder in his case had any triad involvement. The day after his meeting with Four-Finger Loo, the publicity junkie OCCI gave a press conference stating that an ex–triad member was assisting in the investigation of a case monikered the Yee Sang Murders. The very same night, Four-Finger Loo was viciously attacked while having dinner at his usual restaurant and hacked to death.

When the news was relayed to him by his boss, Mislan blamed himself for the old man's death. He was standing on the balcony, shaking with anger and frustration, when Dr. Safia hugged him from behind. Her body warm, her whispers soothing, she told him it was not his fault. He didn't know why, but he kissed her and she responded. They ended up in bed making passionate love. He remembers how they ravished each other's bodies and, when spent, rolled apart, panting in the dark. No words spoken, none needed.

Mislan wonders where she is and who she is seeing. Does she make love to him as passionately as they did? Does she remember or think of him, or has she moved on?

There are times, just like he is experiencing now, when he is so overwhelmed by loneliness and weakness that he wants to track her down. But somehow he gets over it and never does.

17

ARRIVING AT THE OFFICE the next morning, Mislan is surprised to find Inspector Reeziana in full uniform at her desk. Inspector Tee, the outgoing investigator and his assistant, are enjoying breakfast at their desks. Inspector Khamis and his assistant are nowhere to be seen.

"Missed us?" Mislan teases Reeziana.

"Yeah, especially your charm," Reeziana mocks. "Brought you guys breakfast," she says, pointing to a stack of plastic containers on the pantry table. "I know you guys are starving with all the stalls closed."

"How did you manage to buy them?" Mislan asks.

"I didn't buy them. There're given by the public to show their appreciation to us, the frontliners. For risking our lives to protect theirs," she says, enunciating the words to emphasize their importance, and follows it with a laugh. "Unlike you cowards, hiding in the office."

"It's better to be a coward and live than be a hero and die," Tee says pragmatically.

Johan arrives, and he too is surprised that Inspector Reeziana and her assistant are present. Then he notices the pantry table.

"Woah, is that food for us?" Johan asks.

"From the people to us," Reeziana replies and adds, "those of us who are the frontliners."

"That's us all right, frontliners," Johan says, heading for the pantry. From there, he calls out to Mislan, "There's nasi lemak. You want one?"

"Really? It's been days since I had some," Mislan answers, beaming.

"It's just plain with boiled egg," Johan tells him.

"I don't care as long as it's nasi lemak."

The officers and their assistants sit at their respective desks, respecting the social distancing guidelines, and are talking across the open office when Superintendent Samsiah walks in. The small talk stops as they greet-wish her.

"Morning," Samsiah says, returning their greetings. "I thought I heard your voice as I was coming here," she says to Reeziana. "What are you doing here?"

"Feeding these hungry boys," Reeziana replies. "There's a lot more, ma'am, if you want."

"No thanks, I already had breakfast. How was it out there?"

"Humid and tiring, but fun. You should hear some of the excuses the MCO breakers came up with. They put our detectives' bullshit to shame."

They all laugh.

"Yes, I watched some of it on FB," Johan says. "There was one guy who said he needed to go to the office to water the plants. Damn, I couldn't come up with such an excuse even if I tried."

"We caught two of the food delivery boys delivering drugs, cannabis and meth," Reeziana says.

"Drugs are essential too," Mislan deadpans. "MCO or no MCO, they still need their daily fix."

"Tee, anything to brief?" Samsiah asks.

"No, ma'am, all quiet," Tee says.

"OK. Nice of you to drop by, Yana," Samsiah says and leaves her officers to their chat.

———

Inspector Reeziana updates the rest on what she heard from the ground, about the likelihood of the MCO being extended for another fourteen days. The government termed it Stage Two. As the number of infections is still rising and many people are defying the lockdown, the army will be deployed to assist the police. The Inspector General of Police issued orders for the police to take firmer action against those defying the MCO. Those stopped for breaching the MCO without valid reason will be issued with a summons for a thousand-ringgit fine.

"People will starve," Johan says. "Another fourteen days will kill them."

"Yes, but the infection rate and death tolls are increasing. The health ministry said we're not yet in the clear, and if stricter measures are not implemented, well, I don't know what to imagine," Tee says.

"It's easy for you when you are receiving your salary," Johan stresses rather emotionally. "Think of the families that are daily wage earners. No work, no money, no food. I heard some of them may be kicked out of their houses for not being able to pay rent."

Mislan watches his assistant, hearing the pent-up anger in his voice. Sees the concern he is expressing over the fate of people he doesn't even know. He understands what his boss meant when she said Johan is a people-person.

"Yesterday I bumped into the woman that sells nasi lemak near my place. I get Inspector Mislan's nasi lemak from her. I know her husband is ill and isn't working, and they have three school-age children. You think she can survive if this MCO drags on?" Johan pauses to calm down. "I know there're NGOs and individuals working to help, but with this extension, is it enough?" Johan moans.

The investigators and assistants look at Johan, feel what he's feeling but say nothing.

"Hey, I heard one of the men at the roadblock saying that when he was on inquiry counter duty, he got a report from a woman claiming her NGO received twenty K from an unknown donor," Reeziana says.

"No shit," Tee exclaims.

"Why would she lie?" Reeziana replies.

"I wish someone would donate twenty K to me so I can use it to help all the people in need," Johan says.

"Check out the report. I heard the unknown donor called the NGO and asked for their account number. Maybe his phone number is stated in the report."

"Dang Wangi, right?" Johan asks.

Reeziana nods.

———

Mislan is at the emergency staircase enjoying his cigarette when Johan appears at the door, handing him his cell phone. It's Chew from Crime Forensics.

"Morning, Inspector," Chew greets him.

"Morning, Chew, any good news?"

"Afraid not, sorry," Chew says. "I examined the plasticuffs Detective Sergeant Johan gave me, and I still have to say it's inconclusive. I even put the thing on me and wriggled hard to get the impressions on my wrists, but I still can't say the markings are identical to those in the photos. Sorry."

"No problem," Mislan answers, sounding frustrated.

"But for the purpose of investigation, I can safely say you can go with the theory that the victims' wrists were bound using something similar to the plasticuff or cable-binder. I don't think you'd be wrong in that sense."

"Thanks, Chew."

"Inspector, if you do find something similar in the possession of a suspect, we can do a swab on it to see if we could get skin cells for touch DNA testing."

"You mean those used on the victims?"

"Yes. By the way, Inspector, do you want the plasticuffs back?"

"No, why?"

"Remember I told you I even used it on myself? Well, I have to cut it off from my wrists," Chew says, and Mislan can hear him chuckle before the call is terminated.

———

Mislan redials Chew's number.

"Yes, Inspector?" Chew answers, sounding surprised.

"Chew, your contact at Ballistic," Mislan states.

"What about him?"

"Can you ask him if he can differentiate if a bullet was shot using a suppressor?"

"You mean a bullet shot without and with a suppressor using the same gun?"

"Yes, that's it."

"I'll give him a call. You think the killers used suppressors? I thought suppressors are banned here."

"So is porn, but the internet is littered with it," Mislan says.

"Yes," Chew says with a chuckle. "Stupid question, eh?"

———

That afternoon around 3:30 p.m., Detective Sergeant Johan enters the office excitedly waving a piece of paper. As he marches to Mislan's desk, he says, "You're not going to believe this."

Mislan stares at his assistant, thinking he must be waving a notice for his car repossession or house eviction. He says nothing and waits for Johan to reach his desk.

"The unknown donor Inspector Reeziana was talking about—" Johan says.

"—is an Arab prince who wishes to remain anonymous like in Najib's case," Mislan says, cutting off his assistant midsentence.

"No, not an Arab prince," Johan says, not catching the joke. "The phone number he used is the cell phone number of our vic, Ajimullah," he says, placing the copy of the police report in front of Mislan.

"What the hell!"

"Exactly what I said."

Mislan reads the police report. The complainant was Chuah Guat Eng of the Forgotten Children of Kuala Lumpur Foundation. She claimed to have received a call from a Chinese male identifying himself as Peter Lai, who wished to donate twenty thousand ringgit to the foundation. He asked for the foundation's bank account number, saying he would bank in the money immediately.

Skeptical of the call but always in need of donations, Chuah gave the foundation's account number. True to the caller's word, she received a text message from the bank informing her that RM20,000 had been banked into the foundation's account.

As the foundation's account is subject to public audit, she lodged a police report to cover the large deposit received without documentation.

When Mislan puts down the police report, the two officers stare at each other as if saying *"Can you believe this shit?"*

"I called the number twice," Johan says, "couldn't get through. Just the recorded voice telling me to try again as the number may not be in service or out of coverage." To prove his point, Johan presses the redial button. Instantly the call goes to the voice message. Johan terminates the call.

"What's the number?" Mislan asks.

Johan reads it out to him as he checks against the police report.

"We need to talk to this Chuah lady," Mislan says. "In the meantime, I need ma'am's assistance. Let's go to her office."

———

Superintendent Samsiah is having a cup of tea, which she brewed herself in the office. Seeing the two officers, she waves them in.

"A cup of tea?" she offers.

"Thanks but no thanks, ma'am," Mislan answers for both of them. He places the police report on the desk, pushing it closer toward her.

"What's this?" Samsiah asks, putting down her cup. She puts on her reading glasses and starts reading. When she puts the report down, she says, "So, we have a philanthropist who wished to remain anonymous. Another Arab prince, I suppose," she adds with a sly smile.

Mislan laughs, but Johan still does not catch the joke.

"What's with the Arab prince?" Johan asks, curious.

"The ex-PM Najib. Remember the 2.6 billion in his account he claimed to be from an Arab prince who wished to remain anonymous?" she explains.

"Ooo, yeah," Johan says, followed by a chuckle when he finally gets the joke.

"The phone number of the donor is that of my vic, Ajimullah," Mislan says.

"Are you sure?"

"Yes," Johan replies, showing her the victim's cell phone number, which he'd obtained from Ismail Sabri, the chicken seller who was not only the victim's ex-employer but the registered tenant of the crime scene house.

"What's the meaning of all this?" she asks, puzzled.

"A game," Mislan says. "The Seremban 2 killers used the vic's phone to call in the incident shortly after killing the victim. The same MO with our case, which only goes to point to the same perpetrators. Then, for some sick reasons, the killers used the same phone to call this foundation to make a donation of twenty K. How sick is that?"

"You came to see me because . . .?"

"I need to do an IPRS search, I can't access nonserious crimes reports. If my hunch is right, there may be other reports of a similar nature."

"Your hunch says these unknown philanthropists are your killers?"

Mislan shrugs.

"They may or may not be the killers, but the phone numbers used to report the incidents to 999 and now this say they are connected one way or another. You see, the Myanmar- —by the way, what do you call a Myanmar national?"

"Myanmarian or Myanmarese, I don't know," Samsiah says.

"Anyway, the guy, I can't remember his name, the one we picked up at the wholesale market—Azara, yes Azara, he claimed the vics sometimes kept large amounts of cash in the house. He said between two fifty to three hundred K. I think the killers weren't interested in the drugs but in the cash. The druggie Adham said he saw one of them carrying a large backpack when they came out of the house. It could be the cash."

"And then they donate the money to the needy," Samsiah says. "Modern-day Robin Hood, a bit farfetched but interesting."

"I like the term 'philanthropist' better."

"Philanthropist it is. How far back do you want this search?"

"Just one month."

Samsiah arches her eyebrows.

"The Seremban 2 case was about a month back. I couldn't find anything going further than that."

"By the way, speaking of Seremban 2, I received feedback from NCID, Negeri Sembilan Contingent. The vic is listed in one of Narco's watch lists. The vic's alias is Thailand Chai. He hailed from Penang and was said to have lived in Thailand for several years, thus the alias. It was suspected, but nothing concrete, that the vic sometimes acted as a mule for drugs from Thailand."

Mislan nods.

"So your hunch was right, well done."

"But that doesn't prove the vic had drugs in the house when he was killed."

"No, it doesn't, but it increases the probability."

18

LORONG TIONG NAM 4 is in the old section of the city, separated from the infamous Chow Kit by Jalan Raja Laut. From the 1960s to the 1990s, Chow Kit and Tiong Nam were known triad hotbeds and playgrounds. In the 1980s, the Kelantanese from the East Coast and Indonesians from Aceh started making footholds, especially in the food and roadside stalls. On the surface, the triad activities seem to have decreased, and the area looks cosmopolitan albeit predominately Chinese. The triads' presence can still be seen if one knows what to look for. It is not a place one goes to wander aimlessly late at night.

As they drive out of the contingent headquarters to meet Chuah Guat Eng, Mislan gets a call.

"Hey, Chew."

"Inspector, can you talk?"

"With you, anytime," Mislan answers.

"Waa, you sound cheerful," Chew comments. "Catch a break in your case?"

"Hopefully."

"I called about the ballistic question you asked earlier. Well, my friend said yes and no. He said some suppressors use, let me check—ah, here it is—a rubber starfish outlet port, I really don't know what that is all about—well, if the suppressor used it, the rubber starfish outlet port, then there's a possibility of traces or residue of the rubber on the bullet. Otherwise, no, you can't tell if a bullet is shot using a suppressor."

"And in my case?" Mislan asks.

"No rubber residue traced, sorry."

"It's OK, Chew, I knew it was too much to hope for. Thanks."

"No sweat, Inspector, stay safe."

"Yeah, you too."

———

The Forgotten Children of Kuala Lumpur Foundation is housed in one of the old buildings next to the Ah Heng Food Center. It is a walk-up three-story building, run-down and in dire need of maintenance. The staircase, however, is clean and brightly lit. As the officers climb the staircase, a group of boys ranging between the ages of nine to fifteen emerges from the second floor into the stairwell. Seeing the officers, they immediately back up into wherever they came from.

"They must have made us for cops," Johan remarks.

"They learn from a young age, don't they?" Mislan says. "Which floor's she on?"

"Second floor, where the kids came out from."

The officers stand at the doorway of the second floor and peek inside. It looks like a class or discussion room with a few foldable Formica dining tables and red plastic chairs arranged in two rows facing the window where a whiteboard hangs. The children they saw earlier are standing in a tight group at the far corner, staring at them. He sees fear in their eyes. Mislan guesses it's because he and Johan are Malay and the foundation does not get Malay men visiting it. Therefore, these two men have to be from the government, which means trouble.

"Hello," Mislan says with a warm smile, "is Mrs. Chuah's office here?"

One of the elder boys points to the open door next to them. A petite woman probably around the age of seventy appears from the room. Her hair is cut short. She wears a wide smile and holds a cigarette in her hand.

"Inspector . . . ?" she asks.

"Mislan, and this is Detective Sergeant Johan. We're from D9, KL."

"Yes, Inspector Mislan, come, come," she invites them and at the same time shoos the kids away.

Mislan notices that she doesn't proffer her hand for a handshake; the new normal fast becoming normal. Taking their seats, Mislan asks if he is permitted to smoke. In reply, she pushes the almost-full ashtray across the table closer to the inspector.

"You mentioned you needed to ask about the donation?" Guat Eng says.

"Yes. Mrs. Chuah, you said in your police report—" Mislan starts.

"Call me Guat, all my friends do," Guat interrupts him.

"OK, you said in the report the money was banked into the foundation's account?"

Guat nods. "Cash."

"You know at which branch?" Mislan asks.

"No, but I'm sure you can check with my bank to find out."

"There'll be a lot of red tape, but if you accompany us, that would make the process easier," Mislan suggests.

"The foundation's account is with the Maybank down the road, but they're closed now."

"We can do it tomorrow morning, if that's OK with you," Mislan prods.

"Yes, we can. I'm normally in the office by ten."

"Thanks. Is there anything you can tell me about the donor's voice or something he may have said that you remember?"

"Ummmm," Guat drags out the word, recollecting. "Actually, he was quite soft-spoken and sounded educated. He spoke English to me, but he had a Chinese accent, and he did say his name was Peter Lai," Guat says with a smile. She puts out her cigarette and lights another. "Is the police confiscating the money?" she asks.

Mislan spots concerns written all over her face.

"I don't know, but I doubt it," Mislan answers.

"I hope not, because part of it was already used to buy food for the children. People are not able to help much during the MCO. I don't blame them. They need the money to put food on their own tables. They have to be frugal—we don't know how long this MCO or pandemic's going to last."

Johan nods in earnest.

"Have you called the donor to thank him?"

"I tried, but the call didn't go through. The service provider said it's not in service."

"Do you know why the donor picked your foundation?"

"No, I have no idea why, but I'm grateful."

"Sorry to ask, where are these kids from? I mean how did they end up here?"

"They're from everywhere in KL. You don't have to look far, they're around every corner, under every bridge, in every alley. We pretend not to see them, but they're certainly there."

"Who're they? I mean, are they orphans?"

"Not necessarily. Most are abandoned or neglected by parents who are drug-dependent. They're left to wander the streets, to fend for themselves. Some of them were exploited by unscrupulous men and women in our great city as beggars, manual labor, petty thieves, and some even as drug peddlers."

"Why isn't the government taking care of them, I mean the welfare agencies?" Johan asks.

"They do, but—I don't know if I should say this to government servants, especially police officers, but I shall," Guat says, taking a long drag on her cigarette. "The government agencies are selective in who they save from the streets."

"Meaning?"

"For whatever reason, they prefer to pick or assist the Muslims. I'm not saying the Malays but the Muslims."

"Shit," Johan exclaims. "Sorry."

Guat smiles. "Don't be. Hearing concern coming from you officers makes me think there's hope still."

———

When Mislan and Johan get back to the office, there is an envelope waiting for them at the front desk. It's from Superintendent Samsiah. Mislan glances at his cell phone to check the time. It is 6:10 p.m. During the

MCO, his boss leaves the office between 5:30 to 6 p.m., an hour or hour and half earlier than her usual time.

At his desk, he opens the envelope to find four copies of police reports, with a note from his boss saying these reports are similar to that of the Philanthropists. Mislan smiles at the term *philanthropists*, coined by his boss for this case.

He reads the four reports and passes them to Johan. When his assistant is done, he asks, "What do you think?"

"These two," Johan says, holding up two reports, "the phone number belongs to the vic in Seremban 2, Thailand Chai. This," he holds up another report, "belongs to Ajimullah, but this—" holding up the last report, "the number is unknown."

"Could belong to our other vic," Mislan suggests.

"Could be, I need to check with Azara if he has the other vic's phone number."

"All the reports say the donor offered twenty K. So that's a hundred K plus the foundation's donation. Remember Azara claimed there could be two hundred fifty to three hundred K? Where's the rest of the money?" Mislan ponders out loud.

"Don't forget the cash from Seremban 2," Johan reminds him. "The donation started immediately after that case, so they would have gotten money from there, too."

"These guys must be sleeping on money, spending it like oil sheiks."

"There could be more of them who received money but didn't report it. I mean, not all of us are law-abiding citizens," Johan reasons. "If you see from the reports, all of them are registered organizations, meaning their accounts are audited. What if it was given to an individual or an outfit that's not registered? I doubt it would be reported."

Mislan nods.

"We need to talk to all of them. We need to see if there's a pattern as to how these organizations were selected or qualified for the donation."

Johan makes fresh coffee for them as Mislan lights a cigarette.

"It's too late now, but tomorrow there're several things we need to do. One, we need to get records for the three cell phones. See if we can track down all the calls that were made using them."

Johan gazes questioningly at his boss.

"To check if there're others that received donations from our mystery donor. Maybe we'll get lucky."

"Lucky how?"

"I don't know, just lucky. The next thing, we need the telco to give us the locations of the phone. You said Ajimullah's phone is off."

Johan nods.

"But when it was used to make the call, the service provider can tell us where the call was made from, right?"

"I think so," Johan says, unsure.

"Yes, they can," Mislan says, more like trying to convince himself. "I'll ask ma'am if she can assist. She's good at these things. We also need to go to the bank with Guat. Find out where the money was deposited from. I hope it was deposited over the counter, but that's just wishful thinking. I don't think these guys are dumb. Most probably the money was deposited through a CDM, cash deposit machine."

"The machines have cameras too," Johan says.

"Yes, but these guys know that too. Jo, I'll WhatsApp you a video. When you have time later, call your workshop friend. He has a machinist working for him, right?"

Johan nods.

"Show the machinist the video and ask if he can fabricate one as shown in the video."

"Fabricate what?"

"A suppressor or silencer."

"You crazy or what?"

"I'm not asking you to ask him to *fabricate* one. I'm asking you to ask him if it's *possible* for him to fabricate one."

———

Mislan looks at the time on his phone. It is 7:45 p.m. It should be 6:45 p.m. in Bangkok, Thailand. *She must have left the office for the day,* Mislan reckons, and he decides to make the call. After several rings, a woman answers.

"*Sawadee ka, khun* Mislan," Dr. Suthisa Ritchu answers.

"*Sawadee krap,* doctor, how're you?" Mislan answers, now familiar with the Thai greeting after his short stint in Thailand. That's one of the two Thai phrases he has remembered from his last adventure there.

"I'm fine, *kap kun ka.* How about you?"

"I'm fine, *kap kun krap,*" Mislan replies, using the other phrase he knows.

"How is *P'*Samsiah?" Dr. Suthisa, also known as Sophia to them, asks.

"She's fine. Doctor, may I ask you something?"

"Yes, of course."

"Is it possible to purchase gun silencers in Thailand?"

"Gun silencer, I don't know. Maybe Police Sergeant Sharky knows."

"Can you ask for me? Sergeant Sharky doesn't speak English, and I can't speak Thai," Mislan says with a chuckle. "It'll be like chicken and duck talking."

Dr. Suthisa lets out a hearty laugh. "Yes, it almost certainly will be that. I'll give him a ring and ask. If it's not classified, may I know the purpose of your inquiry?"

"It's a case I'm working on. The neighbors claimed they didn't hear any gunshots and I'm working on a theory that the killers used suppressors or silencers. In my research, it was reported that guns are easily available near the Thai-Myanmar and Thai-Laos borders."

"Sadly, that's true. Give me a day, and I'll get back to you. Please give my regards to *P'*Samsiah and *khun* Jo."

"I will, and give my warm regards to Police Sergeant Sharky."

"*Sawadee ka,*" Dr. Suthisa wishes, ending the conversation.

"*Krap sawadee krap.*"

Johan raises his eyebrows at his boss when he hears the Thai phrase. "Was that Dr. Sophia?"

"Yes, and she sends her regards to you."

"How is she?"

Mislan and Johan worked on two cases with Dr. Suthisa Ritchu. The first was a case monikered UTube. When they were investigating the case, Dr. Suthisa, who is a behavioral scientist and criminal profiler with the Royal Thai Police, was on attachment to the Royal Malaysia

Police in Bukit Aman. She heard of the case and asked if she could study and assist with the investigation.

The second case was monikered Soulless and involved cross-border investigations. Mislan and Johan were sent to Thailand, and unofficially, Superintendent Samsiah had asked if Dr. Suthisa could assist her officers. The request was made purely because her officers can't speak Thai. Dr. Suthisa obliged, took some days off, and flew south to Hat Yai. Her assistance was much appreciated by Mislan and Johan, who were lost when facing the unfamiliar language and culture.

Dr. Suthisa is in her late thirties, well-shaped and curvy. She walks with a slight skip and has an attitude like Stoney in Lobo's song "Happy All the Time."

"She's fine."

"You mean *sabai dee*," Johan says, showing off his mastery of the Thai language.

"Whatever."

———

Johan tells his boss he's going to see his friend from the workshop, and Mislan tries to grab some sleep. Pumped up from the exhilaration of catching a break in the investigation, sleep eludes him. It is 8:20 p.m., and hunger visits him. There are some leftovers from the food Inspector Reeziana brought back that morning. He opens the pack, gives the food a good sniff and determines it is still good to eat.

19

THANK GOD FOR THE caring soul of Inspector Reeziana, who comes in every morning carrying a large plastic bag filled with packs of food. Food that the kind folks of Kampung Baru prepared for frontliners in appreciation for keeping them safe from COVID-19. Mislan makes coffee for Johan and himself, and they sit at their desks and enjoy the home-cooked breakfast.

"Jo, did you manage to get the donor's phone number?" Reeziana asks from her desk.

Johan nods with his mouth full.

"You contacted him?"

Johan takes a sip of the coffee to wash down the food before answering. "Guess what? The phone number is that of our vic in the Sentul case."

"What? You're kidding me!" she exclaims.

Johan shakes his head as he scoops a spoonful of noodles into his mouth.

"Maybe the telco had assigned the number to another user," Tee suggests.

"Not that quick. The number has to have been expired for months before they recycle it," Reeziana replies. "But I don't think they recycle them anymore."

Mislan finishes with his breakfast, lights a cigarette, and passes the pack to Reeziana. Unlike him, Reeziana is a social smoker—if there is such a thing. She does indulge when offered but doesn't buy cigarettes herself.

"Have you heard of killers using their vic's cell phone?" asks Mislan, throwing out a general question.

"No, but it doesn't mean it hasn't happened," Reeziana says.

"Usually in stolen cell phone cases, the culprits will change the SIM card—so, technically yes, vics' cell phones were used by the predators," Tee explains.

"You know I'm not talking about the phone, I'm talking about the number," Mislan retorts.

Just then Superintendent Samsiah enters the office. The conversation stops, and the officers greet her. Mislan and Reeziana automatically drop their cigarette to the floor, stepping on them.

"Morning," she returns their greetings, taking a seat at Inspector Khamis's desk. "I see Yana's Food Delivery Service is keeping my officers well-fed."

"You want some?" Reeziana offers.

"No thanks. Yana, are you sure it's OK for you to take the food away?" Superintendent Samsiah asks, sounding concerned.

"Yes, ma'am. There's so much food, it'll go to waste if it's not shared with others."

"OK, I just don't want the district to complain about you taking their food." Samsiah turns to look around and asks, "Can we start?"

She gets an all-round nod.

"Mislan," she calls, starting the morning prayer.

Mislan shakes his head to indicate there is nothing to brief.

"I suppose this'll be the trend until the MCO's lifted," Samsiah concedes. "Lan, would you like to share your case, or are you keeping it to yourself? Perhaps Yana and Tee can shed some light on it."

The mention of his case reminds him of the greeting sent to his boss by Dr. Suthisa Ritchu.

"Sorry, ma'am, I almost forgot. Dr. Suthisa, aah, Dr. Sophia, sends her regards to you."

Superintendent Samsiah arches her eyebrows at Mislan.

"I spoke to her last night," Mislan offers with a grin.

"And how is she?"

"She's fine. What's the word, Jo?"

"*Sabai dee*," Johan says from his desk.

"Yes, that," Mislan says.

"And may I know why you contacted her?" Samsiah probes.

"Remember, in both the cases the neighbors didn't hear gunshots? Well, I figured there're two plausible reasons for it. One, the neighbors didn't want to be involved with a criminal investigation, or two, the killers used suppressors or silencers."

Superintendent Samsiah gives him a slow nod.

"And you called Dr. Suthisa?"

"I did some research on the internet and discovered that guns are easily available in Thailand, at the Thai-Myanmar and Thai-Laos borders. Thailand is also recorded as having the highest per capita gun fatality rate in Southeast Asia. It's just a wild hunch: if guns are easily available there, perhaps they'll have suppressors too."

"And you asked her to find out for you."

"Yes. She said she'll ask Police Sergeant Sharky."

"Why Thailand, why not the United States? Suppressors are widely available there," she says.

"It's not only about getting hold of a suppressor. It's also about smuggling it into the country. It's easier to do it across the border from Thailand."

"That makes sense."

"I also asked Jo to talk to his machinist friend, to see if one can be fabricated. Jo, why don't you tell us what your friend said?"

Johan stands to come closer and Superintendent Samsiah holds up her hand to stop him.

"Stay where you are, social distancing."

The officers laugh at Johan's embarrassed look.

"I showed my friend the video Inspector Mislan sent me. He told me it's easy to fabricate, as a suppressor has no moving parts. The only difficulty is to know what type of material or metal to use for the barrel in the suppressor. He guessed it has to be as strong or heat-durable as the gun barrel itself, because the bullet and charge create very high heat when discharged. If you get it wrong, the barrel in the suppressor may blow up and cause a backfire injury to the user."

"Interesting," Reeziana says.

"I thought the suppressor is supposed to be screwed onto the front of the gun's barrel," Samsiah says.

"Yes, it is," Mislan answers. "Jo's friend said the thread can be easily cut on the gun's barrel. No problem there."

"And using the suppressor will eliminate the blast?" Tee asks.

"Well, there's this suppressor called the Hush Puppy, which was designed for SEALs. There's a video on YouTube where they test-fired it. The blast was reduced to just a puff," Mislan explains.

"Woah!" Tee exclaims.

"Good work," Samsiah acknowledges.

"Ma'am, what about our Special Force, do they use suppressors?" Mislan asks.

"I don't know, perhaps Ghani knows. By the way, where is he?"

"WFH," Reeziana suggests.

The officers look at her questioningly.

"Working from home," she answers with a crafty smile.

"Shooting tin cans in the backyard," Mislan jokes.

"That's good," Reeziana says, laughing.

"Will you people stop making fun of him?" Samsiah says, hiding a smile.

———

The two officers arrive at the Forgotten Children of Kuala Lumpur Foundation at 10:15 a.m. and find Chuah Guat Eng in her office enjoying a smoke.

"Morning, Mrs. Chuah," Mislan greets.

"Good morning, Inspector and Detective Sergeant. Again, please call me Guat," she says, getting up. As they walk down the stairs, she continues, "Last night after you left, I spoke to one of my counterparts. He runs a private shelter for displaced children. I was told he works with the Tiong Nam Cantonese Association and caters mainly to children of drug-dependent parents. I believe as police officers, you're aware of how bad the drug problem is in this area."

The officers nod. The Tiong Nam area is not only infamous for its secret society or triad activities, but also being a hotbed for drugs and gambling dens. Since the mass arrival of Indonesian workers, the area has been filled with them operating sundry shops, restaurants, and stalls selling food and contraband goods, mainly cigarettes.

"Yes," Mislan says, prompting Guat to continue.

"He told me he received the same call from this Peter Lai. My friend, we call him Gong-gong, that's Grandpa in Cantonese. Well, he doesn't have a bank account because he runs a private shelter. To cut the story short, the day after he received the call, he found an envelope in his letterbox containing 10 thousand ringgit."

"Woah," Johan exclaims.

"Just like that, in a letterbox?" Mislan asks.

"That's what Gong-gong told me."

"Can you arrange for us to meet this Gong-gong?"

"I'll call him and see if we can meet him after we finish at the bank," Guat offers.

"That'll be great, thanks."

———

Outside the bank there is a long line of customers waiting to go in. COVID-19 has made banks put in stringent measures, including limiting the number of people in the public space inside the bank. Mislan whispers to his assistant. Johan walks up to the glass front door, which is manned by a security guard. He says something to the guard, shows his police authority card, and points at Mislan and Guat.

The door opens, and the three of them enter, followed by disapproving stares from the people in the line. They approach a female customer relations officer, or whatever they call themselves, whose face is covered by a face mask, and she warmly greets Guat.

"Aunty Guat, how're you?" the woman with the name tag JESSICA greets.

In Malaysia, every aged person is either an aunty or an uncle to the younger ones in greeting, regardless of race, religion, and blood kinship.

Guat takes a seat, saying, "I'm fine, thank you. Jessica, these are police officers, and they need to know where the twenty thousand was banked from into the foundation's account."

Mislan is impressed by Guat's directness, no pussy-footing around. He guesses when you are of a certain age, you know you don't have much time left and stop beating around the bush. Jessica taps on her keyboard without even asking for the foundation's account number. *Guat must be a regular and well-liked customer in this bank.*

Jessica gives the officers a tense look. "Is there a problem, aunty?" she asks.

"Nooo, no problem. I made a police report of the deposit, and these officers just want to ensure all is done legally," Guat answers with a calm, reassuring voice and smile.

"It was from Maybank Taman Maluri, Cheras," Jessica says, and writes the details on a piece of paper.

Guat thanks her, says her good-byes, and tells her to stay safe. As they exit, she passes to Mislan the piece of paper from Jessica.

———

As soon as they get into the car, Guat asks if she can smoke. Mislan says yes and lights one himself. Johan cuts back into Jalan Raja Laut, an arterial road into the old section of the city. Guat tells him to drive all the way to the junction of Jalan Putra. At the junction she directs Johan to make a left and about seven hundred yards later to make another left into Jalan Ipoh Kecil.

"This road runs parallel to Jalan Raja Laut and will take us back to Jalan Tiong Nam," Johan says.

"Yes, Gong-gong's shelter is just down the road there. Easier to come in this way unless we're coming from my place," Guat says, blowing smoke out the open window. "Turn right here," Guat directs, "the third house from the end."

Johan parks the car in front of the house. There is no signage indicating it's a shelter. The only giveaway Mislan notices are the numerous pairs of children's shoes and flip-flops neatly lined against the wall. The house is an old double-story terrace, with dark water-marked exterior walls, rusting rainwater gutters, and peeling paint.

An elderly man appears at the front door and gives a tiny wave, inviting them in. Guat leads the team. At the front door they greet each other in Cantonese, and Gong-gong turns to give the officers a closer look. Guat introduces Gong-gong as Wee.

"Mr. Wee, please to meet you," Mislan says. "This is Detective Sergeant Johan, my assistant."

Wee nods but no hand is proffered. He invites them in and asks if they'd like something to drink. The officers decline, but Guat says she could use a cup of black coffee. A moment later, an elderly woman comes in from the kitchen carrying a cup of coffee.

Wee introduces the woman as his wife. Wee seems to be around eighty years old, of normal height for a Malaysian, slightly hunched and fast running out of hair, with skin marked by a thousand wrinkles and some age spots. His wife, perhaps a few years younger, seems in much better physical shape.

Mislan observes the surroundings, his gaze questioning. The furniture in the living hall is old and rudimentary. In one corner by the staircase are several folded tables and two stacks of plastic stools. Mrs. Wee notices his expression, and says the small kids are sleeping upstairs and the older ones are helping out with food preparation for the needy at the association's building.

"You want to know about the money?" Wee asks, looking straight at Mislan.

Mislan nods.

"Before I admit to anything, may I ask a question?" Wee asks without taking his eyes off the inspector.

Again Mislan nods.

"Are you here to take back the money?" Wee asks with his small eyes narrowing to just a slit.

"No, I'm not. I'm assured by Guat the money is put to very good use," Mislan replies.

Guat interjects, "You can trust these officers. They know about the money the foundation received too, and they didn't confiscate it."

Gong-gong and grandma—Mislan doesn't know the Cantonese nickname for grandma—smile. The tension eases. Wee is a retired civil servant who worked in the Social Welfare Department, and his wife is a retired teacher. They have no children of their own, which in the early stage of their marriage they deemed as a punishment by their gods for whatever sins they had committed. Now, with all the drugs, illnesses, and suffering around the world, they look upon it as a blessing. After retirement, they decided to give back to the community in whatever small way they could, by providing a shelter for displaced children. They hope to offer these children at least a clean and safe place to lay their heads at night with a full stomach.

Guat lights a cigarette, and Mrs. Wee goes to the kitchen and comes back with an ashtray. Mislan takes the opportunity to light one too.

Wee says Peter Lai asked for his bank account number, but he refused to provide it, stating that it's his personal account. He feared that if a large amount of money was banked in, he might get into trouble with the authorities as he couldn't explain where the money came from.

"Mr. Wee, you're not a registered shelter, are you?" Mislan asks.

Both Wee and his wife shake their heads, gazing at Mislan suspiciously.

"Sorry, I don't mean to cause you any alarm with the question," Mislan quickly adds, seeing the fear in their eyes. "I just want to figure out how this Peter Lai came to know of you," Mislan says. "How do the children end up here?"

"Some were brought in by the temple, some by the association, and some by the community," Wee answers. "Long time ago, the police from the station on Lorong Tiong Nam 4 also brought them here, but now not anymore."

"So you basically know all those that send the children here?"

"Yes."

"And there was never a Peter Lai?"

Mr. Wee and his wife shake their heads.

"Not that I can recall," Wee says.

"What about the children's parents and relatives, anyone by that name?"

"We've never met any of them," Mrs. Wee answers. "Not one of them."

"I suppose they don't care, because if they did care, the children wouldn't have been left to roam the streets," Guat remarks.

"Or they're too high or too, what do they call it?" Wee searches for the word.

"*Gian*," Guat offers. *Gian* is the local slang for being strung out or in a state of drug deprivation.

"Yes, that's it, too *gian* to even remember they have children," Wee suggests. "Drugs do that to you."

There is nothing much that Wee can add to what Guat had told them, except the money in the envelope was in various denominations. Some were in hundred-, some fifty-, twenty-, ten-, and even five-ringgit notes. The notes all looked used. The envelope had already been disposed of by the Wees.

———

After dropping Guat off at the foundation, the D9 officers head back to the office. Mislan is anxious to get cracking. There are many things he needs to do: obtain the cell phone records from the service provider, obtain the CCTV footage of the CDM from the bank in Taman Maluri, and interview the four complainants on the donations.

He heads straight for the head of Special Investigations' office. Superintendent Samsiah is just about to have her lunch when Mislan knocks on the door. She puts her packed lunch aside and signals for him to come in.

"You look like a man on a mission," Samsiah comments.

Mislan grins, taking a seat.

"How did it go with the foundation?"

"Better than expected."

Mislan updates her on the information provided by the bank and on the conversation with Gong-gong Wee.

"So they're giving away cash, too," Samsiah says with amazement. "They're beginning to sound more and more like true philanthropists."

"Ma'am, I need assistance. I know we're short, but can Tee be assigned to help me?"

"I don't see why not. Going by the past two weeks, we don't get callouts. What do you need him for?"

"Well, there are three things I need to do immediately. First, obtain the cell phone records. What I need are the numbers the vics' phones called. I want to contact these people and see if any of them also received donations. I then need the telco to provide the locations of the phones when they were active. For this, I bet you'd be the best person to assist me," Mislan says with a smile. "You have the charm to pry their system wide open."

Superintendent Samsiah smiles at her officer's attempt to coax her.

"Second, I need the CCTV footage of the bank where the donor deposited the cash. Hopefully, this guy was careless enough to show his face. And third, I need to interview the four complainants. See if there's any new information that can be obtained from them. This I feel can be handled by Tee."

"I see you have it all planned out."

"It's just a suggestion, and I still need your assistance and blessing."

"Well, you won me over. Give me the details of the cell phones, and I'll work on it. Tell Tee he's now assisting in the Philanthropists investigation."

"Thanks, ma'am."

20

MISLAN TELLS INSPECTOR TEE what specific information he requires from the interviews of the four complainants and sends him off. He prepares an official letter of request for CCTV footage of the CDM, of any camera that covers the entrance to the automated machines and the external walkway. He expects the bank to be sticky and difficult as they usually are in any transaction with the public. Armed with the letter, he and Johan drive to Taman Maluri, Cheras.

Leaving the contingent headquarters, Mislan tells his assistant to head for Jalan Kampung Pandan. The road through this area is always congested because of the massive MRT construction at the roundabout, but he is certain that during the MCO the roads will be clear. They make a right at Jalan Perwira and then left onto Jalan Cochrane.

Even with the MCO, there is hardly any parking space along the road, and they only manage to get one close to the junction across the Hong Leong Bank. Walking back down the road, the officers observe the shops on both sides of the road. The bank they're going to is located on Jalan Mahkota, sandwiched between a sundry shop and a restaurant.

Again, there is a long queue outside the bank waiting to be allowed inside the building. They approach the main glass door, show their police authority cards, and are allowed in by the security guard. Mislan asks for the manager and is shown the side staircase leading up to the first floor.

Upstairs, he introduces himself to one of the customer relations officers and asks to see the branch manager. The officer invites them to sit while he informs the manager.

A couple of minutes later, a Chinese woman in her early forties appears from the closed section of the floor, making a beeline for the customer relations officer. She is dressed in business attire: dark slacks and a matching jacket over a white blouse with the top two buttons unhooked. Her hair is tightly pulled into a ponytail.

The customer relations officer indicates to the two D9 officers sitting at a small round glass-top discussion table, and the woman makes a detour without breaking her step. Mislan and Johan stand as she approaches them.

"I'm Ms. Liew. I was told you wanted to see me?" she says without offering her hand.

Why do they need to add the prefix Mr. or Ms.? Mislan asks himself. He notes this is a common practice when Chinese men or women introduce themselves but not with other ethnicities.

"I'm Inspector Mislan, and this is Detective Sergeant Johan. Are you the branch manager?"

Liew nods and hands out her business card. She remains standing, and the two officers do likewise.

"I'm investigating a double murder. We have evidence that money was transacted using your branch's CDM. We need to view your CCTV recordings."

"I'm sorry, what proof?" Liew asks.

"I'm sorry. I can't discuss ongoing investigations with nonpersonnel. The information that your CDM was used to bank in the money was provided by Jessica of the Jalan Raja Laut branch. You may call the branch to confirm if you wish."

"Your request to view the CCTV recording is above my authorization clearance. I have to check with my general manager from headquarters and the head of security."

"Please do that," Mislan says.

"Can I call you back once I get the reply from them?"

"We'll wait for you here, if you don't mind."

From the expression on Liew's face, he can see she minds. She knows they're waiting on her floor to apply pressure on her to get a reply from the relevant people. Bank people love to pressure others but don't like to be pressured themselves.

Ten minutes after the manager leaves them, she has yet to come back. Mislan tells Johan he's going downstairs for a smoke and to call him when Liew comes out. Stepping out of the bank, he lights a cigarette and walks up and down the block observing the area. Then he sits outside the restaurant next door and orders an iced black coffee. Looking at his cell phone screen, he notes it has been thirty-five minutes since the manager said she was going to consult the general manager and head of security.

Mislan suspects she's stalling, sitting in her office hoping that he and his assistant will leave after waiting for such a long time. *Well, I've got the whole day if she wants to play that game,* Mislan says to himself.

Another ten minutes pass, and his phone rings; it's Johan informing him that the head of security has arrived.

———

When Mislan gets to the upper floor, he sees a Malay man probably in his late fifties, stoutly built with dark skin and jet-black, closely cropped hair, which most likely was recently dyed. The man is watching him with a smug corporate expression. He is dressed in a long-sleeved shirt and sports the ugliest gaudy-colored tie Mislan has ever seen. *The head of security,* Mislan is dead sure. The lady manager is standing next to him, her face plastered with the same smug corporate expression, only prettier. As he approaches them, Mislan notices the man's security tag around his neck: LT. COL. (R) KHAIRUDIN RAZALI, HEAD CENTRAL REGION SECURITY.

"I was informed by Ms. Liew that you requested to view our CCTV recordings?" the man says without introducing himself.

Mislan has dealt with this kind of arrogant jerk many times in his line of work; people who think very highly of themselves—the narcissists. They're usually from the security forces, where they were used to being feared and obeyed without question, and they expect the same treatment from the public. He also knows this type of person understands power and the consequences of going against it.

"Yes, I did, and you are?" Mislan asks.

"I'm Colonel Khairudin, the central region head of security," he answers, emphasizing on the rank of colonel and his title.

"Retired colonel or half-colonel?" Mislan asks, hiding a grin.

"Retired lieutenant colonel," Khairudin answers, staring at Mislan.

"There's a vast difference between a full colonel and half-colonel," Mislan says, holding the half-colonel's stare. "You shouldn't misrepresent yourself, especially to a police officer, as it can be construed as an act of impersonation. Now that you're in the corporate world, the Companies Act terms that as holding out, which is a criminal offense."

Khairudin blinks and Mislan knows he has yanked the feet of this arrogant corporate prick and his lady branch manager back to the ground.

"Proceeds from a double murder case I'm investigating were banked in through the CDM here. This information was provided by your branch in Jalan Raja Laut. To facilitate my investigation, I need to view the CCTV recordings of all the CDM and cameras in the cash machine area, the entrance to the area, and the sidewalk in front of the bank. Now, do I make myself clear?" Mislan asks firmly without shifting his eyes away from the head of Central Region Security.

"I'll need a written request," Khairudin says hesitantly.

"I expected you people would ask for that. Here," Mislan says, handing him the formal request.

The branch manager closes her eyes and sucks in air, as if saying, "*Shit, they came prepared.*"

"Listen, I can see a magistrate and get a court order. If I have to do that, it won't be a polite request. I'll need to interview your security guards, your staff, and probably take all the CCTV recordings, including the ones that are inside here, which may have no relevance," Mislan says softly, which makes him sound scarier. He allows a few seconds for the two corporate jesters to digest what he just said, then adds, "I don't think your bosses would appreciate the negative publicity. Imagine the news headline: *Bank Branch in Taman Maluri Raided by Police for Refusal to Cooperate in Double Murder Investigation.*"

The branch manager asks if she and the head of security could be excused to discuss privately.

Mislan smiles and says, "Of course. You're not under arrest."

―――――――

It's a brief discussion, and when the two of them walk back to him, they're both beaming warmly with their practiced PR smiles.

"Inspector," Khiarudin says, "I don't think we can get copies of the recordings ready for you immediately. We need our IT people to come and make copies for you, and as you might guess, they're based in headquarters."

Mislan gives them a stare saying *That is not acceptable.* The branch manager immediately jumps in.

"We promise you we'll get them ready by tonight and hand them over to you first thing tomorrow morning."

"Wonderful," Mislan says. "I'll send one of my detectives to collect them tomorrow morning. Thank you to both of you. You've been very cooperative, and it's been a pleasure meeting you," Mislan says with just a hint of sarcasm hidden behind a smile.

―――――――

On the way back to the office, Johan says, "That was fun. Did you see the security guy's face when you corrected him on his rank? His height shrank by one foot—it was priceless."

"I'm sure he goes around introducing himself as 'Colonel' instead of 'Lieutenant Colonel.' " Upgrades himself by one rank," Mislan says.

"The public wouldn't know the difference."

"Yes, but to those that know, it does matter. It's like a lance corporal going around claiming to be a corporal. That's just not right, is it? You haven't earned it."

"Is it true what you said back there about it being a criminal offense in the Company Act?"

Mislan flashes his assistant a sly smile.

"You pulled a fast one on him, didn't you?"

"It's for him to find out."

"What about our PI introducing themselves as 'Inspector'?" Johan asks.

"A probationary inspector is an inspector except that he or she is on probation, but his or her substantive rank is inspector."

"OK, understood."

Mislan makes a call to Inspector Tee and asks how he's doing. Tee informs him he is in Damansara Jaya interviewing a complainant. He says another of the complainants will be going to the office to be interviewed. Mislan tells Tee he's heading back to the office and they might as well conduct the interview.

Arriving at the office, Mislan asks the front desk if the interviewee has arrived. The front desk clerk points to a man sitting at the waiting area. He tells the clerk to give him a couple of minutes to put down his things before sending the interviewee in.

"Jo, you want to talk to him?" Mislan asks his assistant.

"OK."

Detective Sergeant Johan calls the front desk to send the interviewee in. Mislan observes the man; he is in his mid-thirties, medium height and build, dressed in a sort of a thobe—the long Arabic gown the locals call a jubah, an outfit that has become very popular among the Malays now with their goatee and a white or green skullcap. He nods to Mislan, mumbling the greeting of *Assalamualaikum,* which has also turned into a standard Malay greeting. Mislan points to Johan and sits back to watch.

He listens to his assistant interviewing the skullcap man for a moment and then walks to Superintendent Samsiah's office.

"How did it go with the bank?" Samsiah asks.

"As anticipated, full of bureaucratic bullshit," Mislan says, feeling exhausted. "How did yours go?"

"I'll get them by tomorrow."

"Same."

"In that case, why don't you go home and get some rest," she suggests.

"I suppose I should."

"By the way, Amir told me his team did some digging into the Seremban 2 case . . ."

Mislan gapes at her questioningly, stopping her in midsentence.

"Don't worry, it has nothing to do with you," she explains with a grin. She's aware that the ISCD and Mislan just do not mix well together. "They got wind of some noncompliance by the MPV that responded to the scene."

"Like?"

"Like your hunch of the presence of drugs at the scene."

"You mean the MPV personnel took them?"

"One of the personnel tested positive for illegal substances. ISCD has taken him into custody and is talking to him. We'll know more soon."

"It seems like these killers were targeting drug dealers," Mislan muses aloud.

"And donating," Samsiah adds.

"Noble criminality," Mislan coins. "Oxymoron."

"There's no nobility in criminality."

———

When he returns to his office, Johan is concluding his interview. The skullcap again wishes him *"Peace be upon you"* before leaving. Johan briefs him that the skullcap man is named Jais, and he runs an orphanage in Bandar Tun Razak, Cheras. He said the caller identified himself as Mohammad, a Muslim convert, and the amount of twenty thousand was banked into the orphanage's account in Bank Islam.

"Why did he say the caller is a convert?" Mislan asks.

"He said the caller's accent was like a Chinese speaking Malay, so he asked and the caller said he's a mualaf, a Muslim convert."

"So the caller could be Peter Lai pretending to be a convert?"

"Could be, but unless we have voice recordings to match them up, it's just speculative."

Mislan laughs. "Watching a lot of *CSI* again, eh?"

Mislan then tells his assistant to knock off and get some rest.

21

WOKEN BY HUNGER, MISLAN looks at the time on his cell phone. It is 8:12 p.m., and he has slept for almost five hours upon returning home. Freshening up, he puts on jeans and a crew-neck T-shirt and mulls where to go to get dinner. He remembers that all essential shops are to close by 8 p.m. and wonders if that includes restaurants.

He makes a call to Inspector Reeziana.

"Yes," Reeziana answers.

"You on duty?"

"Yes."

"Where?"

"Kampung Baru, Jalan Raja Abdullah, why?" she asks curiously.

"You got food there?"

"Lots of it. You want to come?"

Mislan can hear her giggling.

"I'm starving. Be there shortly."

———

Turning left onto Jalan Raja Abdullah, he drives about half a mile before spotting the red-and-orange construction lights on the road. The roadblock is at the junction of Jalan Raja Abdullah and Jalan Raja Alang. A large white tent furnished with tables and chairs sits on the sidewalk outside the Jamek Mosque. Mislan stops at the roadblock, identifies himself, and asks for Inspector Reeziana. The policewoman points to the tent and instructs him to park the car on Jalan Raja Alang about thirty yards away.

Walking to the tent, he sees Inspector Reeziana gaily chatting with a sergeant and a corporal. All of them are in uniform, looking fresh and smart.

"Come in," Reeziana greets him as he stands at the tent's opening. "Join us. Inspector Mislan's my colleague," she introduces him. The sergeant and corporal stand to leave, and she tells them it's OK and there is no need for them to go. She introduces the sergeant as Jamal and the corporal as Sherran.

"What would you like to have? We've got noodles and I think chicken fried rice."

"I'm starving, no lunch. I'll have the fried rice."

Sherran gets up and comes back with a pack of chicken fried rice and a bottle of mineral water.

"Thanks. You guys ate?"

"Several times," Jamal replies and laughs.

"Sir, go ahead, there's plenty more," Sherran says.

Sherran looks young, Mislan estimates maybe in her mid-twenties. She has short hair and a fair complexion, rather sexy and beautiful for a policewoman. She speaks good English, with Eastern Malaysian diction. As he eats, he steals looks at her discreetly, which Reeziana notices.

"Sherran is Sarawakian," Reeziana says.

Mislan nods, pretending not to be interested.

"Aren't you, Sherran?" she asks the corporal.

The corporal nods. "I'm an Iban from Sibu. My full name is Sherran Shondara Minggu."

Mislan raises his eyebrows hearing the name because "minggu" means "week" in Malay. He wonders why the word "week" is part of her name. Most likely, it means something else in Iban.

"Beautiful name," Mislan says. It was all he could think of saying.

"My name was supposed to be spelled 'Sharon' but the policeman made a mistake and spelled it Sherran," she explains. "People who don't know me call me 'Sher–ran.'" She smiles wryly.

"What matters is that people who know you say your name correctly," Jamal offers.

———

After Mislan finishes his meal, Jamal and Sherran leave the two D9 officers to themselves. Mislan lights a cigarette and offers the pack to Reeziana.

"What actually brought you here?" she asks, lighting up. "What's bothering you?"

"Food."

"That's the official line, but what's the real reason you came here?"

"I don't know," he says, taking a long drag on his cigarette. Blowing out the smoke, he says, "Maybe the MCO, you know the self-quarantine, the isolation."

"Hmmm. From what I've heard, that's how you've lived all this while. I'm sorry to get into your personal life, but since Dr. Safia went AWOL—"

"AWOL?"

"Absent without love," she says, and breaks into a hearty laugh.

The way she put it, Mislan just had to laugh along with her.

"Let's not go there, OK?" he says after they stop laughing.

"Look, Lan, until you face your demons, you'll never slay them. I'm here if you want to talk, but I leave that decision to you."

The two officers remain quiet. Mislan turns in his chair to watch the roadblock where Sergeant Jamal and Corporal Sherran are supervising the personnel.

"She's pretty, eh?" she says.

"Who?"

"Sherran Shondara Minggu."

Mislan doesn't answer. He knows Reeziana hit the nail right on the head about him being lonely. It's true that he mostly kept to himself, but Dr. Safia was just a call away. Since his wife left, he was alone but never lonely. He is trying to picture Dr. Safia, or Fie to him, what she looks like, her smile, her laughter, and her anger, the smell of her perfume. His memory of her is slowly but surely fading.

He used to often wonder why she left the way she did—without a word or a goodbye. It sometimes angered him when he thought about it, comparing her actions to that of his ex-wife. She too left without notice or explanation. Yet when his anger subsided, he blamed himself—there had to be something wrong with him. Why else would two wonderful women just up and leave if there's nothing wrong with him? They didn't just wake up one morning and say to themselves, *Time for me to go.* He knows he's not perfect, but sometimes he believes he's more than just imperfect—he is repulsive.

Reeziana was right; he isn't willing to face his demons. His ex-wife left more than ten years back, yet he still clings to the hope they'll one day be back together. Fie left about a year back, and he isn't willing to let it go. Deep down inside, he knows he has lost both his ex-wife and Fie. Yet he's unwilling to move on. As Reeziana says, he has to slay the demons first.

He can't let go of the hope of being with his ex-wife, for that will end all hopes of getting back his son—Daniel—of having a family again. He will let the thoughts of Fie go. Having made the decision, he feels an emptiness in his heart, but he knows he'll have to fill it somehow.

"Lan, are you OK?" Reeziana asks.

"Yeah, sure."

"How's your case coming along?"

Reeziana changes the subject to one she knows will almost certainly bring life back into her colleague.

"It's coming along but too slow. We managed to track the bank branch where the cash was deposited. Ma'am found four reports in IPRS of similar donations, and Tee is tracking the complainants down. I guess tomorrow we'll be able to move a bit faster on the leads."

"This's my theory: your unsubs knew who to hit—" Reeziana starts but is stopped by Mislan's interruption.

"*Unsub*, woah, I feel like I'm acting in *NCIS*," Mislan says, grinning.

"Yes, unsub, unknown suspect, great terminology, eh?" She says, "Leave it to the Americans to come up with such things. Anyway, your *unsubs*"—she emphasizes the word—"knew who to hit and more importantly when to hit them."

"Meaning?"

"The vics were dealers, and the unsubs hit them when they had cash, lots of cash. If they'd hit the vics at the wrong time, there'd be drugs but no money, which is not what they're after. Even worse, if the vics weren't even home."

Mislan gives her theory a slow nod of acknowledgment.

"They, the unsubs, could stake out the house to make sure the vics are home," Mislan rebuts.

"Yes, they could, and probably that's what they did. You said the unsubs weren't interested in the drugs, just the money."

Mislan nods.

"That tells me the unsubs themselves aren't users or dealers but somehow connected with the drug world. If they're not connected, they wouldn't have such information."

"Connected like how?"

"I haven't figured that out yet," she admits with a smile.

Mislan purses his lips, nodding. "Interesting theory."

22

HE STAYS AWAKE HALF the night toying with Reeziana's theory but just can't come to grips with it. She theorized the killers are connected to the drug world but not users or dealers. The best he can come up with is vigilantism. If these were the acts of vigilantes, then it has to be a very organized group. The group would need to have people inside the drug syndicate to get detailed and reliable information. The members have to be professionals with sound knowledge of weapons, police crime scene forensics, and investigation. It terrifies him to imagine that such a vigilante group exists and is going around executing drug dealers.

At 7 a.m., Mislan is already in the office. To his disappointment, Inspector Reeziana and her packs of food aren't to be seen. He gestures to her empty desk, and Inspector Tee, the outgoing investing officer, shrugs. Putting his backpack at his desk, he hears the cheery voice of Reeziana joking with Detective Sergeant Johan coming from the corridor. Johan is carrying a large plastic bag of packed food.

"Are you serious?" Johan asks excitedly.

"I'm not lying. She said she's not ready for something serious, not just yet. Just wants to have fun with no commitment. Enjoy life to the fullest before tying the knot."

"My kind of woman," Johan says and beams.

"—until she decides to tie the knot," Reeziana completes his sentence.

When the two of them notice Mislan staring at them, they kill the conversation. Johan greet-wishes the officers and lifts up the plastic bag to indicate that food has arrived.

———

While having his breakfast, Mislan reminds his assistant to collect the CCTV recording from the bank.

"I'll check with ma'am on what time she's getting the telco reports," Mislan adds.

"What about the complainants Inspector Tee interviewed?" Johan asks.

"I saw his summary on the desk, but I haven't read them yet."

"I heard you were with Inspector Reeziana's roadblock last night," Johan says, changing the subject.

"Yeah, I was hungry, and the restaurants were all closed. I knew they'd have food, so I went there. What did she tell you?" Mislan probes.

"There's this corporal from Sarawak, Inspector Reeziana says she's cute—"

"I thought you're with what's-her-name, Julia," Mislan says, cutting his assistant off.

"We split up, one of the thousands of relationship casualties during this MCO," Johan says, followed by a chuckle.

"Yeah, right."

———

Reeziana tells them that some of the men and women manning the roadblock at Jalan Tuanku Abdul Rahman have tested positive for COVID-19.

"Wasn't there an announcement by the IGP that some of our personnel have been infected?" Tee says. "The IGP was appealing to the public to abide by the MCO and stop going out unnecessarily. Their disregard for the MCO is increasing the risk we face."

"Most people will heed the call, they're not the problem," Mislan sneers. "The problem is those thickheaded people—politicians and their family members who think they're above the law. Until we start taking stern action against them, this shit will continue. We'll be at risk."

"I agree," Reeziana says. "I'm there with them. I see them bend to speak to the drivers, and some of the drivers weren't wearing masks, behaving like this whole pandemic is a hoax."

"Why aren't they provided with PPE like those at the hospital?" Tee asks.

"You nuts or what?" Reeziana replies scornfully. "You know how bloody hot it is in the PPE? Our men and women wouldn't last an hour in the hot sun."

"You better be extra careful," Mislan advises her. "I don't want you quarantined and not bringing us breakfast anymore."

The investigators and assistants laugh.

"I second that," Tee quips.

———

After the investigators and their assistants leave, Mislan spends a couple of hours acting like a pregnant cat looking for a place to give birth. Four cigarettes and countless glances checking the time on his cell phone later, he breathes a sigh of relief and calms down when he sees his assistant walk in with the CCTV recording disc from the bank.

"Was it difficult?" Mislan asks.

Johan shakes his head. "You really put the scare into them yesterday. It was ready when I arrived."

"Jo, you use your computer to view it and note the timing. Then we'll go over them together."

The phone on Mislan's desk rings, and he instantly snatches the receiver. After a moment, he says, "OK, thanks," and puts it down.

With his eyes, Johan asks him what that was about.

"Ma'am, she just got back."

Mislan hurriedly walks to Superintendent Samsiah's office. She has just reached her door when she hears his footfalls.

"How did you know I'm back?" Samsiah asks, curious.

"Front desk," Mislan answers, flashing an impish grin. "You got it?"

"Let me at least get into my office first," she chides.

"Sorry, ma'am."

Superintendent Samsiah takes her seat, pulls out an envelope from her handbag, and hands it to Mislan.

"The telco techy said we're lucky, as the phones were smartphones equipped with GPS. According to the techy, the locations indicated are quite precise, to a yard. But if they were to locate the phones using transmission-tower triangulation, it would not be as precise. It can be as wide as about a hundred-yard radius," she explains.

"Shit—sorry—they really can pinpoint your location that precisely. I thought that's only in movies, you know, like movie-science," Mislan says, surprised.

"Technology has its pros and cons."

"In this case, it's pros."

Mislan thanks his boss repeatedly. Standing and holding up the envelope, he says he needs to go through the report and see what it reveals.

———

Walking into his office, he looks at his assistant. Johan shakes his head, indicating he isn't done yet. Mislan sits at his desk, staring at the telecommunication service provider's envelope. Heart racing, he asks himself, *Is this it, or is it another dead end?*

He rips the envelope open and pulls out the single sheet of paper. His eyes take in its contents in one swift read. He takes a pink highlighter pen from his desk and marks Ajimullah's cell phone number. There were six calls made.

- The first call was recorded at 1:35 a.m. to MERS on the night of the murders from the main road of Taman Sentul Jaya.
- The second call was at 3:40 p.m. to a cell phone. The call was made from Jalan Tuanku Abdul Rahman, next to the old UMNO Building. The receiving cell phone number looks familiar to him.

He checks Gong-gong Wee and Chuah Guat Eng's numbers. It was Gong-gong Wee's number.

- The third call was at 10 a.m. the next day, to a cell phone. He's unfamiliar with the receiving cell phone number. The call was made from Cheras Police District headquarters.
- The fourth call was at 10:22 a.m. to a cell phone. The receiving phone number belongs to Chuah Guat Eng from the Forgotten Children of Kuala Lumpur Foundation. The call was made from Spicy Thai restaurant in Sunway Velocity shopping mall in Cheras.
- The fifth call was at 10:11 a.m. the next day to a cell phone number. The receiving number is unfamiliar to Mislan. The call was made from Jone's Café, Sunway Velocity shopping mall in Cheras.
- The sixth and last call was at 12:45 a.m. the next day to a cell phone number he isn't familiar with. The call was made in front of Maybank, Taman Maluri, Cheras.

Mislan stares at the piece of paper with the pink highlights. His heart is pounding in his chest, and his thoughts are running wild. Reeziana's theory is ringing like a church bell going wild in his head. He lights a cigarette to calm himself. He steals a glance at Johan, afraid his assistant may have noticed him shaking. Johan is engrossed with the CCTV recording. Ugly thoughts are running in his head, thoughts he is unwilling to entertain but needs to share with someone with a cooler head.

When he calms down, he goes through the report again to check if he got it right. Satisfied that he did, he gets up and walks to Superintendent Samsiah's office.

"Ma'am, I need your advice," Mislan says, taking a seat.

Samsiah goes through the report, arching her eyebrows at the high-lighted parts and says, "The third call is interesting."

Mislan nods. "The third, fourth, fifth and sixth are all interesting. They were all made in Cheras, in close proximity to each other."

"What're you thinking?"

"Yesterday Yana suggested a very interesting theory. She believed the killers are not drug users or dealers but someone connected to the drug world."

"She came out with the theory based on?"

"The information needed by the killers. One, they need to have information that the vics were dealing, and two, which is more crucial to their objective, they have to know when exactly to hit the vics. If they just go in blindly, the vics might not have the cash that the killers were after."

"That could also be the reason the killers didn't touch the drugs," Samsiah adds.

Mislan nods. "Last night, based on Yana's theory, I thought it could be the work of vigilantes but discarded the idea based on two reasons. One is the crime locations. Vigilantes usually protect their own turf or community, a housing development or village. Our cases are too far apart: one in Sentul and one in Seremban 2, about fifty miles and two state lines apart. Two, the killers were pros, knew about weapons, crime scene forensics, and investigation. Vigilantes are just a bunch of hot-headed, testosterone-driven men with insomnia."

"The last statement may not be entirely correct," she says, stifling a smile. "And now your suspicion is on . . . ?"

Mislan remains silent while staring at the report from the telecommunication service provider. Superintendent Samsiah sees the pain in her officer's face, the refusal to utter the words to his thoughts. As if by saying the words, it will all become true. She also sees anger in him. Anger at the thought that one of his kind has betrayed the oath they have taken, to serve and to protect. Mislan without a doubt is a certifiable maverick, but no one can question his dedication and loyalty to the Force and the oath he has taken.

"The drug-world connection, I believe the killers tapped our connection into it," Mislan finally says without looking at his boss. "I . . . I think we're the ones feeding them the intel and telling them when to hit and what to do at the crime scenes."

"You're saying the killers were in cahoots with one of us," Samsiah says, almost a whisper.

Mislan lifts his eyes, looking at her, and acknowledging this with the slightest of nods.

———

Superintendent Samsiah slowly stands. She goes to the wall cabinet and takes out a crystal ashtray with the police logo. Putting it on the table in front of Mislan, she says, "Go ahead, you earned it."

Mislan lights a cigarette, grateful for her understanding. His phone rings; it's Johan informing him that he is done viewing the CCTV.

"Jo, I'm with ma'am. You can bring the DVD here," Mislan suggests.

Johan knocks on the door and sees Mislan smoking. Instantly, he knows something major has developed for Superintendent Samsiah to allow smoking in her office. Taking a seat next to his boss, Johan gazes at him, making eye contact as if asking what is going on.

Reading his assistant's eye signal, Mislan flashes him a smile and says, "Brief us on what you got."

Superintendent Samsiah swings her laptop to face Johan. He loads the DVD and after he works the mouse to the relevant time, he turns the screen so that she and Mislan can view it.

"OK, this is the CDM camera. According to the record given by the bank, that's the person depositing the twenty K to the foundation's account. You can't make out his face because he's wearing a face mask," Johan says. "But you can make out that he has short graying hair and is wearing a blue polo shirt with dark blue pants and a blue face mask. No distinguishing features, like specs or facial marks. The clothing is all we have to identify him." When the individual completed his transaction at the CDM, Johan moves the cursor to the timer and cues it to a new timing. "Now, he's seen here from the entrance camera, leaving the cash machine area. Blue polo shirt, dark blue pants, and blue face mask." Johan pauses the video. "See what you make of this."

"OK, that's good enough, because I don't see anyone else with similar clothing in the video?" Mislan asks.

Both Superintendent Samsiah and Johan nod in agreement.

Johan lets the video run and they see the individual move out of camera coverage, and seconds later he reappears on another camera.

"This is from the main entrance camera," Johan explains.

They see the main door open and the individual step in. He stops to talk to the security guard for a brief moment and then disappears to the left, out of camera coverage.

"He went to the upper floor—the banking area," Mislan says.

"Yes," Johan replies and waits, looking from his boss to the head of Special Investigations.

Superintendent Samsiah asks, "What?"

Johan scrolls back the timer. "Watch him when he steps into the bank."

He lets the video run again.

"Stop, play it back," Mislan says.

Johan pulls back the time and lets the video run.

Mislan smiles.

"The security guards know him. The guards give him a wave, a half-salute of some sort, and opened the door even before the individual identified himself."

"That's what I thought too. Remember when we were there? The queue was long and we had to identify ourselves before the guard opened the door to let us in," Johan explains.

"They know each other," Samsiah says. "There, look at him giving the guard a friendly pat on the shoulder. That gesture may be nothing to us, but to a security guard, that's an act of recognition for his service. I'm sure he remembered the moment. Good job, Jo."

Johan beams from ear to ear, and Mislan lights another cigarette. Superintendent Samsiah cautions Johan that nothing shall leave her office before bringing him in. She briefly touches on Reeziana's theory and the telecommunication service provider records highlighted by Mislan. She notices the change in Johan's expression from that of pride a moment ago to disbelief and then anger.

"Who outside the drug world has solid intel about the vics' activities but us?" Mislan says.

Johan gazes at his boss.

"We have our informants, we shake down druggies, and we know what crime scene forensics is all about. Don't forget we know weapons. Dr. Suthisa said that, according to Police Sergeant Sharky, Thai criminals do use suppressors, and most of them were obtained from the Thai-Myanmar or Thai-Laos borders. And we the police can go in and out of Thailand without much hassle. The moment we flash our authority cards, the customs officer will wave us through—interagency courtesy."

"What's your next move?" Samsiah asks.

"We need to ID this individual. I believe the security guard can assist us," Mislan says.

"OK, I want this to be done discreetly. We have nothing to implicate him with the killings. The cash deposit may have an acceptable explanation."

"Like what?" Mislan asks.

"Doing an innocent favor for a kindhearted friend," she offers.

Mislan smiles.

"For the time being, until we're absolutely sure of this individual's involvement, it'll be just the three of us who know about this. Not even our team members need to know. Do I make myself clear?"

Mislan and Johan nod.

23

A CAR IS JUST pulling out of a parking spot on Jalan Mahkota about fifty yards from the bank as they turn onto the road. Johan pulls up close to it, waits for the car to pull out, and takes the slot. They notice the long queue of customers waiting to get into the banking hall. They walk up to the glass front door, and before Mislan can pull out his police identity card, the security guard manning the door opens it. The police officers step in, giving him a quizzical gaze.

"I recognize you from yesterday," the security guard says.

"Good memory," Mislan comments. "What's your name?"

"Bahdur."

Johan shows him the printout of the individual from the CDM camera. "Do you recognize this man?" he asks.

Bahdur takes a close look at the printout. "No, sir, cannot see the face."

Johan shows him the printout of the man putting his hand on Bahdur's shoulder. "Remember this?"

"Yes, I remember this, maybe five or six days ago."

"You know the man?" Mislan asks.

"Yes, policeman. He always come here, very friendly, and this is first time pat me on shoulder, I remember."

"Policeman!" Mislan remarks. "What's his name?"

"Yes, sir, policeman, sir. Sorry, sir, I don't know his name."

"How do you know he's a policeman?" Mislan continues.

"Sometimes he comes wearing a police uniform, sergeant, I remember."

Mislan looks at his assistant with an expression of disbelief.

"How do you know it's a sergeant uniform?" Johan asks.

"I was Nepalese Army. I was a sergeant, and we also use three stripes for sergeant like British Army," Bahdur says proudly. "Malaysia police rank is the same as British and Nepalese Army."

"Do you know which police station he's from?" Mislan asks.

"Sorry, sir, he never told me. Always, he ask how I am, if I've eaten, and is the boss in? That day he talked about corona and told me to be safe."

"Boss? Who did he always come to meet?"

"Bank manager, Ms. Liew."

"Is the boss in?"

"Yes, sir."

"Thank you, stay safe," Mislan says. As they're stepping away, he asks, "What race?"

"Chinese."

———

After waiting a few minutes, Ms. Liew appears from the door behind the teller's counter. Seeing the two D9 officers, her expression changes to one of *"Oh my god, not these assholes again."*

"Inspector, Sergeant," she greets them, gesturing to one of the discussion tables.

Stepping up to her, Mislan suggests that they speak in her office or a private room instead of the open discussion table.

"Why? I'm fine with discussing here," Liew says, seemingly uncomfortable with having the officers poke around in her office.

"This is a private and serious matter, and I'm sure you wouldn't like your staff to overhear what we're discussing," Mislan warns.

Her expression instantly changes to one of defiance.

"I have nothing to hide from my staff."

"So be it," Mislan says, taking a seat. With a voice slightly louder than normal he says, "In regards to the case of the double murder, I need to interview you on your involvement."

The customer relations officer seated closest to them lifts her head, openly staring at them upon hearing the words "double murder" and "your involvement." Her stare catches the attention of the branch manager, who immediately holds up her hand to stop Mislan.

"I'm sorry, I think we better go to my office and discuss."

Johan grins.

———

Driving out of Taman Maluri, Johan asks where they're heading, and Mislan tells him to go back to the office.

"This is too big for us to go in alone. I need to consult ma'am," Mislan admits.

In the many years he had been with the Special Investigations Unit, he has never investigated a serious crime that involved police personnel. This is not to say that no police personnel were ever involved in serious crimes, but he has never been unfortunate enough to be involved in the investigation. He has investigated cases of policemen extorting money from foreign workers, policemen gambling, disorderly conduct in public, but never anything this serious. He recognizes the intricacies and procedural complexities when it involves one of their own.

"What do you think she'll do?" Johan asks.

"I don't know, but I'll be damned if I let someone else take over this case."

Johan nods. He knows his boss's thoughts about cases being taken from him. They almost had one of their cases taken over by the Gaming, Secret Society, and Vices Department (D7) once. And it was for all the wrong reasons. Mislan fought to keep the case. Fortunately, he was backed by Superintendent Samsiah at the risk of her own career.

They go straight to Superintendent Samsiah's office. The expressions on their faces are enough to tell her that trouble is imminent.

"Problems?" she asks.

"Yes, but not the kind you're thinking," Mislan answers, as they take their seats.

"And what kind of problem was I thinking?"

"The kind that Inspector Mislan always gets himself into, where the ISCD has to be involved," Johan replies.

"So, it's good problems, then."

"Not good either," Mislan says with a wry grin.

"Let's hear it."

"The individual, or unsub as Yana termed it, was positively identified by Bahdur the security guard and Liew the bank branch manager. He's a regular at the bank, and this is the problematic part: he's a police sergeant."

"What?" Superintendent Samsiah asks, eyes wide in disbelief.

"Yes. His name is Lai Kwang Kee. Can we check his service records?" Mislan asks.

"How do you know he's a police sergeant?"

"Bahdur claimed he had been to the bank before in uniform. Being an ex–Nepalese Army man, he's familiar with rank insignias. This was later corroborated by Liew, the branch manager. Both of them don't know where he's stationed. His banking record gave his house address, not the office."

"How did the branch manager know him?"

"She said about four months back, a man, one of the bank's customers, was creating a scene, a lovers' tiff with one of the female tellers. The man was loud and scaring the other customers. Lai was there, and he took care of the situation and escorted the man out. From that incident on, whenever he came to the bank, he would pop by the manager's office to say hi."

"You got his service number?"

Mislan passes a slip of paper to her.

"It's from his savings account record. Jo said that's quite a senior number, maybe thirty years of service," Mislan says.

She looks at the clock on the wall. The time shows 4:20 p.m.

"Why don't you go and have your smoke? I'll call you when I have some answers," she suggests.

––––––––

After her officers leave, Superintendent Samsiah walks over to the new building and takes the elevator to the Personnel Department, which is part of the Contingent Administrative Office. She asks for ASP Saraswathi, the officer in charge of personnel service records.

ASP Saraswathi is a slim woman of about five foot two, in her mid-forties, and single. Samsiah heard that she's reading law in the evenings as a mature student, perhaps looking at an early retirement.

"I have a favor to ask," Samsiah says. "There's this sergeant, well, I knew him from my days in the district. He called me and asked if there's an opening in my unit. Before I make a decision, I'd like to view his service record."

"Where's he stationed?"

"I think Cheras, but I'm not sure. You know *lah*, when you get old, you forget so many things," Samsiah lies, polishing it with a warm smile.

"Do you have his service number?"

"Yes." Samsiah reads the name and service number.

Saraswathi keys it into her computer and says, "Cheras Police district headquarters. Give me a second. I'll get his file."

"Thank you," Samsiah says, thinking, *That was easy.*

After a few minutes, Saraswathi comes back carrying the service book and records of Sergeant Lai Kwang Kee. Although she is bursting with curiosity, Superintendent Samsiah stays composed and opens the service book slowly. Sergeant Lai joined the police as a trainee in 1990. He was recruited through the special program conducted by the police to bring in more non-Malays into the force. After graduating, he served in general duty attached to Penang. Subsequently, he was transferred to Klang Selangor, then to Negeri Sembilan contingent headquarters in Seremban, and then to Ipoh, Perak. In 2003, he made detective and was attached to the NCID strike team based in PGA Central Brigade before they moved to PULAPOL. In 2016, he was promoted to sergeant and was stationed as assistant investigating officer at Cheras Police district headquarters.

His personnel records say that he hails from Penang, is married, and has two children. He lives in Bandar Tun Razak, Cheras.

"May I snap his photo from this file?" Samsiah asks.

Saraswathi looks at her questioningly.

"So that when he comes to see me I can recognize him. I don't want him to feel embarrassed when I don't recognize him," she says, flashing a smile.

"Oh," Saraswathi says as if she understands. "That's an old photo. Give me a second, I'll print from his digital record, which is updated annually."

When Saraswathi hands Samsiah the printout, she thanks her for being very helpful.

"Are you bringing him on board your unit?" Saraswathi asks.

"He has a solid career and was in NCID, which could be useful to my unit. Yes, we'll probably pick him up."

———

Mislan jumps off his chair in expectation upon seeing Superintendent Samsiah walking into the office.

"Did you get it, ma'am?" he asks impatiently. "Did Personnel suspect anything?"

"Give me some credit, will you," Samsiah says. "No, Personnel didn't suspect anything. I told her I knew Lai from my days in the district and that he'd asked if there's an opening in the unit. I, of course, needed to view his service records before I decide."

"That's the best bullshit I've ever heard," Mislan says, followed by a chuckle.

"I'll take that as a compliment, thank you." She hands him the printout of Lai's photo. "I got this for you."

"Wow, thanks."

Mislan and Johan stare at the photo of Lai, for the first time seeing what their suspect looks like. It is a standard facial shot. Lai looks pleasant, his eyes clear, short hair, salt-and-pepper at his temples and posing with a tiny smile. Nothing in his look would indicate he's capable of murder, such as a psychopathic leer. But then you only notice those looks for a microsecond when they're arrested and when cornered while being interviewed up close and personal.

Samsiah asks Mislan for his notepad and writes down Sergeant Lai's particulars that she memorized and passes it back to him.

"Height five feet, six inches, weighs 140 pounds, slender. That's about the height and size of the individual we saw in the bank's CCTV. Now this is interesting. Narco's strike team detective. He was at one time stationed at Negeri Sembilan contingent headquarters in Seremban. Now an AIO in Cheras Police. Everything fits like a glove," Mislan confirms. "Can we pick him up?"

"Nooo," Samsiah says.

"Why not?" Johan is puzzled. "The telco said the call was made in front of the bank. The CDM camera and record confirmed he banked in the money."

"Like I said earlier, we have nothing on him. Everything is circumstantial. So he banked in the money; he can claim he was going to the bank and a friend asked him as a favor to bank it in."

"What about the calls made using the vic's cell phone?" Mislan challenges.

"Have you considered that there could be many others in front of the bank making calls not captured by the camera? How do you prove it was him making the call using the vic's phone? Can you put the phone in his hand when the calls were made?"

Mislan and Johan look at each other.

"Just as I thought," she says.

Mislan takes a cigarette from the pack, and looks at his boss. She gives him a nod of approval, and he lights it.

"Give Jo and me ten minutes with him, and he'll spill it all out," Mislan brags.

"He's a police sergeant with tons of experience, he'll come up with a hundred excuses if you interview him without concrete evidence. You need to put him at the scene, or put the vic's phone in his hand," she stresses. "Until you can do that, I'm not, I repeat, I'm not authorizing any move against him."

"Can I put a tail on him?" Mislan asks.

"How're you going to do it with the MCO? At every roadblock, you'll be stopped and you'll have to identify yourself. By the time you're cleared, he'll be long gone or would have made you," Samsiah says.

Mislan purses his lips, turning to his assistant.

"Anyway, what're you expecting, another hit?"

———

A long sulking night ensues, with Mislan chain-smoking and Johan glued to his social media. Superintendent Samsiah's words spin around in his head: *Put the phone in his hand or put him at the scene.* He asks himself, *How the hell do I do that?*

"Jo," Mislan calls out. "You know anyone in Cheras Police you can trust?"

"Trust how?" Johan asks, looking up from his Facebook page.

"Trust to do something, you know."

"Something what?"

"On the quiet for us."

"Like?"

"Get into the suspect's office and car. Have a look-see."

"You mean break in," Johan says, followed by a laugh. "You're scary when you're desperate. No, I don't know anyone that's crazy enough to do it. Even if I do, I won't be a party to it."

"You and your morality," Mislan sneers. "This fucking guy's a killer."

"This fucking guy's a police officer, and ma'am's right, we don't have anything concrete to tie him to the killings."

"Not yet, but I promise you we will—one way or the other."

24

THAT MORNING, AFTER THE brief morning prayer, Mislan asks Superintendent Samsiah if they can do a check on Lai's bank account.

"What're you expecting to find?" Samsiah asks.

"Hopefully a lot of money."

"I don't think he's stupid enough to keep it in his account."

"He may have several other accounts and maybe even use his wife's account."

"Hmmm."

"Can't CCID check to see if he has other accounts?" he asks, referring to Commercial Crime Investigation Division.

"I don't know. Don't they have to seek the National Bank's approval for such things?"

"You're asking me?" he says with a chuckle.

"I'll check with them and see."

———

After leaving Superintendent Samsiah's office, Mislan stops at his office and signals for his assistant to follow him.

"Where're we going?" Johan asks, catching up with him at the elevator lobby.

"Ma'am said she wants us to put the vic's phone in the suspect's hand. That's what we're going to do," Mislan answers as he steps into a waiting elevator.

"By the book, I hope."

"I only do things by the book," he says, flashing his assistant a sly grin.

"Your book, you mean."

They head out toward Jalan Pudu, turn off into Jalan Peel, and enter the Sunway Velocity Shopping Mall. The parking lot is almost empty, as most of the shops in the mall are closed except for eateries and banks. Mislan parks closest to the staircase leading up to the shopping floor.

Coming up into the open-air courtyard between the two wings, he searches for Spicy Thai Restaurant. The restaurant has the bright royal-yellow and bloodred signage and decorations typical of Thai restaurants here. It's located at the far end of the north courtyard.

There are only two staff at the restaurant, a bored-looking waitress and an even more bored-looking male cook. He knows that F&B workers depend on tips from customers for extra income. With restaurants allowed only to do takeout business, tips aren't forthcoming, therefore the bored expressions on their faces.

As it's a Thai restaurant, Johan tries to impress them with his mastery of the Thai language. He enthusiastically greets them with "Sawadee krap." The female staff smiles and replies with a "Sawadee ka." Then the problem starts.

"Sawadee krap," the cook replies followed by, "ja hai pom chouy lear a'rai die'bang."

Johan blushes, embarrassed.

"Sorry, what did you say?"

"How may I assist you?" the cook translates.

Mislan laughs at his assistant's awkwardness and decides to take over.

"I see you have CCTV here," he says, pointing to the ceiling above the counter and at the corners of the dining area. The two staff follow with their eyes the directions Mislan points to, and nod. "Where's the monitor?"

"In the manager's office," the waitress answers.

Mislan introduces himself, shows his police authority card, and tells her he needs to view the recording.

"I have to check with the manager," the waitress replies.

"OK, give him a call."

"Her."

"OK, give her a call."

The waitress makes the call, and after several yeses and nos, she terminates the call and beckons for the D9 officers to follow her. The manager's office is barely the size of a toilet cubicle. *Rental must be very expensive,* Mislan figures. A tiny table pushed against the wall, a folding chair pushed under the table, and a wooden IKEA file rack constitute the furnishings. Even then, only one and a half people can fit into the office. The waitress flips open the laptop on the tiny desk and keys in the password. It comes to life, and the four camera feeds appear.

"Can you bring it to this date and time?" Mislan asks, writing down the details on the notepad beside the laptop.

The waitress punches in the date and time in the parameter setting, and four still images appear on the screen. From the images, Mislan can make out that camera #1 covers the cashier counter and the rest cover the dining area. He nods to the waitress to run the video. The restaurant was empty, but he catches a glimpse of a leg that was moving away from the cashier counter.

It strikes him that the video timing may not be synchronized with that of the telecommunication service provider. He checks the time on his phone and compares it with the video timing; his suspicion is right. He tells the waitress to bring the time back to two minutes earlier and run the video again.

When the video starts, camera #1 shows a man roughly the height and build of their suspect standing in front of the cashier counter with a cell phone to his ear. With his free hand, he passes money to pay for his food. The cashier returns his change. He picks up the plastic bag on the counter and walks out.

"Can you go back again? This time make it four minutes," Mislan tells the waitress.

"There," Johan says, pointing to the screen, "that's him walking in. See the dark blue pants and black shoes? He's in half-uniform."

Mislan inhales deeply. The man's face is covered with a blue face mask, and nothing distinctive can be seen of his features except for his graying hair. But what his assistant pointed out was right. Most police-men would replace their uniform shirt with a civilian one but not their pants when going out for lunch or for a short spell. It's known to them as half-uniform and is against regulations. He produces a thumb drive from his backpack and asks the waitress if she could copy the recording into it. She agrees, and he asks her to make it ten minutes before and after the clip they just watched.

Waiting for her to copy the video onto his thumb drive, Mislan walks out to the courtyard and lights a cigarette. After a while, Johan comes out holding the thumb drive. Mislan gives the waitress a wave of thanks and walks away in search of Jone's Café. He stops abruptly.

"Jo, can you go back and ask the waitress if she can print out a copy of the suspect's purchase receipt?"

"OK."

———

Jone's Café is located in the middle section of the left wing. Mislan sees three customers seated at the chairs spread one yard apart lining the outer glass wall. Johan walks in to the cashier counter as Mislan observes the surroundings for CCTV cameras. He spots one behind the cashier counter, one at the entrance, and one at the far deep end of the dining area.

Johan motions for his boss to follow him behind the counter. Mislan stubs out his cigarette in a flower pot and walks into the café. A com-puter monitor sits on the lower counter with the images of the three cameras. Mislan gives him the date and time he needs to view, and the cashier, a young Chinese male with multiple earrings, punches on the keyboard next to the monitor. Still images of the three cameras for the date and time appear.

A man about the same height, hair, and build as their suspect and wearing half-uniform was captured on camera entering the café.

Mislan asks the cashier to run the video.

The man was wearing a face mask and talking on a cell phone. He reached the cashier counter, cupping his hand on the phone as he addressed the cashier. The cashier said something to him, probably confirming the orders. All of a sudden, the man pulled his face mask down to his chin and spoke to the cashier. The cashier nodded, the man pulled his face mask back up to cover his face and continued talking into the phone. Then he moved away from the cashier counter and out to the line of chairs.

Mislan's and Johan's eyes almost pop out of their sockets at the suspect's action.

"Did you see what he just did or was I imagining it?" Johan asks.

Mislan asks the cashier to run the section again, frame by frame. When the suspect's face appears, he tells the cashier to pause the frame. The smiling Sergeant Lai's face is clearly seen on the screen, with his left hand holding a phone and his right hand cupping it.

"Got you," Mislan declares.

When Mislan and Johan go to Superintendent Samsiah's office, they find ASP Amir there. Mislan is about to turn away when Superintendent Samsiah calls, "Mislan, Jo, come in."

"Ma'am, sir," Mislan and Johan greet them.

"Sorry to interrupt, I'll come back later," Mislan says.

"You're not interrupting," Amir says. "In fact, we were just about to call you to join us."

"I'll go then," Johan offers.

"You too, Jo," Samsiah says, "both of you." Seeing the worried expressions on her officers' faces, she adds, "And it has nothing to do with any misconduct allegation against you."

Superintendent Samsiah and ASP Amir see the look of relief on Johan's face and laugh.

"Take a seat, Lan. Jo, pull a chair in," Samsiah instructs them, "and close the door behind you."

Superintendent Samsiah explains the presence of ASP Amir from ISCD. He had come to update her on the Seremban 2 MPV response compliance inquiry. In an interview conducted by ISCD, the patrolmen admitted there were drugs found at the scene. The drugs were removed before the investigating officer's arrival and later sold off for 12,000 ringgit. ISCD will be charging the two patrolmen in due course.

The frustration and disappointment on Mislan's and Johan's faces are apparent. To them, these are the type of police personnel that the court should throw in prison for the maximum length allowed by law. The Malay saying "Harapkan pagar, pagar makan padi"—you depend on the fence, but it's the fence that's destroying the rice plants—is so apt.

"We also discussed your earlier request to check the suspect's and his spouse's bank accounts. In my view, since this involves our personnel, ISCD should be doing it and not CCID."

Mislan nods.

"I'm glad you agree," Amir jokes.

"I'm always supportive of ISCD as long as they're not investigating me," he says with a naughty grin.

"By the way, why are you two still in the office? I thought I asked you to go home and get some rest," Samsiah asks, gazing at her officers.

"We just came back," Johan answers.

"From?"

"From putting the vic's phone in the suspect's hand," Mislan answers triumphantly.

"What did you do, beat a confession out of him?" Samsiah jests.

"I wish, but no, I used my mojo," he jabs back. "Jo, you want to give ma'am the thumb drive?"

Superintendent Samsiah slots in the thumb drive, and the rest of them move around behind her. Mislan presses Play, and they wait anxiously. Two minutes in, the suspect, talking on a cell phone, appears at the entrance of Jone's Café wearing a face mask. The suspect steps up to the cashier counter, cups his hand on the cell phone and speaks to the cashier. The cashier responds to him, and suddenly the suspect pulls his face mask down to his chin. Mislan presses the pause button, and the suspect's face can be clearly seen on the screen. A man in his mid- to late fifties, graying hair, clean-shaven, thin face, with slit clear eyes.

Mislan stops the video. Superintendent Samsiah turns to look at her officers over her left shoulder and then to Amir over to her right.

Expressions of shock, surprise, elation, and anger are reflected on their faces. One by one, they silently move back to their chairs.

Mislan is dying for a cigarette, but he knows with the ISCD representative here, he'll be putting his boss in a bad light if he asks for permission to smoke. It would breach policies and procedures in the presence of their custodian and enforcer.

"The video is from Jone's Café," Mislan says. "The time and location of the call made by the suspect coincide with the telco report on the vic's cell phone."

"Playing the devil's advocate," Amir says apologetically, "what if the suspect was coincidentally talking on his own cell phone at the same location and time but another person was on the victim's cell phone at that place and time too?"

"What's the chance of that happening?" Mislan asks. Then he turns to look at his boss.

"I don't know," Samsiah admits. "Amir?"

"Going by the video, none, I guess," Amir answers, killing his own supposition.

"How do you want to proceed?" she asks Mislan.

"You know how I want to proceed, but I'd like to hear your thoughts." Superintendent Samsiah glances at the clock on the wall.

"Amir, are you free to join us?" she asks.

Amir nods.

"I'd like to call upon the OCPD. I don't want him to be caught with his pants down on this. But I also want the search of his house to be conducted simultaneously to eliminate any opportunity for evidence to be removed. I'll get Ghani to lead the search team."

The OCPD is the Officer in Charge of Police District. In the case of Cheras Police District, he holds a rank of assistant commissioner of police (ACP), one rank above hers.

The officers nod their agreement.

25

THE POSSE OF D9 and ISCD arrive at Cheras Police district headquarters on Jalan Cheras at 2:10 p.m. ASP Amir introduces himself to the inquiry counter and asks for directions to the OCPD's office. He is directed by the female corporal to level one. As the posse turns the corner to the staircase, they hear a voice calling to the head of Special Investigations.

"Ma'am, Superintendent Samsiah, how are you?" a female sergeant calls, accompanied by a salute.

The posse stops, and Superintendent Samsiah turns to see a woman in sergeant's uniform.

"Zaiton, what a surprise to see you here. I'm fine. How're you keeping?"

Sergeant Zaiton was once a D9 detective under her command. About a decade back, she took a bullet during a raid at a sleazy bar on Lorong Tuanku Abdul Rahman 2, where one of their armed suspects was spotted. She and Johan were teamed as a couple to go into the bar to snoop and confirm the suspect's presence. The suspect made them, drew his gun, and fired. Johan managed to shove Zaiton away, but the shot still hit her on the shoulder. Johan immediately returned fire, killing the suspect before he could take a second shot at her. After her recovery, she was assigned to general duties.

"I'm OK. Ma'am, you know *lah*, here every day is routine, not much excitement. That's why *lah* all this," Zaiton says, running her hand up and down her rotund body. "Inspector Mislan, Jo, *waa*, why D9 IO and AIO are all here?" Zaiton asks, curious. "Sure something big is happening."

It is common for district personnel to be suspicious or to assume something big is happening in their district when officers from Contingent or Federal headquarters descend on them, especially in numbers. Special Investigations (D9) and Integrity Standard Compliance (ISCD) would seem a lethal combination for a hunting team on their turf.

Sergeant Zaiton's excited voice is attracting curious stares and glances from surrounding personnel and those passing by. In ASP Amir's view, it's bringing unwanted attention to the posse's presence.

Stepping forward, he says, "I'm ASP Amir from ISCD. We're here to meet with the OCPD. If you'll excuse us, we're already late."

Sergeant Zaiton raises her eyebrows at the word ISCD and steps aside, saying, "I'm sorry."

The posse continues up the stairs to the OCPD's office and are followed by wary eyes.

———

Stepping into the OCPD's external office, ASP Amir introduces himself to the personal assistant. She apologizes, saying her boss is on his way and should be here shortly. She invites them to take a seat and asks if she can get them any drinks. ASP Amir declines on behalf of all of them. A few seconds later, they hear footfalls on the stairs, and the OCPD, ACP Rusdi Abd Rashid, appears. He's in early fifties, clearly balding with gray hair on the sides, slightly overweight, and is panting like a horse after a grueling race.

The officers stand to greet him, and he replies with a wave, inviting them into his office. The personal assistant comes in with a pitcher of cold water and several glasses. She pours a glass and offers it to the officers, but they decline. ACP Rusdi, obviously thirsty from being in the hot sun checking on his men manning the roadblocks, drains the water in one long gulp. He then pulls a face towel from one of the drawers to wipe his face and neck.

"It's burning hot out there," he says, pouring another glass of water for himself. "The beauty of our country, it's either too hot or too wet, nothing in between," he continues with a chuckle.

Superintendent Samsiah nods and lets the OCPD catch his breath before starting. She introduces ASP Amir and her two officers.

"D9 and ISCD, this has to be serious," Rusdi says with a dry chuckle, trying to hide his anxiety. "My PA didn't say why you needed to see me, she just said you said it's important."

"Sir, may we close the door?" Samsiah asks.

"Yes, yes. Now you're really frightening me," Rusdi says, trying to keep his tone light. "What's this about?"

Johan gets up to close the door. Superintendent Samsiah turns to ASP Amir, indicating for him to take the lead as ISCD. Amir gives the OCPD a summary, with as little information as he can provide on the Seremban 2 and Sentul killings. The brief centers on the donations made to the Forgotten Children of Kuala Lumpur and Mr. Wee.

"We have strong evidence that one of your personnel may be involved," Amir says. "At this moment, his involvement may be coincidental or indirect," he adds to lighten the blow, "but we, D9 and ISCD, are of the opinion we need to take him in for clarification."

"If that's the case, why is D9 involved?"

"This is not yet confirmed, but we're working on the possibility that the large amount of money donated came from an illegal source or sponsor," Samsiah answers for Amir. "At this point, sir, I think it's best if we don't go into it until we're sure."

The OCPD nods his agreement.

Amir turns to look at her, curving a minuscule grin of *Thank you for saving my ass*.

"Who's this person?" Rusdi asks. Clearly, he looks disappointed that one of his personnel could be associated with criminal activities.

"Sergeant Lai Kwang Kee," Samsiah says.

"Lai! Impossible! He's one of the best AIOs we have. I don't buy it," Rusdi snaps, while glaring at Mislan and Johan. "You're the IO?" Before Mislan can respond, he says, "You must be mistaken."

"Yes, we may be, that's why I asked for ISCD to come along. We'd like to keep this internal until we can verify every detail," Superintendent Samsiah butts in. "Sir, to avoid any unnecessary embarrassment to Sergeant Lai, would you like to call him to your office?"

ACP Rusdi picks up the phone and tells his personal assistant to call Sergeant Lai to the office. He leans back in his chair and closes his eyes. Superintendent Samsiah and ASP Amir feel the pain he's experiencing. They turn to look at each other, and Amir lets out a sigh of anguish.

His friends in the police think his job is easy, just office work and getting rid of the bad policemen or women. Yes, it may be physically easy, but it's mentally and emotionally taxing. Having to witness the pain and suffering of those whose trust was broken. Like what he is seeing in ACP Rusdi. He also knows the bad apples need to be taken out before their decayed attitude contaminates the rest of the apples in the barrel. They need to be weeded out and acted upon to safeguard the public and the Force.

———

After several minutes, there is still no indication of Sergeant Lai coming. Mislan looks at his boss questioningly. His boss silently signals for him to calm down and wait. ACP Rusdi is still in his leaned-back position, his eyes closed. His chest heaves up and down in controlled breaths, probably some meditation technique he learned to calm his anxiety. Mislan head-gestures toward him, and Johan leans to whisper in his ear, telling him to relax and let the head of Special Investigations handle the situation. Mislan turns to hiss at his assistant.

Suddenly, an explosion echoes through the building. Startled, ACP Rusdi almost slumps forward onto his desk. The personal assistant lets out a terrified scream. Mislan springs to his feet and is already at the door before the rest of them get up. Rushing past the personal assistant's desk, he asks where Sergeant Lai's office is. The personal assistant shouts that the office is one floor above.

With Johan close behind, he runs up the stairs three steps at a time. The staircase is crammed with uniformed personnel, and he pushes his way through to the door where a huge crowd has gathered. Pushing and shoving, he emerges at the doorway.

The office of Sergeant Lai is full of uniformed personnel. Most of them are just standing and gawking. Mislan shouts at the top of his lungs, "Get out! Get out! This is not a bloody show." Seeing most of them holding their cell phones, he barks, "Don't any of you dare take photos of this!"

Johan starts shoving the uniformed personnel aside, with shouts of "D9, stand back!" A few officers in uniform stare defiantly at him, and Johan stares back as if saying, *Back off.* ACP Rusdi, Superintendent Samsiah, and ASP Amir arrive and the officers step away.

Sergeant Lai Kwang Kee is slumped to his right in an all-too-familiar standard light-blue velvet swivel police chair. His head lolls onto his right shoulder. His right hand hangs limply from the chair, with the tips of his fingers barely touching the floor. Blood is oozing from a gaping hole under his chin, dripping into a dark pool on the floor directly below his head. There is a dark wet patch on his head, coloring part of his gray hair bright red. Mislan notices the bullet had gone through, penetrating the skull. Blood is still running down his chest, soaking his uniform shirt. Lai's eyes are wide open and bulging out of their sockets. *It had to be caused by the bullet's impact, or the pressure of the brain exploding,* Mislan thinks. The dead eyes are staring out across the room. Mislan follows the line of sight to the glass window. *Probably he was looking outside, at the freedom he will never have again.* A Walther PPK pistol is lying on the floor under the desk a few feet from the body. The wall behind him is clear of blood, but Mislan notices a few specks of blood and pinkish-white substance stuck on the ceiling around a tiny hole in the white asbestos. A bullet casing is stuck at the leg board of a desk opposite to his.

He hears ACP Rusdi angrily barking orders to his men to clear the floor, and soon the floor is quiet and free of uniformed personnel.

Mislan looks around the office, and notices a box of latex gloves on top of the steel cabinet. He pulls one out and slips it on. He examines Lai's left hand lying across his stomach for a pulse but feels none. He did not expect to feel any, what with the gaping hole under the chin and another on top of the sergeant's head.

"Who shares the office with him?" Mislan asks.

"I don't know," Rusdi replies.

Mislan steps to the other desk, and the name plate reads SERGEANT FAUZI.

"Is Sergeant Fauzi around?" Mislan asks.

One of the remaining officers standing outside says he's on road-block duty.

"I have to inform the OCCI," Rusdi says. "Has anyone called Forensics?"

The same officer says D10, which is the contingent crime scene forensics team, is on the way and so too are the paramedics.

"He's dead, we don't need paramedics," Mislan says. "Ma'am, can we get Chew from Forensics to handle this?"

"Why?"

"I'll feel better if he does."

"Let me make a call."

"Let's wait for the paramedic to certify he's dead and the crime scene boys to finish first before we do our part," Mislan suggests.

ASP Amir tells the rest of the officers to clear the corridor and let D9 and ISCD do their work. Mislan steps out from the office into the corridor. He lights a cigarette, receiving a glare from Amir.

"Sorry, sir, really need one," Mislan says.

"Why don't you go to the window there? Less obvious," Amir suggests.

"Thanks."

Johan notices his boss walking with a slight unsteadiness in the knees and recalls the misstep at the Sentul crime scene. Blood and gun-shots are still traumatic for him.

"What do you think led to this?" Amir asks Johan.

"Don't know."

Superintendent Samsiah tells Mislan that Chew and his team are on the way. She informs him Sergeant Zaiton wants to see him. Mislan looks at her inquiringly.

"I don't know, maybe she knows something. Are you up to it?" she asks.

"Sure, let me finish this," he says, holding up the cigarette. "Why don't you sit in too? You know, to make her feel more comfortable."

"I will, and I'll get Amir to sit in, too."

Superintendent Samsiah leaves her officer by the window and walks back to Amir and Johan.

"Jo, you stay here. Tell D10 to wait for Crime Scene from headquarters," Samsiah instructs him.

"OK, where will you be?"

"We'll be with Sergeant Zaiton, over there."

———

Sergeant Zaiton is clearly shaken by the incident, possibly remembering the trauma of being shot herself in the sleazy bar. Superintendent Samsiah and ASP Amir are already in the office when Mislan enters. He leans against the table facing them.

"What do you want to tell Mislan?" Samsiah asks.

"I don't know if this is relevant," Zaiton starts tentatively. "Lai saw me talking to you at the staircase earlier. Then when I was in the office, he came barging in, which is very unlike him. The many years that I've known him, Lai was a humble, courteous, and friendly person. Extremely helpful whether it's work or on a personal matter. He's a real team player." She pauses, inhaling several times. The officers can see tears welling in her eyes. "Several years back, he heard about me needing some money for my daughter's admission to college; he lent me the money without asking when I could pay it back. That's the kind of person Lai was."

The officers remain silent, allowing Zaiton a few moments to deal with her grief, to sort out her thoughts.

"But today, today I saw a different side of him," she continues timidly. "The rude side that I never knew he had. As I said, he barged in, no 'hi,' no 'sorry, you got a minute,' no 'are you busy,' nothing. He slammed the door with a bang, staring at me and asking who you guys were. I don't know how to describe it, I mean the manner he asked the question. It was like, I don't know . . . scary. His eyes were red with anger. I told him you're D9, my old boss and colleagues, and ASP Amir from ISCD. Then he specifically asked, 'Is that Inspector Mislan and Detective Sergeant Johan?' When I replied 'yes,' he asked in an accusing way, 'Why are D9 and ISCD here? What did you tell them?' When I said I didn't know and I didn't tell you anything, he got angry, threatening, not with words but his body language. He tensed up, his hands in fists. Suddenly, he dashed out saying, 'They're after me, aren't they?'"

Samsiah looks at Mislan, then at Amir.

"Did he say why he thought we were after him?" Mislan asks.

Zaiton shakes her head. "I saw anger, and fear too in his eyes. His hands were shaking, and for a moment there I thought he was going to attack me."

"Lately, how has he been behaving?" Mislan continues.

"Normal, I guess. I saw him about two days back: he seemed to be his usual self. He asked me about the roadblock duties and seemed OK."

"How close is Sergeant Fauzi with Lai?"

"They shared an office. I guess they're close, but if you mean are they buddies, I don't think so."

"Who do you think is Lai's buddy here?" Mislan probes.

"He was friendly with everybody, but buddy, I don't know. From what I heard, Lai was not the typical Chinese man in the force that we stereotyped. He didn't smoke, and didn't drink or gamble."

"Affairs?" Amir asks.

"Haven't heard of those either. I don't know what he's alleged to have done that brought you here, but as far as we here are concerned, Lai was a good man," Zaiton says.

"I'm sure he was," Samsiah says.

26

DETECTIVE SERGEANT JOHAN KNOCKS on the door, pokes his head in, and informs them the paramedics have certified the death of Sergeant Lai and left. Chew and his team are now doing their examination. Mislan tells him they'll be there shortly.

"Jo, has Sergeant Fauzi been called back?" Mislan asks.

"Yes, on his way."

"Don't let him into his office until I say so."

"OK."

They continue probing Sergeant Zaiton on what she knew of Lai, which was not much. Superintendent Samsiah thanks her, and they leave her to mourn her dead colleague. Outside in the corridor, Mislan asks if he can access Lai's service and personal records.

"Amir, can you assist?" Samsiah asks.

"I'll get them for you. What do you hope to find in them?" Amir asks Mislan.

"From Zaiton's description, one would think he's a saint, but we know what he was involved in. I'm hoping his files could show me what triggered him to go wayward," Mislan says, taking out a cigarette to light. Superintendent Samsiah gives him an admonishing gaze, and he puts the cigarette back into the pack. "Sir, is it possible to get ahold of the SB vetting on him?"

"You mean the Special Branch recruitment vetting?" Amir asks, curious.

"Yes, I'd also like to know his family's background, his upbringing."

"For what purpose?" Samsiah asks.

"In my case, there were two killers involved. If Lai was one of them, I need to know who his accomplice was. It could be from his old boys' network," Mislan explains.

"No promises, but I'll check with recruitment and see if they still have it," Amir replies.

"Thanks. Excuse me while I get my fix by the window. I'll join you later."

———

Superintendent Samsiah and ASP Amir stand in the doorway to Lai's office, watching Crime Scene Forensics Supervisor Chew and his team going about their work. Lai's face is literally turning white, with most of the blood drained out of his upper body. Chew takes a close look at the gunshot wounds, angles his head to look at the ceiling, then back again to the wound on top of the skull. He slowly fishes out the contents of Lai's pockets and places them neatly on the desk.

Mislan joins the two officers at the doorway. He asks where Johan is and is told he went down to the vending machine for some drinks.

"Chew, sorry to make the special request for your assistance," Mislan says, greeting the forensics supervisor.

"Inspector, no problem, always happy to be working with you. How come you're on this?" Chew asks, curious.

"Long story, I'll tell you as we go along."

Johan arrives with some pack drinks. He passes them around. Superintendent Samsiah and ASP Amir inform Mislan they're leaving. She needs to brief the OCCI, and Amir needs to work on getting Lai's service and personal records.

"What time do you think you'll be done here?" Samsiah asks.

"Don't know. I'll be here as long as it takes."

"You're on tomorrow, right?"

Mislan nods.

"I'll get Yana or Khamis to take over your shift. I want you to get some rest and stay on this for the time being. I almost forgot I need to tell Ghani's team to stand down, unless you still want him to do the house search."

"No, I don't think the family knows about this yet, and I certainly don't want them to be informed of their loss by Ghani. Best we let the district handle that part."

"OK, if you say so."

"Thanks, ma'am."

After the head of Special Investigations and ISCD leave, Mislan and Johan enter Lai's office. The stench of clotting blood fills the room.

"Chew, can we open the window?" Mislan asks.

Chew tells one of his boys to open the window, switch off the air-conditioner, and switch on the ceiling fan.

"That's much better," Mislan says.

"Can never get used to the smell, can you?" Chew remarks.

"It's not so bad in an open area. Are you done with the body?"

"Yes. Straightforward. Entry here," Chew says, pointing under the chin, "and out here." He points to the top of the skull. "The bullet went through and hit the ceiling." He points to the spot scattered with pink-white substance and with a puncture hole.

"Can we move him out?" Mislan asks, head-gesturing to Lai's body.

"Yes."

"Jo, can you get the OCS to arrange for the body to be sent to the morgue?"

"Where, HKL or HUKM?"

"Anywhere, it doesn't matter. Chew, you found any cell phone?"

"Yes." Chew points to a cell phone on the desk.

"Have you tried to check it?"

"Locked. We'll have to do it at the lab."

"So you don't know whose phone it is?"

"I assume it's his, found it in his pocket."

"Hang on."

Mislan steps out to Sergeant Zaiton's desk and asks her for Lai's cell phone number. Returning to Lai's office, he makes a call. The cell phone on Lai's table rings, a Chinese-song ringtone.

"Is that the only one?"

"So far. You expect more than one?"

"Hoping."

"Are those his car keys?" Mislan points to a bunch of keys on the desk.

"Yes, and house and office keys, I think."

"Can you get your boys to check the car?"

"Now?"

Mislan nods. "Maybe split your team. Save time."

Chew instructs his assistant and the cameraman to examine the car while he and the rest finish the office.

"Check with Detective Sergeant Johan—he's downstairs—which one is the deceased's car," Mislan tells Chew's assistant. "Johan will be in attendance there."

Mislan watches as Chew swabs Lai's hand for gunshot residue, GSR. Then he picks up the bullet casing and dusts it for prints before placing it in an exhibit bag.

"Have you done the gun?"

"Dusted."

Mislan snaps on the latex gloves and handles the Walther PPK. He ejects the magazine and clears the chamber of the bullet before placing them on the desk. He cocks the gun and examines the end of the barrel.

"Threaded," Mislan says.

Chew looks at him questioningly.

"Thread on the barrel to hold a suppressor."

"But that's a police-issued gun?"

"Yes, but how many policemen check the guns issued to them? I mean really check it, that's apart from making sure the guns are cleared. Unlike the general duty personnel, sidearms issued to officers and detectives, even AIOs, are usually theirs for the long term."

"Meaning?"

"Once issued to them, they get to use the same gun until it's returned for whatever reason, like being transferred or to replace it with a new model. The general duty personnel are issued with guns when they come on duty, and at the end of their duty the guns are returned to the armory."

"The next day they are issued a gun again," Chew says.

"Yes, and it may not be the same gun."

Chew nods.

"Anyway, even if Lai returned the gun and was issued with a new gun, the GD personnel that was issued with Lai's gun wouldn't spot any difference. Even if he or she noticed the thread on the barrel, they'd assume it's a normal thing." Putting back the gun, Mislan asks, "Can I smoke?"

"Yes, we're done actually except for up there," Chew says and points to the hole in the ceiling. "Need to get a ladder to go up and recover the bullet."

Mislan lights a cigarette.

"Why do you say our policemen would think a threaded gun barrel is normal?" Chew asks.

"Our police personnel aren't gun-savvy like the Americans, and suppressors aren't used here. The only time Malaysians, including police personnel, see suppressors being used is probably in the movies. Even I didn't know much about it until I researched them on the internet. I know of officers and personnel who haven't fired a single shot, except at the shooting range, their entire career. When it comes to guns, all they know is to load, shoot, and unload or clear the chamber. So if they see something on a gun, they'll think it's part of the design. I'm talking about our general duty personnel. The Special Force personnel, well, I'm sure they know a lot about guns."

"You're kidding, right?"

Mislan smiles, seeing the baffled expression on the forensics supervisor's face. His cell phone rings; it's Johan telling him he needs to come down.

"Why, what did you find?"

"A bloody treasure trove."

————

The car is a metallic gray Proton Waja 1.5 sedan, one of the earlier national car models, probably about ten years old. Yet it looks in mint condition. All the four doors, hood, and trunk are wide open. The seat covers seem to be original, and so is the interior. Johan and Chew's assistant are standing at the open trunk when Mislan and Chew arrive.

"What did you find?" Mislan asks again.

Johan points into the trunk. The spare tire has been removed and placed by the side. In the depression where the spare tire is normally kept is an opened black plastic bag and an unwrapped piece of brown cloth. Through the opening in the plastic bag, Mislan sees bundles of cash. In the middle of the unwrapped cloth is a five-inch black cylinder; it must be the suppressor.

Mislan and Chew stare at the two items unblinkingly.

"What about the vic's phone?" Mislan asks his assistant.

"There's a cell phone in the glove compartment. I also found some receipts, which I'm sure will match the ones we got from the restaurant and café."

"Have you checked if the phone belongs to our vic?"

"Not yet. I wanted you to see it first."

Mislan and Chew move to the front passenger door, and Johan points to the cell phone in the open glove compartment.

"I don't understand why would he keep the money and suppressor in the car? I mean, what if he's stopped at a roadblock and his car inspected? The exhibits would directly link to him," Chew says.

"He's a police sergeant. Who's going to inspect his car at a roadblock? It's the safest place for him to hide the exhibits. He stashes them at home, his wife or kids may find them. Chew, can your guy dust the phone so Jo can check it out?"

Chew gives the instruction to his technician, and they walk back to the trunk.

"Chew, you can get prints from the plastic bag, right?" Mislan asks. "Yes."

"OK, good. What about from the money?"

"That too, but a bit difficult, very much depends on the condition of the money."

"Can you do it here?"

"Yes, but it's tedious, and I prefer to do it at the lab."

"OK, can you do the suppressor and phone here?"

"Not a problem."

Chew instructs his assistant to carry out the dusting and to do the car exterior too. Mislan steps away and lights a cigarette. The time is almost 6 in the evening, but he decides to make a call to Superintendent Samsiah. He needs instructions and guidance.

"Ma'am, sorry, have you left the office?"

"Not yet. Lan, just for your info, the OCCI held a PC on the suicide at 5."

"What did he say?"

"I don't know, Amir was there. For the time being I want to keep D9 out of the picture. I don't want our link to the suicide to be known to the public, not just yet."

"Good. How did he take your absence?" Mislan means the Officer in Charge of Criminal Investigation.

"I don't know, I passed the word through Amir," she replies again with a tiny chuckle.

"Smart."

"Yes. Anything, Lan?"

"We found the money, suppressor, and most likely the vic's phone in Lai's car."

"Good job."

"About the cash, Chew says he prefers to dust the plastic bag and the money back at the lab. How do I go about it?"

"I forgot, this is your first case involving a large amount of cash," she says. "You and Chew take the cash into a room, use the deceased's office if you wish, then the deceased's ghost can be your witness too—" she lets out another chuckle. "I'm joking, OK? After you count the money, ask Chew to sign for it."

Mislan notes that the head of Special Investigations is in good spirits, probably brought about by managing to escape the press conference. Mislan suspects, apart from the publicity junkie OCCI and his PR dolls, any officer who is serious about investigating and solving crime doesn't fancy talking to the media. These are the real officers, never going after glory. They prefer to be left alone in the shadows to do their work.

"OK, will do that."

"Oh, Lan, don't forget to put gloves on."

"Sure."

"And record the amount counted and not the amount you both agreed," she says, followed by more chuckles.

Mislan smiles. With all the pressure she must be currently experiencing, it's nice to hear his head of Special Investigations laugh.

"Good one, ma'am."

As soon as he terminates the call, his cell phone rings. It is Audi.

"Inspector, where're you?"

"None of your business. Just because you did me a favor once, doesn't mean you're now my mother wanting to know my whereabouts," Mislan jokes.

"I was told you're at Cheras Police headquarters. Are you investigating the suicide?"

"You should know D9 doesn't handle suicides."

"That's what I thought, but you're at the suicide scene. How come?"

"I'm at the office," Mislan lies.

"Really, then I must be seeing a double," Audi says, followed by a hearty laugh.

Mislan turns toward the headquarters building and spots her by the porch waving at him.

"Shit," he cusses.

———

Mislan excuses himself from Chew and walks over to meet Audi halfway, to stop her from coming to the car they're examining.

"What's with the car?" she asks, trying to sidestep Mislan standing in her path.

"Jo's looking to buy it," Mislan says, grabbing her arm and directing her back to the porch. "Let's talk under the porch. It's too hot out here."

"And he needs crime forensics guys to look over the car for him," she says mockingly.

"Oh, him, he's mechanical forensics, just assisting Jo." Mislan pulls her lightly to follow him, saying, "Do you want to talk to me or to Jo?"

"To you, of course, and because of that I swallow your bullshit about Jo buying the car."

"Then let's go to the porch."

Audi relents and follows Mislan to the porch. "So what's with the suicide?"

"What did the OCCI say?"

"The usual crap, the deceased was depressed, was in some sort of marital difficulty, blah, blah, blah."

"What did ASP Amir say?"

"How did you know ASP Amir was there?"

"Lucky guess."

"So you knew about the PC and you know it was all bullshit. Tell me what's really going on, and why is Special Investigations involved?"

"This is strictly off the record."

Audi nods.

"We think he's connected to my case, but we're not sure how yet. It's premature for us to conclude anything, and it's unfair to the deceased," Mislan lies.

"Shit, you're talking about the Sentul double murder? How is he connected?"

"I just said it's too early for us to confirm his connection. We're still checking out a few leads. It may just be a tenuous link and he's innocent of any wrongdoings. Look, I need you to keep this under wraps for the moment. You splash what I just told you, and my case is flushed down the toilet."

"OK, but how soon will I know something?"

"I'm hoping sooner rather than later. The suicide will hit the news tonight. That in itself will cause the killers in my case to be wary and put up their guard. If you report anything that could be interpreted as tying this with the Sentul double murder, then my case is as good as freezing cold."

"I understand."

"Good, now let me continue with my work. I'm really beat. Jo and I have been up since yesterday, and in a few more minutes, I'll turn into a grumpy middle-aged man."

"We don't want that, do we?" Audi says with a laugh.

———

After Audi leaves, Mislan walks back to the car, and Johan tells him the cell phone found in the glove compartment belongs to their victim—Ajimullah.

"How do you know?" Mislan asks

"I turned on the phone and made a call to Ajimullah's number. The phone rang."

"Good work."

Mislan asks Chew if he can have the deceased's cell phone. Chew tells him it's with his technician at the deceased's office.

"I thought you wanted me to unlock it," Chew says.

"It's a four-digit passcode, right?"

Chew nods.

"Let's try his service number. If I can unlock it, that'll give us the chance to work on the call and message logs tonight."

With Chew carrying the black plastic bag of money, they head back to the deceased's office.

27

AT THE LOBBY, SERGEANT Fauzi stops them and introduces himself. Mislan tells Chew to go ahead and do the necessary while he has a quick chat with the sergeant. Fauzi is in his mid-thirties, average height, with a slim build and fair complexion. He looks more like a schoolteacher. The heartache and frustration of being an assistant investigating officer haven't shown on his face; Mislan figures he must have just been promoted to sergeant and assigned as AIO. The sergeant suggests they use the office of the AOCS (Assistant Officer in Charge of Station). The office is at the rear of the ground floor behind the inquiry counter. Fauzi knocks on the door; no one answers but the door is unlocked. He opens it, and they go in.

"How well did you know Lai?" Mislan asks once they are seated.

"We shared the same office, pretty well I guess," Fauzi answers matter-of-factly.

"I mean outside of working hours."

"The occasional teh tarik or lunch, nothing more than that. Lai, or the late Lai's, not the huu-haa type."

"His friends?"

"I met a few when they stopped by our office to say hi to him and have a brief chat. I don't know them and most of the time wasn't introduced to them. I don't mean Lai was being rude or hiding something by not introducing them to me, they were just very brief encounters, you know what I mean."

Mislan nods.

"Did you hear of him experiencing money problems?"

"Lai," he smiles, "he's the go-to man if you need money or any assistance."

Mislan narrows his eyes at the sergeant.

"Not what you're thinking. He's not an Ah-Long—loan shark. He assists with no interest, just helping a fellow officer."

"What about his family, wife, et cetera?"

"Never met them. His wife, from what I understand, is a home-maker. Two kids, both grown up, married, and working."

Mislan waits for more but there's nothing. Mislan figures it has something to do with some unwritten, misguided brotherhood rules that they subscribe to from watching too many Hong Kong cop movies. The sergeant seems not to want to volunteer anything, not wishing to be involved.

After going the long way around the silly unwritten rules of loyalty, Mislan feels the sergeant is comfortable with his soft questioning and is by now reassured that he's not on a witch hunt to implicate others. He starts asking more probing questions.

"How was his manner, behavior, these past few days?" he asks.

The sergeant seems to give the question a little thought, lights a cigarette himself.

"Usual, the same friendly Lai." He pauses, taking a long drag on his cigarette.

Mislan senses there's something the sergeant wants to get off his chest but is holding back. "And?" Mislan probes, looking at the sergeant intensely.

"I don't know what happened, but yesterday, he seemed, mmm, like he was agitated or—" Fauzi hesitates.

"Agitated how?"

"Not like cursing or swearing or anything like that. It's not his style. We were talking about COVID and all the infringements by the ministers and politicians when his phone beeped, incoming text. After he read it, his manner and face instantly changed, I don't know, like he was angry or frightened. I was watching him from my desk as he read the text: he was agitated. As he looked, or more like stared, at his phone, he became angry then frightened. In the few seconds, his expression changed from one to the other. He abruptly stood up and left. As he stepped out, I heard him asking over the phone rather insistently, 'When?'"

"Do you know or have any guess who he called?"

Sergeant Fauzi shakes his head.

"Did he come back in after he made the call?"

Again, Sergeant Fauzi shakes his head.

"I didn't see him again until this."

"And this—I mean, the change in his manner—happened yesterday about what time?"

"Afternoon, around 3 or 4 p.m."

———

When Mislan joins Chew, the latter has already started counting the money and noting the amount, organizing by denominations and arranging them in neat stacks. He asks Chew for the deceased's cell phone. Sitting at Sergeant Fauzi's desk, he tries punching in the first four digits of Lai's service numbers. The phone screen does not unlock. He tries the last four digits of his service number, still to no avail. "Fuck," he swears. Chew stops counting and flashes him a smile. Mislan knows if the third attempt fails, the cell phone security system will go into automatic block mode.

"Switch off the phone first, then reboot it. You'll get another three tries," Chew says.

"Really?"

"I think so," Chew says with a smile, and continues with his counting.

"If I screw it up, your IT guy can still unlock it, right?"

"Yes."

Mislan switches off the cell phone and switches it back on again. The lock screen appears. Lai's service number is eight digits and he tries punching in the middle four numbers. To his delight, the screen unlocks.

"Got it," he exclaims.

Immediately, he opens WhatsApp and scrolls to read the latest chats. One catches his attention. It was from Liew (MBB), and it reads: *2 police came asking about u.* The chat was dated yesterday at 3:31 p.m. He checks the call records and, sure enough, he finds an outgoing call made to Liew (MBB) yesterday at 3:32 p.m.

"I know why he took his life," Mislan says to Chew.

Chew lifts his head with a questioning expression.

"He knew we were closing in on him."

"How?"

"Sergeant Fauzi said yesterday between 3 to 4 p.m. when they were talking, the deceased received a text message. Reading the message, he flipped, became angry or fearful according to Fauzi. The deceased stepped outside of the office and made a call, and left." Mislan shows the WhatsApp chat from Liew.

"Here, read this."

"Who's this Liew (MBB)?"

"Branch manager where the deceased deposited the money."

"They know each other?"

"Yes."

"So he believed he was made and chose the easy way out," Chew says.

"As a police officer, wouldn't we all?"

———

By the time the crime forensics team clears up, it is almost 8 p.m. Outside, the sky is dark. Mislan and Johan are exhausted, having been up for the last thirty-six hours. Mislan drives his assistant back to the contingent headquarters where his car is parked. He tells Johan to get some rest, and there's no need to come in early as Superintendent Samsiah will be calling either Inspector Khamis or Inspector Reeziana to replace them.

On his drive home, Mislan stops at a Kentucky Fried Chicken in Kampung Pandan and orders a takeout snack plate set of spicy chicken. After a refreshing long, cold shower, finger-licking spicy chicken, a mug of strong black coffee, and a cigarette, he is reenergized and wide awake.

He starts pondering about the late Sergeant Lai Kwang Kee, a fifty-seven-year-old man with three years to serve for a full pension. A man with more than thirty years of unblemished service. A man his coworkers described as humble, friendly, helpful, and a team-player. A man with no known vice.

But now he knows the late Sergeant Lai had lived a double life, that of an outlaw and brutal killer. What puzzles him is: What was Lai's motivation? What made him, after dedicating thirty years to serving the public, suddenly decide to go on a killing spree? What triggered it? Was it the money? If it was the money, why was he donating large amounts of it? He makes a mental note to know more about the late Sergeant Lai. To understand what motivated him to commit the despicable acts of taking other lives.

His next question is: Who was Lai's accomplice—or were there accomplices? In his Sentul double murder, two 9mm guns were used. Could there have been three or more of the killers? But Adham the druggie claimed he saw two men getting out of the black SUV and two men come out of the victims' house. Lai was issued with a Walther PPK .32, or did he also own a 9mm stashed somewhere? Or could it be that the two men didn't include Lai but were part of a band of men like him? In the Seremban 2 case, the gun used was a .32. He needed to send Lai's gun for ballistic matching.

"Shit," Mislan cusses aloud.

With Lai's death, it'll be more difficult to get his accomplice or accomplices. Lai didn't have social media accounts, at least not on his cell phone. Hell, he didn't even have a laptop at the office. Mislan had earlier done a quick check of his cell phone but couldn't find any social media apps. Maybe he had a laptop at home. He makes a mental note to ask his boss if ASP Amir can check on it.

Putting his thoughts aside, Mislan unlocks Lai's cell phone and starts reading the SMS messages. As he expected, there are very few SMSs, mostly promotional spam and MCO notifications. He then opens WhatsApp to reread the chats. Some were written in Chinese characters, but most were in the commonly used mixture of Malay and English.

Most of the WhatsApp chats were with his coworkers; some Mislan thinks were from his wife and children. Nothing incriminating or suspicious draws his attention. Fatigue finally catches up, his eyes become watery with a burning itch and his mind unfocused. He decides to call it a night.

28

ALTHOUGH HE KNOWS HE doesn't need to come in early, Mislan is already in the office at 7:30 a.m. Inspector Reeziana greets him warmly and points to the pantry table. Inspector Tee and his assistant are already enjoying the breakfast she brought.

"Are you on today?" Mislan asks.

"Yes," Reeziana answers. "By the way, Sherran says hi to you."

"She did?" Mislan asks, surprised yet tantalized.

"Yeah, she was on duty."

"I thought you were playing Cupid between her and Jo."

"I am, but she said hi to you," Reeziana says, giving Mislan the "*You know what I mean by that, right?*" grin.

"You just finished your shift there?" Mislan replies, changing the subject.

"No, I just swung over there to get some breakfast for you guys. I'm your replacement today."

"Don't they mind, I mean, you're not stationed there but you still take the food?"

"Naaaw, they have lots of food. Most of the time it goes to waste," she says, taking a pack of fried noodles for herself. "Ma'am said you got one of them. The unsubs."

"Sort of. He actually beat us to it. He got to himself, and he's not an unsub anymore," Mislan says, walking to the pantry.

Reeziana and Tee look at each other at Mislan's reply. They remember how he felt in one of his cases when his primary suspect committed suicide, breaking the link to the accomplices. How he felt cheated of the satisfaction of nailing those responsible.

"Cheated of another closure," Tee joshes.

"Not if I can help it," Mislan replies, making a mug of coffee and selecting a nasi lemak pack.

"Who's handling the suicide?" Reeziana asks.

"I don't know, but I'm guessing ISCD, ASP Amir," Mislan answers.

———

Superintendent Samsiah enters the office and joins her officers. Tee briefs her on the callout for the last twenty-four hours, which as expected was zero. Superintendent Samsiah informs them that, according to figures announced by the Director of Criminal Investigation Division, the crime rate dropped by 60 percent during the first phase of the MCO. In the early stage of phase two, it dropped to about 70 percent. The MCO has achieved what the police force had failed to do: significantly reduce the crime rate.

Superintendent Samsiah thanks Reeziana for coming in to replace Mislan and hopes it will be a temporary situation so that she can go back to assisting at the roadblock. Just then, ASP Amir appears carrying a file under his arm, and he's invited by Samsiah to join them. Tee's assistant excuses himself, leaving the officers to their discussion.

"Lan, since we're all here, and your case, I mean the suicide, is out in the open, would you like to share with us what you discovered after we left?" Samsiah asks. "For the time being, I asked Amir to keep the two separated."

"I'll do the best I can, but I can't promise you it'll be separated for long," Amir responds with a gesture upward to indicate the OCCI.

Mislan nods, takes a sip of his coffee, and asks if he can have a quick smoke before he starts. Samsiah and Amir laugh at his request.

"Ma'am, I believe Mislan has earned it. Can we allow him to smoke this time here in the office?" Amir asks.

"I think so too," Samsiah says.

Mislan lights a cigarette and passes the pack to Reeziana.

"I didn't know you smoke," Samsiah says to Reeziana.

"She smokes, but she doesn't buy," Tee says.

"Social smoker, only when offered," Reeziana replies with a grin.

Mislan updates them on the recovery from the deceased's car: the cash, the suppressor, his victim's cell phone, and the receipts from Jone's Café and the Spicy Thai restaurant. Chew had also recovered the bullet from the ceiling. The bullet, gun, and suppressor will be sent to Ballistic for testing. He tells them he inspected the gun and found the barrel to be threaded to accommodate the suppressor. Chew will dust for prints on the plastic bag and cash to see if there are other prints apart from the deceased's.

"Ma'am, I've sent Jo to Ballistic to lock in the evidence. Can you ask them to bump the test up the waiting list?" Mislan asks.

Superintendent Samsiah looks at him questioningly.

"Need Ballistic to confirm it's the gun used in Seremban 2. Don't want to be tripped up by tunnel vision and later be told by Ballistic it wasn't a match."

"What's the probability of a non-match?"

"See, in the Sentul case, two 9mms were used, so there is a likelihood these guys might have two .32s," Mislan replies.

"Both with suppressors ready?" Reeziana asks. "Slim but not impossible."

"OK, I'll give Ballistic a call after this," Samsiah says.

"If it matches, it'll allow ASP Rohimmi to close his case," Mislan says.

Superintendent Samsiah and ASP Amir nod their agreement.

"I heard you found money. How much cash was there?" Tee asks.

"Exactly 315,900 in used hundred, fifty, twenty, and ten notes."

Tee lets out a low whistle.

"That's a lot of money," Amir says.

"It is, and if we take into account the amount that was given or donated, which so far we've managed to trace at 110 K, that's almost half a million."

Detective Sergeant Johan arrives and informs his boss the exhibits have been locked in at Ballistic. He hands the Ballistic slip to him, and Mislan in turn passes it to Superintendent Samsiah. She snaps a photo of it with her cell phone and returns the slip. Johan is about to leave them to their discussion, thinking they were still in the morning prayer session, but the head of Special Investigations asks him to join them.

"You think there's more?" Reeziana asks.

"Possible. We'll only know for certain if we can get hold of the Seremban 2 vic's phone. So far, even with the telco location report, there's nothing that can give us a glimpse of the individual using it, or as Yana terms him, the unsub."

Samsiah and Amir nod their understanding.

"Mislan," Amir says, "ISCD will be handling the suicide inquiry. Before I forget, here're the service records and personal file you requested. We'll need them back as soon as you finish," he says, passing Mislan the documents. "Just curious, have you figured out why the deceased decided to end his life?"

"I believe he opted for the easy way out. Remember Sergeant Zaiton's statements? She said the deceased demanded to know who we were and specifically mentioned Johan's and my name."

Samsiah and Amir nod.

"I interviewed his office mate, Sergeant Fauzi. According to him, between 3 and 4 p.m. the day before the incident while they were having a casual chat, the deceased received a WhatsApp text. Fauzi said that upon reading the text, the deceased flipped. He appeared angry or frightened. The deceased rushed out of the office while making a call. Fauzi said he sounded tense and heard the question, 'When?' After that, the deceased didn't reenter the office, and that was the last he saw him." Mislan pauses, taking another sip of his coffee. "Here," he continues, "this is the WhatsApp he received."

Samsiah takes the phone, reads it, and passes it on to Amir. It is the WhatsApp sent by the branch manager Liew.

"Immediately after that, Fauzi said he made a call." Mislan scrolls the call list and passes the cell phone back to Samsiah. "Here."

"Can I see the phone?" Reeziana asks.

"So you think he knew we were closing in on him?" Amir surmises.

"Most likely. I'm confident if we check the bank's CCTV, we'll see him paying a visit to the branch manager. She most likely showed him the CDM CCTV recording we requested. He put two and two together and knew he was in our crosshairs. When he saw us at the station, he knew it was game over for him, and he took the easy way out."

"D9 and ISCD, a hell of a powerful combination, eh," Amir says.

"To police personnel, nothing more lethal," Reeziana quips. "Like a submarine."

The head of Special Investigations and contingent ISCD look at her inquiringly.

"Submarine—beer with a shot glass of vodka inside. The last drink to end a wonderful night out," she explains with a smile.

They just have to laugh at the manner in which she puts it.

"His suicide has, however, made our chances of identifying his accomplice—or accomplices—more difficult. This guy, I mean the deceased, as I said earlier, lived a life like a monk. No vices, no social media, no nothing. Hell, he didn't even have a laptop in the office," Mislan says getting back to business.

"Really? That's so un-police-like," Samsiah comments.

"Initially, I took Zaiton's description of the deceased with a pinch of salt, she being a woman and maybe not included in the men's world. On top of that, she was financially assisted by him, and also, you know how we as Malaysians don't like to say bad things about the dead. Then, when I interviewed Fauzi, he too said the same of the deceased. So, I guess it had to be true."

"Jekyll and Hyde," Amir says.

"Exactly. Sir, since ISCD's handling this inquiry, may I tag along to meet the family, check out his house? Maybe he has a laptop at home. I really need to know him and his activities. I need to know what his double life was. To understand why he flipped, I mean thirty years of service with three years to full pension, what made him give it all up?"

"Money, retirement plan?" Tee suggests.

"If that's true, why give the money away?" Reeziana rebuts. "Mislan said they've given away more than a hundred thousand."

"I don't think it's money," Johan joins in. "His car is a ten-year-old Waja. With that kind of money, you'd think he'd be driving a Honda at the very least."

"Complex," Amir admits. "I'll let you know when we'll be visiting the family."

———

The late Sergeant Lai's house is a unit in a government-subsidized low-cost apartment building. The building of two-bedroom apartments is probably two or three decades old. These were the first housing projects initiated by the state and federal government to shelter the city's low-income dwellers. There are many such projects on the city's fringes, which by now have turned into the city limit itself. The boxy structures are eyesores and not well-regarded by the residents and owners of newer condominiums that surround the areas.

The deceased's unit is on the second floor. It is sparsely furnished but very tidy and organized. No sign of lavish living at all. A red Chinese prayer altar with burned-out joss sticks is about the only colorful and probably most expensive fixture in the house. Mrs. Lai is in her early fifties, skinny like a pencil, with short hair. She is dressed in a pair of dark brown baggy skirt-pants and a worn-out black T-shirt. She looks a mess, with bags under her red eyes, probably from weeping and lack of sleep, but she tries hard to maintain a brave smile for them. The station must have already informed her of her husband passing, Mislan figures. After the formalities of introductions and condolences, Amir starts inquiring about her late husband.

"Kee," which is what she called him, "seemed normal, but with him it was difficult to know if anything's wrong. He doesn't talk about his work or whatever was bothering him." Mrs. Lai adds ruefully, "After almost thirty years of marriage, you'd think I'd know him well, but the truth's I don't."

"I understand you have two children," Amir says.

"Yes, both grown up and married. They're at the morgue to make the necessary arrangements."

"I saw some kids' shoes outside," Mislan says. "Whose are they?"

"Oh, those are Kee's nephews. They're staying with us." She notices the blank look on Mislan's face and adds, "Kee's brother Peter's in prison, and we're taking care of his kids."

"Kee's—I mean, Lai's brother is in prison? So, your sister-in-law is staying with you too?" Mislan asks.

Mrs. Lai purses her lips, shaking her head. "Yes to your first question, and no, my sister-in-law is not staying with us." She hesitates a moment before saying, "I don't know if I should tell you, but I suppose it's all right, now that Kee's gone. And anyway, I'm sure you'll find out about it sooner or later. Peter was convicted of killing his wife about four years ago." Again she pauses, inhaling deeply before continuing, "I believe that was the only time I saw Kee break down."

The officers can see that she's struggling to continue. The pain of witnessing her husband break down must have hurt her as much as it hurt Lai. The two officers remain silent and wait for her to continue if she's up to it.

"Ever since that day, he sort of kept all his emotions bottled up. I guess he was ashamed. You know, being a policeman, and his own brother was imprisoned for . . ." Mrs. Lai leaves the sentence hanging.

"Where did this happen, I mean with Peter?" Mislan asks.

"Penang. They were living in Penang. Peter was an accountant, and so was his late wife. Somehow Peter got mixed up with drugs, lost his job, and then one night in a heated argument, he struck and killed his wife."

"And this was four years back?" Mislan asks.

Mrs. Lai nods. "I know it was heart-shattering for Kee, because, as the eldest, he supported his siblings. He was not a highly educated man, I mean he was not a university graduate, just a Chinese school secondary form 3. He was working as a fisherman for many years, then he worked in the market and did odd jobs supporting his family. That was where we met, I was working at the market too." Mrs. Lai allows herself a tiny smile before continuing. "When he was offered to join the police, he was so proud and happy and told his family that from then on he would take care of them. With his small police salary, he put his two younger sisters through school and Peter through college. His father was a manual laborer at a shipyard warehouse, so it was Kee who supported them. He placed high hopes on Peter to care for the family once he retired."

"How old is Peter?"

"He's the youngest in the family. I think he's twelve years younger than Kee; that puts him around forty-five or forty-six."

"Mrs. Lai, does your husband have any close friends, I mean, like buddies that he hangs out with?" Mislan asks, changing the subject.

"I don't really know, but I suppose the men at his workplace are his close friends."

"Outside of the police force?"

"Some of his school friends, but I really don't know them that well to tell you who or where they are. After he was transferred from Penang, he saw less and less of them."

"Are his parents still . . ." Mislan asks letting the last word hang.

"His father passed away about two years back, and his mother is living with one of his sisters in Penang."

Mislan points to the framed pictures on the wall and asks if he may take a closer look at them. Mrs. Lai takes all three of them down and brings them over. The photos are old and in fading color. All are of Lai in his younger days with his police friends.

"Did your husband own a computer or a laptop?" Amir asks.

Mrs. Lai shakes her head. "Kee was not into all that," she says with a tiny smile. "He always said they're distracting and too much time is wasted on social media and playing games on them."

After answering Lai's widow's questions about what will ensue with her husband's demise, ASP Amir and Inspector Mislan again offer her their condolences and thank her for the meeting.

29

Superintendent Samsiah left instructions at the front desk for Mislan to see her upon returning to the office. When ASP Amir and Inspector Mislan report to her office, she calls for Inspector Reeziana to come and join them.

"While you were away, Yana made a stunning discovery," Samsiah says. "Yana, you want to tell them?"

"The deceased's cell phone—" Reeziana starts.

"Oh shit," Mislan utters, unzipping his backpack, "I must've left it in the office."

"I have it," Reeziana says, holding the cell phone up. "You passed it to me to read the WhatsApp, remember? Anyway, after you left, I went through it, reading the chats and messages. There was nothing interesting there. Then I checked the call list and found something quite intriguing."

Amir and Mislan regard her questioningly.

"There's this number—actually there are a few numbers that don't have a name or identity attached to them and are listed as 'unsaved' by the service provider. But there's this one number that was regularly recorded as called-out or called-in, but strangely, there's no name or label attached to it."

"So?" Mislan asks.

"Now, if that number is from a caller that made numerous calls to you or you to him or her, wouldn't it make sense to name or label it? The name or label makes it easy for you to recall the number when making a call or to know who was calling."

Amir and Mislan nod their agreement.

"Here, I've listed down the dates, times and number of calls made or received from the number," Reeziana says, handing Mislan a piece of A4 paper. "That's just going back two months."

"Woah, that's a lot!" Mislan exclaims, passing the paper to Amir.

"Forty-eight in and out calls. I'm sure the telco can give you a longer list."

"Have you called the number or checked with the telco?" Mislan asks.

"Ma'am said to hold on, wait for you to come in."

"I asked Yana to hold on because I'd like to avoid another suicide on our hands," Samsiah says. "By now, whoever the deceased's accomplice or accomplices are will have known about his suicide. I hope I'm wrong, but it did cross my mind, they could have made a suicide pact. Anyone cornered would blow his head off to cut any link to the rest of them."

"I like that thought," Mislan says.

Samsiah, Amir, and Reeziana wince at his morbid response.

"Before we discuss how to go about this discovery, would you like to tell us how it went with the widow?" Samsiah asks.

Amir tells them about the low-cost apartment and modest furnishings. There was no indication that money had been lavishly spent on their lifestyle. He tells them about the deceased's brother, Peter, who is serving a prison sentence for killing his wife. About the deceased taking care of Peter's two young children, aged fifteen and thirteen. About the deceased not owning any computer or being into games and social media.

"Looks like Lai lived a simple life," Samsiah remarks.

"Yes, it does look like it," Amir agrees.

"What drove him to this?" Samsiah asks, meaning the killings.

"In my opinion, he flipped when his brother, Peter, was hooked on drugs and killed his wife. According to Mrs. Lai, the deceased had been supporting his family, putting his siblings through school and college. He had put his hopes on Peter—who, by the way, was an accountant and so too was his wife—to care for the family, his aged parents, when he retired. But all that went down the toilet when he got involved with drugs and then got jailed for killing his wife. Mrs. Lai said the deceased broke down when it happened and that was the first time she witnessed him doing that. The deceased had always been reserved, but after that breakdown, he turned into an emotional vault. Ma'am, can we confirm the case and sight the IP?" IP is the police term for Investigating Paper.

"When did this happen, this Peter thing?" Samsiah asks.

"About four years back in Penang."

"I'll try and see if Penang can release the IP for us to sight."

"Come to think of it, I think that was why the deceased used his brother's name to give away the money. Remember, Gong-gong Wee and Chuah Guat Eng from the foundations both claimed the caller identified himself as Peter Lai."

"Redemption for his brother," Amir says.

———

Inspector Reeziana is tasked with obtaining information from the telecommunication service provider. Superintendent Samsiah suggests that all dealings with the telco are to be done at management level and not with their customer service. In the meanwhile, no call shall be made to the numbers concerned.

After the discussion, Mislan makes a call to Chew.

"Any luck with the prints?" he asks.

"Managed to lift several but mostly partial. We're running them through the system. I'll call you once we're done," Chew replies.

"What about the money?"

"Still working on it, but it won't be that fast, there are too many and the notes are used, and mostly what we got are smudged prints. By the way, the super at Ballistic said on preliminary examination, the bullet recovered from the ceiling looks like a match with the one from the Seremban 2 case."

"That's not surprising. The prints in the car?"

"I think they'll be done soon."

"Thanks, Chew, keep me posted please."

"Of course. Stay safe."

30

SITTING AT HIS WORKSTATION in the bedroom, Mislan switches on the television to world news. It's filled with depressing news. Countries all over the world are in lockdown, with the COVID-19 infected cases and death toll on the rise. The economic and humanitarian crises, even in developed countries, are at an unprecedented level, bleak and scary. The marginal income earners are going without food and medical assistance. When the news shifts to the poor of undeveloped countries, Mislan decides to turn off the TV. The news and images are too disheartening to stomach.

In his mind, the poor around the world were already suffering even before the pandemic, and with the pandemic, the suffering multiplied a hundredfold. The irony of it all is that it is the poor who are helping the poor while the rich and politicians just provide lip service.

He remembers there was this one politician who made a video of himself telling the people to stay home and adhere to social distancing. This politician made the call while holding a wineglass and standing in his indoor swimming pool. *Can you fucking believe this jackass?* Mislan reflects angrily. *Didn't he know that most Malaysians can't even afford to own a house, and most of them are sharing a tiny, cramped rented house or room with their whole family?* Mislan sighs.

He lights a cigarette and removes Sergeant Lai's service files from his backpack. His cell phone rings; it's Inspector Reeziana.

"Yes, Yana."

"Just got back from the telco, got the report."

"That took a hell of a long time."

"They're on skeletal staffing."

Mislan glances at the time on his phone. It is 8:45 p.m. "OK, give me thirty."

Mislan calls his assistant and tells him he is going to the office if he wants to join him.

———

The cell phone number is registered to Jaafar Abdul, and the billing address is 24, Taman Air Panas, Setapak, Kuala Lumpur.

"What about his IC number?" Mislan asks.

"We need a court order for personal details," Reeziana answers.

"No shit."

"Yes, shit, something about data privacy laws introduced by the government."

"Bloody bureaucratic bullshit." Speaking to his assistant, he asks, "Jo, feel like going for a drive?"

"Where're you guys going?" she asks, concerned.

"Getting some fresh air. Been cooped up too long," Mislan says with a grin.

"Yeah, right. Don't you go spooking the guy. Remember what ma'am said," she warns.

"Not going anywhere near him. Just out for some fresh air, right, Jo?"

"Yeah, like you expect me to believe you."

———

Mislan asks his assistant to drive. He pulls out his cell phone and taps on Waze, keys in Taman Air Panas. Waze indicates it is seven miles north and will take seventeen minutes to reach. He tells Johan to make a left on Jalan Pudu. In front of Tung Shin hospital, they hit a roadblock. After identifying themselves, they're waved through and head for Jalan Kuching. When they exit onto Jalan Pahang after Kuala Lumpur General Hospital, they hit another roadblock. Clearing the roadblock, they head in the direction of Kuantan and take a right slip road to Taman Air Panas.

The housing development is MCO-level quiet and deserted. Not a single vehicle or human being on the road. Through the glass sliding doors in the front, he can see most of the houses are lighted, and some of the occupants are gathered in the living rooms around their television sets. Just the way Mislan likes it— everyone staying indoors. He observes the upstairs windows to see if any busybody is peeking through the curtains watching them driving at this hour in front of their houses. Nothing catches his eyes. He tells Johan to switch off the headlights and drive slowly as he tries to read the house numbers.

"That one on the right," Mislan says, pointing it out to his assistant.

Johan inches the car forward. The house is a double-story intermediate lot with a short driveway and a porch. Except for the porch light, the lights downstairs where the living room is are all off. The lights in a room above the porch are on, and the windows are closed and the curtains drawn. Through the thin curtains, he doesn't see any shadow or silhouette move in the room, which he figures is most likely the master bedroom. Unlike other houses on the block, which have undergone major external renovation or additions, the house looks to be in its original state. The standard design when it was bought from the developer. *Probably a rented house*, Mislan thinks.

"Are you picking him up?" Johan asks apprehensively.

"No, I just need—" Mislan stops whatever he is about to say. "Look, a black SUV."

Johan drives past the house.

"It's a Nissan X-Trail, but the druggie said a Harrier or Lexus."

"They all look the same to a druggie," Mislan says. "Go up to the end and make another pass. I need to get the plate number."

Johan drives for another two hundred yards and makes a U-turn. As he approaches the house, he slows down, and Mislan jots down the SUV plate number. Driving back to the police contingent building, he tells his assistant to check with the transport department.

"Do it first thing tomorrow morning before coming to the office," he says.

"Are we on tomorrow?" Johan asks.

"I think Tee is on, why?"

"Nothing, just asking."

———

The excitement of their new lead keeps him awake. He's eager for the morning to come and to get going. He lights a cigarette and pulls out Lai's file thinking to give it another read, but the euphoria of the latest lead makes it difficult for him to focus. Closing the file, he stubs out the cigarette and climbs on the bed. Since his visit with Reeziana at the roadblock and deciding to let go of the hope of reuniting with Dr. Safia, he has been able to sleep—not well, but well enough. He supposes his feelings for her were more than he was willing to admit. His aloofness must have hurt her and made him lose her. When he finally sleeps, no demon pays him a visit.

———

The next morning when Mislan arrives at the office, there is no breakfast waiting for him, just Inspector Reeziana with a wide grin savoring the disappointed look on his face. He puts down his backpack and walks to the pantry to make a mug of coffee.

"Had your breakfast?" Reeziana inquires teasingly.

"Nope, why don't you be a good girl and get some from the road-block?" he asks grumpily.

"Once, I don't think they'd mind, but making it a habit would be embarrassing, don't you think?"

Inspector Tee walks in and, to Mislan's disappointment, is empty-handed.

"You spoiled us. Look, Tee's also expecting breakfast," he says.

"No breakfast today?" Tee asks.

"See," he says to Reeziana.

"What did you find out last night?" she asks, changing the subject.

"What made you think I went looking for anything?"

Reeziana laughs.

"This is exactly what gave me a bad reputation," Mislan says, pretending to be hurt. "You guys keep thinking and hinting I'm up to no good even when I'm doing nothing wrong. By behaving this way, you guys planted the idea in ma'am's mind."

"Planted what?" Superintendent Samsiah asks, standing in the doorway.

"Nothing. Morning, ma'am," Mislan greets her.

"With you, Lan, it's never nothing," Samsiah retorts. "What have you been up to?"

"Me and Jo, we went out for a drive last night . . ." Mislan starts.

"To?" Samsiah asks, cutting him off midsentence.

"Setapak."

"Where exactly in Setapak?" she asks, staring at him.

"Air Panas."

"Yana, isn't that where the cell phone number owner lives?" she asks, turning to Reeziana.

Mislan looks at Reeziana, his eyes asking, *How did she know?*

"Yes, ma'am."

"Didn't I tell you to stay away, no contact to be made? Which part of my instructions don't you understand? Do you want another suicide on our hands?" Samsiah is furious.

"No, ma'am."

Just then, Detective Sergeant Johan arrives, excitedly waving a piece of paper. He greets Superintendent Samsiah.

"You're not going to believe this," he says, placing the piece of paper in front of Mislan.

"What won't we believe?" Samsiah asks.

"He's a police officer," Johan states excitedly.

"What?!" the officers exclaim in unison.

Superintendent Samsiah turns to look toward the door, to ensure there is no one listening or coming.

"Jo, close the door," she instructs and makes a phone call.

Mislan excuses himself, goes to the emergency fire escape staircase and lights a cigarette. His hand is shaking. *Police officer, what in heaven's name is going on? Is there a death squad within the force like in the Philippines? Is this how we're fighting drug dealers? Am I going to have another suicide on my hands?* Sickened by the new information, he starts to tremble with anger. Yes, police personnel have been known to commit crimes, even murders. Yes, they too are human and succumb to human weaknesses and evils, but that's no excuse for despicable conduct. *For fuck's sake, we took an oath to uphold the law. Yes, admittedly the law and the people who administer it are not perfect, but it's better than being lawless.*

Halfway through his cigarette, he hears a soft knock on the door. It's Johan telling him Superintendent Samsiah wants him back inside. He squashes the cigarette under his feet, and when he reenters the office, ASP Amir is sitting at Inspector Khamis's desk reading the transport department report.

———

ASP Amir puts down the motor vehicle report and looks at Mislan as if asking, *Now what?* Mislan goes to his desk to sit and looks at his boss as if saying, *Your call.*

"I don't have to impress on all of you how delicate of a situation we have here," Samsiah starts, giving each and every one of them an intense gaze. "I want us to keep our cool and evaluate all the evidence we have. I want a solid damning connection between him and the deceased, if not the case itself."

Mislan's cell phone rings; it's Chew. He holds up his hand, saying he needs to take the call.

"Yes, Chew."

"Inspector, just called to let you know we're done with the money and car. I'll be running the prints through the system."

"Chew, can you scan the prints and send them to me? Only those from the plastic bag."

"Sure, what do you want to do with them?"

"I don't know yet, but I want to try something."

"OK, will get my IT guy to do it."

"Thanks, Chew, stay safe."

"What do you have in mind?" Samsiah asks, after hearing Mislan's request.

"I'm thinking if ASP Amir can check the prints against our personnel database," Mislan says.

Turning to Amir, she asks, "Can you?"

"I can't, but Bukit Aman Personnel Department can."

"Worth a try," Samsiah admits. "Let's go to the meeting room. We'll need to use the whiteboard."

––––––––

Reeziana acts as the whiteboard maestro, holding a blue, black, and red marker each. On one end of the whiteboard, she writes the name *Lai* in blue, circling it with a cloud. Below the name she writes *PPK .32, suppressor, Sentul double murder victim's cell phone*, and *money.* On the opposite end, she writes the name *Jaafar* in red and circles it with a cloud. Below it she writes *black SUV*, and the registration number. In the middle, slightly below the two clouds, she writes *unnamed cell phone number* in black and draws an arrow to each of the clouds.

"That's about all the connection between them we got, the unnamed cell phone number," Samsiah says.

ASP Amir nods.

"And that's not strong enough to make a move on him," Samsiah continues. "Remember, he's a police officer, and by his service number, he's a senior police officer."

The room goes silent.

"Any suggestions?" Samsiah asks, just to break the dead silence.

"I think we need to learn more about him," Amir suggests, "discreetly."

"That's going to be a problem," Mislan says. "You know the police's favorite pastime is gossiping. The moment we do a check on him, he'll get wind of it. That's if he's not in the personnel department itself. As it stands, we don't even know where he's stationed."

"Amir?" Samsiah asks.

"Mislan's right."

"I can find out where he's stationed," Reeziana offers. "I have a friend in the Bukit Aman personnel department. I can ask her a favor, saying I'm hooking up with this guy and need to know a little about him."

"You think your friend will buy your story?" Samsiah asks.

"She's a pushover for romance and marriage crap. She will."

They all look at her, trying to match the confidence in her voice against her expression.

"Trust me," Reeziana says, grinning back at them.

"OK, we'll leave it in your good hands. Once we know more about him, we'll see where it leads us."

"Can I check on the prints from Chew?" Mislan asks, excusing himself.

The first thing he does, stepping into his office, is light a cigarette. He boots up his computer and checks his email. Clicks on the email from Chew and prints the attached documents. There are five prints.

ASP Amir and Inspector Reeziana are on their cell phones while Superintendent Samsiah, Inspector Tee, and Detective Sergeant Johan are engaged in small talk about the pandemic. Johan is telling them that one of his school friends had been infected and is hospitalized. Mislan hears Amir saying "yes" a few times before saying, "I'll see you soon, and thank you, sir." Reeziana in the meantime is giggling into her cell phone, cheerily chatting and taking notes. *She must be talking to her Bukit Aman friend*, he thinks. *By the sound of it, she can really cook up a fairytale—girl stuff.* When she terminates the call, she's beaming from ear to ear.

"We girls, when it comes to men, we know how to find out about them," she brags.

"What have you got?" Samsiah asks with a grin.

"He is a DSP with the NCID Intelligence Unit based in Bukit Aman. He's forty-three and divorced."

"Deputy Superintendent of Police, whoa," Johan says.

"More interestingly, he's NCID Intelligence," Mislan states. "Narcotic."

ASP Amir looks at Superintendent Samsiah, concerned.

"This is getting from bad to worse by the minute," Samsiah admits. "Lan, have you got the prints?"

Mislan hands them over to her, and she passes them to Amir.

"What did recruitment says?" she asks Amir.

"He says the prints are digitized, and if I can provide the name, he can forward the prints to me. We can get our fingerprint staff to make the comparison."

"Can you trust him not to leak the name?"

"I've asked for six individuals' prints just to throw him off. Anyway, I've known him for many years; I think I can."

"Good."

"Ma'am, can we get Chew to do the comparison? I trust him, and he has no interest in police politics."

"Amir?"

"I'm fine with it."

"Good, let's get to work."

31

CHEW CALLS TO INFORM Mislan that he matched two of the five prints to one of the digital prints sent to him. One of the prints has a fourteen-point match, and the other a seventeen-point match. Both are deemed a positive match.

"Who?"

"Jaafar Abdul. The rest no match."

"Chew, sorry, I thought you needed a twenty-point match to be positive," Mislan says.

"Between twelve and twenty. You got the suspect?"

"Soon, I hope."

"Good luck. Stay safe."

Mislan hurries over to Superintendent Samsiah's office with the good-bad news. She's on the phone and waves him in. The instant she puts down the phone, Mislan says, "We got him."

"The prints?"

"Yes, two matched prints from the plastic bag with the money. Can we pick him up?"

Superintendent Samsiah remains quiet for a moment, deep in thought. "I was just talking to my squad-mate in NCID. Just a courtesy call and dropped Jaafar's name. He said Jaafar is on emergency leave for two days."

"Since when?"

"Yesterday."

"Does he know where Jaafar is going?"

"I didn't ask. Didn't want to raise any suspicion."

"Maybe he went back to his hometown," Mislan suggests.

"Did Yana say where his hometown is?"

"No, I don't think so."

Superintendent Samsiah picks up the phone and calls Reeziana.

"Did your friend say where the suspect is from?" she asks.

"No, I didn't ask—that question would blow my cover story. I mean, dating someone and not even knowing where he's from," Reeziana replies.

The head of Special Investigations chuckles, "True." Putting down the phone, she informs Mislan that Reeziana doesn't know where their suspect is from.

Mislan sighs.

"I'm sure he heard about Lai's suicide and probably took leave to—I don't know, maybe cover his tracks. Was he home when you went for some fresh air last night?"

"The bedroom lights were on, but I didn't see any movement."

"So you did go to his place last night," Samsiah says, shaking her head at her officer.

Mislan grins. "But his SUV was in the driveway."

Samsiah makes a call to ASP Amir. Mislan excuses himself to have a quick word with Jo. When he returns, ASP Amir is already in the office.

"So you want to pick him up?" Amir asks.

"Before he vanishes or covers his tracks," Mislan answers.

"Ma'am says he's on emergency leave. Do you know where he is?"

"No, but I'll try his house first. With the MCO, I don't think he's going anywhere."

"He's a police officer, I'm sure he can get through the roadblocks. He may not be able to check in to a hotel, but what if he has a place where he can bunk?" Amir asks.

"That's the risk I have to take," Mislan answers.

"I suggest we put eyes on his place before we make our move in," Samsiah suggests. "In the meantime, you get your team ready."

"That's a good suggestion," Amir agrees.

"I'll get Jo to organize it. Can I use the standby detectives?" Mislan asks.

Superintendent Samsiah nods. Mislan makes a call, asking his assistant to join them. When Johan arrives, he briefs him on the stakeout.

"Jo, they'll go on bikes, and make sure they stay invisible."

Johan nods and leaves.

"Do you need Ghani's team to back you up?" Samsiah asks.

"I'd rather have Yana as backup. There've been enough deaths already."

Samsiah nods. "Amir?"

"It's best if I stayed out of it. It'll give the impression of impartiality if I'm to conduct the compliance inquiry later. I need to give Dato's CP a heads-up on this before he finds out from you-know-who." The CP mentioned by Amir is the state Chief of Police.

Samsiah nods.

"Take two detectives with you," Samsiah instructs and pauses. "Lan, he's armed, and I hate dead heroes."

"Understand."

"Good luck, and be safe."

Inspector Reeziana, Detective Sergeant Johan, Detective Sergeant Reeze, Detective Syed, Detective Zain, and Mislan are waiting in the meeting room for Superintendent Samsiah and Assistant Superintendent of Police Amir to join them. The officers and detectives have all been issued bulletproof vests and walkie-talkies. Mislan had drawn a sketch of the area and marked the target with a red marker. When Superintendent Samsiah and ASP Amir join them, Mislan gets the nod to start the briefing.

"The target's a double-story intermediate house. We've put eyes on it to confirm the suspect is home. Once confirmed, we'll approach the target through this road," he points to the sketch. "Yana, you'll drop Reeze and Syed here. Reeze and Syed will proceed on foot behind the houses and cover the back door. As you are from behind, you won't be able to see the house number. It's the second to last house on that row. After dropping the blockers, Yana and I will proceed slowly. I'll park here, before the target, and Yana, you'll pass the target and park here. Reeze, once you're in position, alert me. The rest of you won't leave your vehicles until you receive my instruction. Any questions so far?"

There are none.

"I'll lead the arrest team. Johan will announce our presence. Yana and Zain will take cover behind the SUV and cover us."

"What if the SUV isn't there?" Reeziana asks.

"If the stakeout says the SUV isn't there, we abort. If the SUV's not there, chances are he may not be home, and I don't want to show our hand. Once the suspect's apprehended, Crime Forensics will be called in. I've already asked Chew and his team to be on standby. Reeze, Syed, and Zain will guard the suspect. After the search is complete, the suspect will ride with me, with Syed guarding. Any questions?"

Again there are none.

"The suspect's armed and known to be dangerous. As ma'am says, she doesn't want a dead hero. Check your weapon, walkie-talkie, and vest. Be safe." Mislan turns to the head of Special Investigations. "Ma'am?"

"The suspect's trained in handling firearms. There's a strong possibility he has killed before, and I don't think he'll hesitate to kill again if he's cornered. As Mislan said, I hate dead heroes. Good luck."

Johan's cell phone rings. Answering it he replies, "OK, hold on."

"Stakeout said the SUV is there, but they can't see any movement in the house," Johan tells Mislan.

"Tell them to keep watching. I'm sure he's there."

Johan relays the instruction and adds, "Let me know if the suspect is seen or is leaving the house."

Mislan looks at the head of Special Investigations, asking if she's OK with his gut feeling. She gives him a slight nod, and he tells the team they move in five minutes.

———

Johan drives out of Kuala Lumpur Police contingent headquarters, taking the same route they took last night. They pass the same roadblocks, but the seven-mile journey seems to take longer than the seventeen minutes it is supposed to. All through the drive, the two officers remain silent, both deep in their own thoughts. The anticipation of how things will go down. This is the first time they'll be apprehending a senior police officer. They don't know what to expect or how to respond should things get nasty. One thing for sure, the suspect will resort to rank-pulling —he is two ranks above Mislan. Should he be placed under arrest, cuffed, and frisked for weapons or should he be treated differently?

When they drive along Jalan Pahang, Johan almost misses the exit to Taman Air Panas. Mislan glances at his assistant.

"Are you OK?" he asks.

Johan nods, flashing him a thin smile.

Mislan takes out his cell phone and calls the stakeout detective, asking if there is any development.

"Nope, all is quiet."

"OK, when you spot us in front of the target, break off and return to the office. We'll take over from there."

"Roger that."

Driving into the housing development, Johan gives the brake pedal two light taps, a signal for Inspector Reeziana in the rear car to stop and drop off the cut-off team. Mislan turns around in his seat and watches as Detective Sergeant Reeze and Detective Syed get out of the car. They casually walk to the back of the row of houses. Johan inches the car forward and stops just before the target. Reeziana passes them, goes ahead a hundred yards, makes a U-turn, and parks as instructed facing the two officers' car.

Mislan observes the target. The black Nissan X-Trail SUV is in the driveway. He notes his assistant is holding the steering wheel with both hands, gripping it tightly. He sees the vein on his neck as he clenches his jaw, tension oozing from every pore. A normal physical and emotional state before stepping into an unknown dangerous situation. Mislan desperately needs a cigarette to calm his nerves. He lights one and gives the surrounding area a once-over. Although it's just around 1 p.m., the area is deserted. This time the MCO is his ally. The walkie-talkie cracks, startling him and his assistant; the cut-off team is in position. He gives the order to move.

Stepping out of the car, he drops his cigarette and steps on it. Suddenly, he realizes he hasn't given the front gate any thought. "Fuck," he swears, thinking, *What if the gate is padlocked? Calling out from the front gate isn't an option. It will be disastrous, and climbing it will expose us as sitting ducks. Whatever it is, there's no turning back now.*

Keeping his eye on the windows above the porch, he approaches the gate and puts his hand through the grille gap. To his relief, the gate isn't padlocked. He slides the slide-bolt latch and opens the gate. Johan quickly moves straight to the front door while Reeziana and Zain take position behind the SUV.

Mislan takes cover opposite Johan at the front door and gives his assistant the signal to announce their presence. He manages to catch his assistant's hand just as he is about to knock on the door. Johan looks at him, surprised. He points to the doorbell button attached to the wall.

Johan presses the doorbell. They can hear the chime from inside the house. The team waits anxiously. The seconds ticks by. Johan glances at his boss, and his boss turns to look at Reeziana. He eye-gestures to his assistant to ring the doorbell again. Another loud chime from inside the house. Their anxiety level increases.

Mislan hears muffled footfalls, probably someone climbing down wooden stairs. Then a strong firm male voice asks, "Who is it?"

Johan jerks his head toward his boss, then turns to the door as if asking if he should answer it. Mislan nods.

"Police, please open the door."

"Police!" the male voice exclaims.

"Yes, police. Please open the door," Johan repeats.

Mislan notices the footfall stops and the voice sounds closer to them. He reckons the suspect must be in the living room, close to the front door. He uses sign language to signal to Reeziana that the suspect is down in the living hall. She acknowledges. Reeziana and Zain draw their weapons and level it to the door.

"What's it about? Where're you from?"

Johan looks at Mislan, unsure if he should answer. Mislan motions for him to step back and take cover beside the SUV.

"D9 KL, and we need to bring you in to assist in one of our investigations," Mislan answers, taking the lead.

"D9, Special Investigations?"

"Yes. DSP Jaafar Abdul, please open the door, and I'll explain everything to you."

A strained hoarse laugh erupts from inside the house. The laughter stops as quickly as it started.

"Assist in your investigation," Jaafar says, followed by mocking laughter. "But what you really meant is arrest me and kill me like what you did to Sergeant Lai."

"Sergeant Lai took his own life—"

"NO, he didn't. He pulled the trigger, but it was you that drove him to do it," Jaafar interrupts Mislan midsentence. "Did you even know him?" he shouts. "Did you know what hell he was going through?"

"We found out about his brother, if that's what you mean."

"Lai was a Narco detective who spent most of his life fighting against drug dealers. Every day it ate him alive, piece by piece. His own brother, a brother he raised as a son, his brother who had made it in the world only to succumb to drugs. Drugs trafficked by those bastards who don't give a damn about other people's lives and suffering, just so they can feed their greed."

Mislan notes that Jaafar's voice has turned to dry anger. "Sir, I'm not here to discuss the right and wrong of Sergeant Lai's actions. I'm here to bring you in for questioning. I beg you to cooperate before Delta Force is called in," Mislan pleads, hoping to calm his rage and strike some sort of sense and fear in him by mentioning Delta Force, which is the special operation strike force.

Silence from inside the house.

"Sir," Mislan calls.

No response. Mislan throws quick glances to Reeziana and Johan. He hears muffled footfalls; he figures it's coming from the wooden staircase, but the sound is fading. He deduces Jaafar must be going upstairs, perhaps to get dressed and give himself up. A few seconds later, he hears the muffled footfalls returning.

"Sir," Mislan calls again.

"Do you know where the money goes, the dirty drug money?" Jaafar asks.

"Some of it, yes."

"If you hadn't killed Lai, all of it would have been put to good use. To help children who were displaced because of those bastards. That's what the money should be used for, not taken by the government to use for themselves!"

"I agree with you, sir."

"Lai and I didn't use one single sen of the money for ourselves. That was the oath we made. Every single sen would be used to help the children, to give them a chance to make it in this world. Do you understand that?"

"Yes, sir, that's noble of you," Mislan says, trying not to sound patronizing and antagonize the situation. He remembers reading: when talking to fools, just say "you're right"—that will end the conversation. It works.

"Thank you."

Silence follows.

———

Outside the house, apprehension is running high, and adrenaline is pumping. Their nerves are on edge and palms sweaty. All eyes are fixed to the front door. The sun is now shining on their backs. The thick and heavy bulletproof vests are making them sweaty and uncomfortable.

Mislan hears the sound of metal friction and instantly knows it's a pistol being cocked: the all-too-familiar sound of a pistol's slide being pulled back to load a bullet into the chamber.

He glances at his team members; they nod to indicate they heard it too. He isn't satisfied with the cover available. But that is the best they have unless they move farther away. Farther away means they would have to move back to where their cars were parked, which was too far from the action, and their effectiveness will be compromised.

Reeziana is half-crouched behind the suspect's SUV. The SUV rear roof is of the same height as she is, and there's no way she can prime her shooting arm over it. The best she can cover herself is at the SUV side rear-left. With her right shooting arm by the SUV side trained on the front door, she is half-exposed. Zain took the right rear and has no line of fire to the front door unless he shoots through the SUV windows. Johan crouches low by the hood, well covered with both his arms resting on it. Gun leveled at the front door, eyes unblinking.

Mislan steps back behind the side wall. He hears the doorknob creak and sees it slowly turn. The wooden door cracks slightly open. Half of a face peeps out. He stares into the peeping eye of DSP Jaafar. It is as clear and bright as the sky outside. For a fleeting moment, he thinks he sees a smile or perhaps a sneer on the half-face.

"Sir," Mislan says.

Jaafar's eyes shift in his direction.

"Sir, please don't make it worse than it already is," Mislan pleads.

"You really think it can be worse?" Jaafar asks cynically. "Your team, what, four or six of you came all geared up for a raid expecting the worst. But you're telling me not to make it worse than it already is."

"You know this is standard gear for—"

"For a raid of an armed and dangerous suspect," Jaafar finishes Mislan's sentence. "I was a Narco Strike Team leader, I know the drill."

"Yes, sir."

Without warning, the door swings open inward and Jaafar stands in the doorway. A man in his mid-forties, tall, dark brown skin, crewcut hair, dressed in a light green polo shirt, dark slacks and barefooted.

"Is there any other way," Jaafar says rather than asks.

Mislan thinks he sounds resigned. He sees a pistol in Jaafar's hand. It is pointing to the floor.

"Gun!" he shouts to his team members. "Sir, please put the gun down."

Jaafar looks straight ahead, ignoring his order. He seems distant, staring out into the sunlight and the trees while taking deep breaths. Mislan notices the clear eyes are watery, not watery like a druggie's on withdrawal, but watery like tears are welling in the lower lids.

"DSP Jaafar, sir," Mislan calls again, "please put the gun down. Please."

He thinks he sees Jaafar curve a tiny smile. Without even looking at him or warning, Jaafar raises his shooting arm, leveling his pistol at Reeziana. Taking dead aim at her. Mislan sees his index finger move from the trigger guard, wrapping it around the trigger.

"Yana!" Mislan shouts a warning.

Two deafening shots rang out in harmony. Jaafar is kicked back into the house. Mislan rushes in. He sees the pistol has been flung to the middle of the living room. Jaafar is lying on his back, his face grimacing with agony. Blood is oozing profusely from his chest and abdomen. His light green polo shirt is turning red. A blood puddle under his back is fast spreading.

Mislan kneels by Jaafar's side, lifts his left hand, and places it on the abdomen's wound. He lifts the right hand and places it on the chest wound. Reeziana and Johan rush in and kneel across him. He tells Johan to press hard on Jaafar's left hand on the abdomen to stop the bleeding while he does the same to the right hand over the chest.

"Yana, call the paramedics," Mislan instructs. "He's still breathing. Syed!" he shouts for the detective. "Find me some cloth to stop the bleeding."

Reeziana steps away to make the call. She notices the neighbors have come out in droves to *kepochi*. After calling for the paramedics, she calls the cut-off team to come to the front and assist with crowd control. When Detective Syed doesn't respond to Mislan's call, Johan dashes to the kitchen and grabs a few face towels, handing a couple to Mislan to press on the chest wound. He uses the rest to do the same to the abdominal wound.

"Yana, inform ma'am," Mislan calls to her, who is outside the house calling for MPV assistance.

Mislan notices Jaafar's eyes flicker and his mouth twitch. Every time Jaafar gasps for air, he hears soft rippling sound coming from his chest. It sounds like water spouting, or a tiny spring in the ground. Jaafar's breath is shallow although he inhales deeply.

"The paramedic is on the way," Reeziana calls back. "I've also asked for assistance from the station for MPV."

This time Jaafar does smile, or tries to smile.

"Why?" Mislan asks.

Jaafar closes his eyes.

"Why not," he struggles to say, opening his eyes. "They killed my child," he laboriously mumbles, "my only child." Taking short deep breaths, he closes his eyes.

Mislan waits; he needs to understand, he needs his closure.

"Lost my wife," Jaafar suddenly says, low as a whisper. Mislan sees a few tears rolling down the side of Jaafar's face. "The bastards killed so many of us. Destroyed our lives," he says with a voice full of anger. Jaafar starts coughing, and Mislan knows he's choking on his own blood.

"Yana, where's the bloody paramedic?" Mislan shouts.

"Almost here," Reeziana calls back.

"The bastards deserve to die. 39B, mandatory death sentence. We, Lai and—"

Suddenly, Jaafar goes into wild convulsions. His mouth is wide open, gasping for air. Mislan holds him down the best he can, saying, "Hang in there, stay awake." Reeziana comes to assist. Blood spouts from his mouth. As suddenly as it started, it stops. Mislan feels for his carotid pulse: nothing.

He hears the wail of the paramedic vehicle in the distance, but there is nothing the medic can do. Jaafar lost the will to live, and no medical assistance can save him.

32

THE PARAMEDICS ARRIVE, CONFIRM the death of Deputy Superintendent Police Jaafar Abdul, and leave. Reeziana is sitting on the stairs staring at her hands covered with dry blood, looking ashen. Mislan has never seen her in such a shaken state. The cheeky, witty Reeziana is gone, replaced by a solemn, somber individual. He looks for Detective Sergeant Johan and spots him outside the house. *Johan is probably distancing himself from the scene,* Mislan figures. *Wise move to get some fresh air and to clear his head and conscience. Nothing can be done to change the course of events; best to step away and let others take over.*

Mislan sits next to her. As far as he can recall, this is the first shooting Reeziana was involved in. Johan has had several experiences and even shot and killed a man in saving Zaiton's life. In this situation, his assistant had to shoot to save Inspector Reeziana's life. He is confident Johan will bounce back in due time. Reeziana, on the other hand, may need more than just time to get over it.

It is never easy to take another person's life, even in a kill-or-be-killed situation. Human life is precious, sacred. There are always the thoughts that keep you awake at night: *Could I have avoided it? What if I did it differently?* They say you will get over it, but the truth is, unless of course you are a psychopath, you never will.

"You OK?" Mislan asks.

Reeziana nods without looking at him.

"Why don't you go wash your hands? Here, have a cigarette," he says, passing her the pack.

"What about you? You look worse than me. Look at your pants," she says.

"OK, let's both go wash our hands and have a smoke."

"He was going to shoot me," she says, jerking her head at Jaafar's corpse.

"Yes, he was, his finger was on the trigger. You did the only thing you could to protect yourself."

"But why? He knew he couldn't outshoot us."

"He lost the will to live."

"Jo shot him too."

Mislan nods.

In the kitchen, he observes as Reeziana scrubs her hands using the liquid dishwasher soap. She scrubs fiercely then rinses. Holding them to her nose, she cringes and scrubs them again.

"It's not on your hands," he says. "It's in your head."

She glances at him inquiringly.

"The smell, it's in your head and will stay there for a few days. I still smell and feel my slimy blood even till now."

Reeziana purses her lips. Then turns off the tap and wipes her hands with the paper towel.

———

From the kitchen where they're smoking, they hear voices, lots of voices coming from the front. Mislan chucks his cigarette and rushes out. He sees Superintendent Samsiah, ASP Amir, and four or five other uniformed senior officers at the front door, about to come into the house.

"Ma'am, sir, please don't come in. Forensics hasn't arrived yet," Mislan says.

"You are?" asks an officer in the uniform of assistant commissioner of police with a name tag identifying him as Raja Ibrahim.

"My officer, Inspector Mislan," Superintendent Samsiah replies.

"Sir, if you wish me to brief you, we can do it at the porch," Mislan offers.

The senior officers stay a moment to gaze at the corpse of DSP Jaafar Abdul before moving out to the porch, followed by Mislan. He gives them a super brief account of what transpired that led to the suspect being shot dead.

"There'll be an inquiry by ISCD," ASP Amir informs.

Mislan nods.

"Was any of your team hurt?" Samsiah inquires.

Mislan shakes his head.

"Thank God."

Just then the Crime Forensics team led by Chew arrives. Mislan excuses himself to meet Chew at the gate. After briefing Chew, he rejoins the officers.

"Why aren't you calling our D10?" Raja asks.

"This team did the Cheras case with us. It's best if they do this too," Samsiah answers.

"The suicide?"

Samsiah nods.

"These cases are connected?"

"Yes."

"How?"

"I'm sorry, for the moment I'm not able to release details of the case yet. I believe the OCCI will give the necessary press release."

Raja gives her a knowing smile, saying, "Yes, don't want to dim his stage lights."

"It's bad enough that during the MCO, the IGP and OCPDs are hogging the media attention. He'll murder you if you steal this from him," one of the officers says, and the rest of them laugh.

Hearing the officers talk and joke makes Mislan wonder if shifting their focus from the tragic incident is a way for them to avoid reality. A refusal to admit that one of their members could be involved in an appalling crime. Dissociating him from them and them from him.

"Then D9 will have another dead-policeman case on their hands," another officer jokes.

The officers chat for a little more and leave the scene. Superintendent Samsiah and ASP Amir cautiously enter the house. Chew is dusting the handgun, a 9mm Cobra Patriot, with Mislan eagerly waiting. Reeziana stands as the two senior officers enter. Samsiah heads straight for her.

"How are you?" Samsiah asks.

"I'm OK, ma'am, thanks."

"You need to talk, I'm always available."

Reeziana nods.

Chew passes the gun to Mislan. He ejects the clip and notices it's empty. He pulls the slide back; the chamber is empty too. He slips the clip into his pocket, pulls the slide all the way back and checks the barrel. It is threaded to fit a suppressor. Showing it to Chew, he tells him to look for the suppressor. Mislan motions to his boss and ASP Amir to follow him to the kitchen.

Out of Reeziana's sight and hearing, he shows them the empty gun and magazine. Samsiah turns to look behind to make sure Reeziana isn't following them.

"Ma'am, I don't think she can take it if she knows," Mislan says softly.

"I agree," Samsiah says. "She'll be devastated."

ASP Amir and Mislan nod.

"I swear his finger was wrapped around the trigger," Mislan says. "We all heard when he cocked the gun."

"We believe you. Inspector Reeziana and Detective Sergeant Johan acted in the belief that Reeziana's life was threatened with death or serious injury. He was aiming at her, to shoot her. I don't see anything wrong in their actions," Amir says. "How were they to know the gun wasn't loaded?"

"Suicide by police," Samsiah says angrily. "What an evil person. Bloody heartless of him to burden their consciences with his suicide. He should have had the balls to take his own life like Lai did."

"He's a Muslim, and suicide is a grave sin," Amir says, trying to calm her anger.

"Sin my foot," Mislan snaps. "It's OK for him to execute others, but not OK for him to blow his fucking head off? Blame his cowardice on religion. What about Yana and Jo, you think they'll be happy to know they were tricked into aiding his suicide?"

"Let's keep this between us until I can come up with how to break it to her and Jo," Samsiah instructs.

———

The *kepochi* crowd has been dispersed by uniformed personnel with the threat of arrest for breaching the MCO. By the order of Superintendent Samsiah, Inspector Reeziana and the rest of the team leave the scene. Only Mislan and Johan are to stay back until all is concluded. Chew's team searched the entire house and car. They found another handgun, a police-issued 9mm Glock. The Glock too was modified to fit a suppressor. They found two suppressors and several plasticuffs. They also found the Seremban 2 victim's cell phone. No cash was found.

It was almost 6 in the evening when the crime forensics team completed their tasks. Johan makes sure all lights and electrical appliances are switched off and locks the house. The two officers drive back to their office in complete silence.

Mislan knows his assistant and friend will talk when he's ready to talk. For now he just needs to be with his thoughts and conscience.

Earlier, Mislan called Superintendent Samsiah requesting that he be put on tomorrow's twenty-four-hour shift. Superintendent Samsiah had asked him the reason. He said he needed to be close to Johan, needed to be physically there for him. She agreed.

33

On reaching the contingent headquarters, Mislan asks if his assistant would like to go somewhere for a drink and talk. Johan says he wants to go home and rest. Sitting in the car with the engine running, he again asks if Johan is all right.

"I'm OK. I'd just like to be alone," Johan says, noticing his boss's reluctance to step out of the car.

"I know. I just want to have a smoke before I go up," Mislan says, making an excuse not to leave his assistant.

Johan lets his boss smoke without saying anything.

"Jo, you know I'm here if you want to talk."

"What's there to talk about? He pulled the gun on Inspector Reeziana—it's either him or her. It's a no-brainer—she brought us food and he executed people."

"Can't argue with you on that," Mislan says, followed by a chuckle. "Not to forget she's fixing you up with that beautiful Sarawakian corporal, what's her name?"

"Sherran," Johan replies with a tiny smile.

"Yes, Sherran."

"You don't have to stick around, really, I'm OK," Johan says.

"I know you are. By the way, we're up tomorrow."

Johan nods.

Mislan flicks his cigarette and steps out of the car, saying, "Stay safe, I'll see you tomorrow."

———

Driving home, his stomach growls and he realizes he hasn't eaten since morning. Now that the adrenaline rush is gone, his normal bodily needs take center stage. Mislan stops at the Thai restaurant near his place and orders fried rice with bulls-eye egg to take away. Waiting for his order, he calls his son.

"Hi, kiddo, have you eaten?"

"Yes."

"What did you do today?"

"Nothing."

"Did you do any schoolwork?"

"Yes, online but it's boring."

"It won't be long before everything will be back to normal. Just do the best you can."

"Daddy, the TV said this year there's no Raya," Daniel says, sounding disappointed.

"Is that so?" Mislan answers. The holy month of Ramadan is about ten days away, and he totally forgot about it. "I'm sure everything will be OK by then."

"Mummy said no Raya, no baju raya."

"She's joking, kiddo. You'll get your baju raya, don't worry."

"OK, Daddy."

"OK, kiddo, love you."

"Love you too."

Terminating the call, Mislan reflects on the coming month of Ramadan. The television has been full of debate on Ramadan bazaars. A whole month of food fiestas that Malaysians are used to enjoying. The sale of delicacies from every corner of the country at makeshift tents pitched along roads in almost every housing development. Starting from 3 p.m., the bazaar will be visited by hundreds, if not thousands, of people for their favorite home-cooked dishes. It isn't only the Muslims that crowd the bazaar for their breaking of fast food, but the non-Muslims also take the opportunity to enjoy the spread.

This year, it will be different, thanks to the COVID-19 pandemic. There is a strong indication that Ramadan bazaars won't be allowed. State representatives are working on introducing online bazaars to stop people from gathering, to check the spread of the virus.

The Ramadan bazaar to the Malays is the celebratory precursor to Raya. Hari Raya Aidilfitri is to mark the end of the monthlong fasting in the month of Ramadan, known as Eid-al Fitr outside of Malaysia. It's celebrated by Muslims all over the world. In Malaysia, it is a grand affair, as 50 percent of its populations are Malay, therefore Muslim. Mislan wonders what it will be like with the cancellation of the bazaars, possibly even Raya festivities. It's something he cannot imagine, especially for the children.

———

Reaching home, Mislan takes a long shower and then makes a mug of coffee and sits down to have dinner. He tries to recall his conversation with Jaafar.

"NO, he didn't. He did pull the trigger, but it was you that drove him to do it."

Did I? Mislan asks himself. *How was I to know he would take that path? I was just following the leads and collecting evidence—how the fuck would I know he was going to blow his brain out? NO, I'm not going to be guilt-tripped by his death.*

He suddenly loses his appetite. Throwing the half-eaten fried rice into the garbage bin, he takes the coffee mug to the bedroom. Lighting a cigarette, he thinks of giving his assistant a call to check on him. Deciding against it, his mind wanders back to Jaafar's words.

"They killed my child . . . my only child. Lost my wife. The bastards killed so many of us. Destroyed our lives."

Mislan cannot begin to imagine the pain and suffering he went through as a father losing his only child. What if it happened to his only son, Daniel? How would he react? Would he have done the same? He has no answer and pushes the thought aside.

Mislan isn't a religious person, but that night before he goes to sleep, he prays to Allah that he doesn't experience what Jaafar did.

34

INSPECTOR REEZIANA IS NOTICEABLY absent that morning. Superintendent Samsiah tells Mislan she had given her a couple of much-earned rest days. ASP Amir joins them, and this time around, he accepts an offer of D9 black coffee from Johan. He tells them he has made a request to D11, the Sexual and Child Abuse Department, which is staffed with psychologists, to keep slots for Reeziana.

"We still need for her to agree to be treated," Amir says. "What about you, Jo? Would you like me to make similar arrangements for you?"

Johan shakes his head. "Thank you, sir, but I'm fine."

"I understand this was not your first shooting, but if you feel a need to just talk with an expert, let ma'am know and I'll make the arrangements."

Johan nods.

"I'll speak to her," Samsiah says. "You know how sensitive it can be when we still think of psychologists as shrinks."

"OK, I'll leave it to you, but if you ask me, I think you're the best unqualified shrink she needs," Amir says, followed with a smile.

"I think Mislan should go and see one," Samsiah jokes. "He has turned down being considered for promotion, what, five years now?"

"I'm happy with what I am," Mislan replies.

"I did some digging into the late DSP Jaafar," Amir says, changing the subject. "In my opinion, he flipped when he lost his only child to drug overdose. His son was sixteen. The loss wrecked his marriage, and soon after his wife left."

"His *only* son," Samsiah says rather than asks. "When did it happen?"

"Six to seven months back. From what I heard, the boy was a straight-A student, a budding footballer. Somehow, he mixed with the wrong crowd and got hooked on drugs. They said the boy's body was discovered behind a dumpster in Petaling Jaya. The autopsy gave the cause of death as heroin overdose and didn't find any sign of physical injuries or foul play. PJ police believed he was dumped there after he overdosed."

"He, I mean he and his wife, must've been shattered."

Amir nods.

"I had the feeling that because of it, he lost the desire to live even before he was shot. When we spoke through the door, there was something in his voice. He sounded like he was resigned to the fact that it was all over," Mislan professes.

"It was over when you knocked on his front door," Samsiah says.

"Yes, but he could have had it out in court and dragged out the case for years. Yet he chose not to, like he wanted to end it all. When he peeked through the door, I thought I saw a tiny smile or sneer, hard to tell."

Samsiah's eyebrows arch.

"I tell you, ma'am, sir, at that moment I asked myself, '*What game is he playing?*' When he was gasping for air, all bloodied, he opened his eyes, and this time he really did smile at me. I don't know what to make of it. He was probably telling me, '*I win, you lose.*'"

"Maybe he did," Samsiah says.

"He also told me about Lai and the living hell he went through after his brother was imprisoned. I figured he was sort of a shoulder for Lai to cry on. Last night, I went through Lai's record. They knew each other when they were both in the Narco Strike Team. In fact, Lai's promotion was based on his recommendation. So, he had always been there for Lai. Again, I'm just theorizing, but after he lost his son, the two of them sort of leaned on each other—consoling and supporting. That was when he came up with a plan to get even. It was Lai's turn to be there for him.

He did say the dealers were committing offenses under section 39B of the Dangerous Drugs Act, which carries the death penalty. They were just administering the sentence. Here is the good part. In their scheme, the money didn't go to the government to be spent on themselves—I guess he meant the politicians. The money was donated to help displaced and abused children of drug-dependent parents. He claimed he and Lai didn't use a single sen for themselves."

"I believe him, I mean, we visited Lai's house and also his house. There didn't seem to be anything lavish there. And they both owned old cars," Amir says.

"How's that for noble deeds?"

Superintendent Samsiah and ASP Amir laugh.

"There's still one thing that puzzles me," Mislan says.

"What's that?" Samsiah asks.

"The two shots to each vic in my case. Why two shots with two guns?"

"It could be a show of commitment," Samsiah replies. "In the Seremban 2 case, only one gun was used, and it was Lai's gun, a .32. So if anything went wrong, we could only put Lai at the scene. Although he may not necessarily be the shooter. In your case, they decided that to seal their commitment they would both shoot and kill the vics. Now both of them could be placed at the scene. That could well be their logic."

"But the two 9mm pistols were recovered at Jaafar's place," Amir reminds them.

"Yes, they were. What could be proven is that both their prints were on the guns," Mislan answers. "The link is the bullets at the scene and the guns with their prints on them. That puts them both at the scene."

"Well, I guess now you have no more loose ends," Amir says. "All wrapped up neat and tidy."

"I guess so."

"Lan, I'm sorry you didn't get the closures you're hoping for," Samsiah says.

"But I did," Mislan answers with a tight grin.

"How so?"